watch me

ALSO BY LAUREN BARNHOLDT

Two-way Street

One Night That Changes Everything

watch me

LAUREN BARNHOLDT

Previously published as *Reality Chick*

SIMON PULSE
New York   London   Toronto   Sydney

SIMON PULSE
An imprint of Simon & Schuster Children's Publishing Division
1230 Avenue of the Americas, New York, NY 10020
This Simon Pulse paperback edition July 2010
Originally published as *Reality Chick* in 2006 by Simon Pulse
Copyright © 2006 by Lauren Barnholdt
All rights reserved, including the right of reproduction
in whole or in part in any form.
SIMON PULSE and colophon are registered trademarks
of Simon & Schuster, Inc.
For information about special discounts for bulk purchases,
please contact Simon & Schuster Special Sales at 1-866-506-1949
or business@simonandschuster.com.
The Simon & Schuster Speakers Bureau can bring authors to your
live event. For more information or to book an event contact the
Simon & Schuster Speakers Bureau at 1-866-248-3049
or visit our website at www.simonspeakers.com.
The text of this book was set in Adobe Garamond.
Manufactured in the United States of America
4 6 8 10 9 7 5 3
Library of Congress Control Number 2009936158
ISBN 978-1-4424-0255-3
ISBN 978-1-4391-0427-9 (eBook)

To my mom, for books, Parcheesi,
and always believing

ACKNOWLEDGMENTS

Thanks so much to my agent, Nadia Cornier, for making things happen so fast, and for loving Ally as much as I do. My editor, Michelle Nagler, for her superb guidance and advice, and for making this book so much better. My sister Kelsey, for reading every word as I wrote it. My sister Krissi, for being there when it happened. My dad, for teaching me about Yankees and March Madness. Kevin Cregg, for taking my word counts. Kiersten Loerzel, for my best high school memories. My grandparents, for everything. Ralph Riccio and Holly Schaff, for letting me steal their wireless internet. Rob Kean, for helping me with writing and life, and always taking my phone calls no matter what time it is. Robyn Schneider, for 9:31, LiveJournal, and everything else you can imagine. And most of all, C. J. Sullivan, for believing I could do it, even when I doubted myself, and for making me the luckiest girl in the world.

NOW

The question people ask me most these days is "If you could do anything differently, what would it be?" This question is designed to accomplish one of two things:

1. To make me break down. The press loves when anyone cries, screams, or loses control in any way. It's why those videos of celebrities going crazy and attacking the paparazzi are so popular on TMZ. The public eats up scandal, and therefore, so does the press.

2. To get a scoop. Every reporter wants to be the first one to break the story, so they try to ask questions that will get you to talk. Notice how they don't ask, "*Would* you have done anything differently?" They avoid "yes or no" questions like Paris Hilton avoids knockoff handbags. Except, of course, when they ask if Corey

and I are still talking. In that case, the "yes" or "no" response is enough of a scoop for them.

When you think about it, "What would you have done differently?" is a pretty shitty question to ask. I mean, even if I *wanted* to do anything differently, I couldn't, so having to think about it serves no purpose other than to drive me absolutely crazy. Which is why I don't. Think about it, I mean.

Well, not that much, anyway, because the truth is, I don't think I *would* have done anything differently, even if I could. I prefer to subscribe to that whole "everything happens for a reason" theory, mostly because the alternative is just too disturbing to think about. If everything doesn't happen for a reason, then we're all pretty much fucked, because each decision we make could be screwing up our lives forever.

No one wants to hear that, though. They all want me to have regrets, to wish I hadn't done certain things, to be upset about the stuff that happened. It's weird thinking people I don't even know are so interested in my life that they want to know who I'm dating or what I'm up to. It's also weird to think that a lot of these same people would love nothing more than to see me miserable about what happened during my time on the show.

The truth is, none of those people really know *what* went on these past three and a half months. I'm not sure *I* even understand it all. The only thing I know for certain is that three months ago I was a completely different person.

Which seems kind of crazy—that everything can change in such a short amount of time. But maybe that's what life is, really—just a bunch of small things that add up to one big thing. And even though sometimes you can't see it coming, you have no choice but to let it happen.

THEN

I'm the last person you'd expect to be out of bed when I don't have to be. My theory is that it's impossible to function properly without enough sleep, therefore getting up early is actually wasting your day being less than productive. So to find me waiting in line at eight in the morning for *In the House* auditions proves just how bad I want to be on the show. I know, I know, it's kind of corny to want to be on a reality TV show, but this is *In the House*. The king of reality TV. The show that launched Tansy McDonald's broadcasting career. She's the one that was on *In the House: Tampa Bay*. The blonde with the big chest? Now she does the TV Guide updates on its preview channel. Or used to.

"This is ridiculous, Ally," my friend Grant says, stomping his Timberland sandals on the sidewalk. "We're here an hour early and there's, like, fifty people in front of us."

4

He shades his eyes from the sun and rises up on his toes, surveying the line in front of us.

"The lines for these things always move fast," I assure him, looking at the people around us and trying to get a sense of the competition.

"How do you know?"

"I read it somewhere," I lie. Grant is one of those people who gets super impatient and cranky. If he thinks we're going to be here for a while, he might decide to take off, and I really don't want to wait by myself. I'm not the best at doing things alone—I always have to have someone with me. Like when I got my license, I had to take my brother Brian with me. And when my wisdom teeth came out, I made my boyfriend Corey skip his basketball practice and stay in the waiting room, even though the dental hygienist, Brandi, assured me that I would be okay to drive home on my own. Like I was really going to—everyone knows girls whose names end in "i" can't be trusted. Last year, for example, Kristi McConnell was always trying to get in my boyfriend's pants—she went by "Kristina" right up until the seventh grade, when she became "Kristi with an i" and lost all sexual integrity, i.e., the ability to stay away from other people's boyfriends.

"It's fucking hot," Grant says, taking a swig from the water bottle he's holding. "I thought Syracuse was supposed to be the snow capital of the world or some shit."

"Not in the summer, dork," I say, hitting him playfully on the arm and trying to distract him from his crankiness. "And it's not *that* hot out. Come on, this is going to be fun.

Me, you, having an adventure . . . I wouldn't want to be here with anyone else." I link my arm through his and give him my most winning smile.

"Ally, you *couldn't* be here with anyone else." Grant says, and disentangles his arm from mine.

"That's not completely true," I tell him. "I could have come with Alicia Billings." This year *In the House* is doing a special season, called *In the House: Freshman Year.* They're filming the show at Syracuse College, so in order to even try out for the show, you have to be a member of their incoming freshman class. Rumor has it that the only reason SC allowed *In the House* to be filmed on its campus was because when MTV's *College Life* took place at The University of Wisconsin, their applications and donations, like, tripled.

Anyway, Grant, Alicia Billings, and I are the only three people from our graduating class who are headed to Syracuse in the fall, and seeing as how I've never said a word to Alicia Billings and Grant and I are very good friends, it made more sense to come with him. Not to mention the fact that I don't think Alicia Billings has a car and we live in Rochester, which is about an hour and a half away from where the audition's taking place, at this bar in Syracuse called Dougie's.

Grant rolls his eyes and swats at a bee that's swarming around his head. "Fucking bees are here too?"

"Ohmigod, Grant, that guy behind us is totally checking you out," I say, grabbing his arm and tilting my head toward the blond cutie waiting in line behind us.

"Really?" he says, showing interest for the first time since we've been here.

"Totally," I lie for the second time in as many minutes. Grant is gay, and obsessed with any guy who shows the slightest interest in him. Actually, if you ask Grant, he'll tell you he's bi, but I've never seen him even look at a girl.

The line starts shuffling forward at a little after nine o'clock. Grant and I are in the second round of kids, and at about nine thirty, we're led into the bar where we're seated at tables of four. A casting assistant with pink hair places a box of pencils and four pieces of white paper down on our table.

"Fill these out," she instructs shortly, turns on her heel, and is gone.

"She was pleasant," Grant says, rolling his eyes again and grabbing a pencil.

"Hey, Grant," I say, jabbing him in the ribs with my elbow. "We're in a bar. Haha." He looks at me like I'm nutso. I try again. "Get it? We're not twenty-one. And we're in a bar. Fun, eh?"

He looks away and wordlessly starts to fill out his application. Geez. Talk about not wanting to have fun. I hope he knows he's really going to have a hard time making new college friends with that attitude.

I pick up my pencil and start to fill out my application, making sure every word is neat and precise. I read somewhere that presentation totally counts when it comes to applications. I think they were talking about job applications, but still.

Name: Ally Cavanaugh
Age: 18
Hometown: Rochester, NY
Hair Color: Dirty blond
Eye Color: Green
Height: Five feet, five and a half inches
Weight: Riiiiiggghhht. I'm not fat and I'm
not skinny.
Why do you want to be on *In the House*?:

Hmmm. What to write, what to write. Somehow "because I think it will be fun and I wouldn't mind being on TV to distract me from the fact that my boyfriend is going to school two thousand miles away" doesn't seem like the best answer. I mean, it's the answer that's *true,* but definitely not the one that's going to get me on the show.

I try to get a glimpse of what the girl next to me is writing. I see the words "enriching experience" before she catches me looking and covers her paper with her arm, a là third grade.

Enriching experience, my ass. Has she ever even seen the show? Last year everyone was naked in the hot tub with two of the girls kissing each other. And that was just the first episode. Not that I plan on kissing anyone—girl or otherwise—in a hot tub. Or anywhere, for that matter. I have a boyfriend.

I'm deciding to skip the "why do you want to be on the show" question for now when a bald man wearing a black polo shirt with the *In the House* logo on the pocket walks up to our table.

"Hi, guys," he says cheerfully. "I'm Al. Just wanted to welcome you to the *In the House* casting call and see if anyone has any questions."

We all look at him blankly. How can we possibly have any questions? We just got here. Suddenly I have a thought. Maybe this is a test. You know, to see who among us has the *personality* they're looking for. Isn't that what they always say about *In the House*? That they're looking for the right mix of personalities? That the cast members don't necessarily have to be the best-looking people (even though it seems every cast looks like a modeling lineup for Fashion Week), they just have to be themselves.

"I have a question," I say to Al boldly.

"Yes?" he says.

"Who do I have to sleep with to get Colin's phone number?" I ask. I toss my hair over my shoulder flirtatiously. He looks at me blankly. "You know, Colin? From *In the House Los Angeles*?"

"Right," he says, clearly not amused. He walks away. Hmm. This is going to be harder than I thought.

Once the applications are filled out, we're herded into a group interview with a casting director. Thankfully, it's not the same one I made the sexual comment to. I look at it as a fresh start.

"Well," the new director says, looking over our applications. "Let me start by introducing myself. My name is Mike Marino, and I'm the head casting director, as well as executive producer of *In the House*." Wow. These people don't fuck around. When they want a job done, they send the head honchos. Mike takes another glance at our applications and then attaches them to the clipboard he's holding. That's it for our applications? So much for agonizing over what to write. "The reason you're put in groups like this is so we can get an idea of how you interact with other people. Interaction with others is, as you know, the most important aspect of being a cast member. Now before we get started, are there any questions?"

This time, I keep my mouth shut. Apparently sexual quips aren't the way to score a spot on the show.

"Actually, Mike, I have more of a comment than a question," the Asian girl in our group says. Fool. "Here." She thrusts a manila folder at him. "This is my headshot and resume." Headshot and resume? What is she, looking for a spot on *The Apprentice*? The ad for the casting call didn't say anything about needing a picture or a resume. I don't have a resume. And the only picture I have with me is a copy of my senior picture that's been in my wallet since before graduation. I was supposed to give it to Lindsay Abrusia, but I never got around to it. On the back, it says, "Hey Linds! It was great getting to know you this year! Have a great summer and good luck at UMass! Keep in touch, Love ya lots, Ally."

"Sure," Mike says, pushing the folder into his gray messenger bag without looking at it. You can tell the Asian girl's pissed, but she tries not to show it.

"So," Mike continues, "why doesn't everyone introduce themselves, and tell us something about yourself." He scans the clipboard in front of him. "Tell us your name, where you're from, and your most embarrassing moment." Most embarrassing moment? That's his idea of telling something about ourselves? When you meet new people, don't you usually tell them your name, where you're from, and maybe a hobby or two? Definitely not something as personal as your most embarrassing moment.

"I'll go first!" the Asian girl announces, and everyone else breathes a sigh of relief. She adjusts her black button-up shirt, smoothes her hair, and smiles. I look around, thinking maybe they're filming us already, but there's no camera in sight. "My name is Jill Bliss," she says, "I'm eighteen years old, and I came all the way from Scranton, Pennsylvania, for a chance to be on *In the House*!" By the end of her declaration, she's almost screeching. I have this crazy vision of her in a tiara and sash. *My name is Jill Bliss, Miss Pennsylvania!*

Everyone in the group stares at her blankly. "And your most embarrassing moment?" Mike prompts.

"Well," Jill ponders, pulling a strand of her hair like it's the most important question she's ever been asked. "I guess it would have to be last year, at my sister's bachelorette party." She looks around, making sure she has our attention. "You see, in the Korean culture, we tend to be very reserved." Grant and I catch each other's eye across the table, and I can tell we're both thinking about Amy Lee, a Korean sophomore at our school who got in trouble for giving Mike Hern a blow job in the auditorium during study hall. Her defense was that in her culture, women were expected to please their men, and when Mike wanted a blow job, she had to give it to him. I bite my lip to keep from laughing.

"So my sister has a male stripper come, of course," Jill says. "And after he gets down to his G-string, he picks me up and throws me over his shoulder!" She looks at us expectantly. "It was completely humiliating! A Korean girl is really more affected by things like that. Korean women are very *conservative* and *reserved*. Which is why I think a lot of girls in my high school treat me differently."

"How so?" Mike asks her, and to my surprise, he looks intrigued. Doesn't anyone else think her most embarrassing moment was totally lame?

"Well," Jill says slowly. "It's like people have a stereotype about you if you're Asian. They think you're subservient to men, and that you're very conservative, and so that's the way they treat you. They don't expect you to stand up for yourself or know what you're talking about. I'm hoping that people at college will be a little more open-minded." Does this girl have a screw loose? Didn't she just say she was conservative and reserved?

"Maybe," I say, before I can stop myself, "people treat you differently because you make such a big deal about the fact that you're Korean."

She looks at me like I'm a piece of gum on her shoe. "I'm sorry?" she asks sweetly, but it's one of those sweet voices that you know isn't good, like when your mom says, "Oh, sweetheart, be a dear and help your old mother by cleaning out the entire garage."

Shit. I clear my throat. "I just think that maybe you bring up the fact that you're Korean, which forces people to notice it about you. I mean, I would never have even thought about the fact that you're Asian if you hadn't mentioned it. But when you bring it up and start talking about it constantly, it forces people to focus on it."

She glares at me. Lovely.

Casting interview, an evaluation:

Number of sexual remarks made that have fallen ridiculously short of their goal: one.

Number of people I've pissed off with my big mouth: one.

Chances of getting on the show: slim to none.

Yup, right on track.

"And you are . . . ?" Mike asks, turning his chair toward mine.

"Oh, um, I'm Ally. Ally Cavanaugh."

"And Ally, why don't you tell us your most embarrassing moment?" Great. Now thanks to my big mouth, I have to go next. I don't want to go next. In fact, I don't really want to go at all.

"Well," I say slowly, debating whether I should tell them my real most embarrassing moment, which I've never told anyone, or my fake most embarrassing moment, which I haven't made up yet. Then I realize that anything I make up is most likely going to be as lame as a stripper throwing you over his shoulder at a bachelorette party, and since I just told off Ms. Conservative, I have to top her. So I go for the truth.

"My most embarrassing moment actually happened

about a week ago, so it's funny you should ask me that, Mike," I say, smiling confidently. I read in a magazine article that using someone's name makes you seem like you're connected to them in some way, even if you've just met them. "See, my boyfriend Corey is away at school already. He actually had to leave about two weeks ago—he's a basketball player at the University of Miami, and his team had to go early for practice." I smile, like I'm totally cool with the fact that Corey's far away, even though I've cried myself to sleep every night since he's been gone. "We've been spending a lot of time on the phone, of course, but when you're used to seeing someone every single day, the phone just isn't the same. So about a week ago, I was feeling a little, um, horny." I almost stop myself. There's something about saying the word "horny" out loud to a bunch of strangers that's kind of sick. Especially if you're using it to describe yourself.

"Yes?" Mike says, leaning forward. I look around the group and see they're all hanging on my every word, even Grant, who's never heard this story.

"So, um, we were on the phone," I say, "and we started, you know, having phone sex."

Mike looks amused, and I gain some confidence. "So I was getting kind of, um, you know, loud, and my mom heard me. So she called from her room, 'Ally, are you okay?' and I was, like, 'Um, yeah, Mom, I'm fine,' and she was all, 'Okay . . . are you alone?'" By now, everyone is laughing. Except Jill. "She never mentioned it the next day, but it was still really humiliating."

14

"How long have you and your boyfriend been together?" Mike asks.

"Almost two years," I tell him, and he writes something down on his clipboard.

"How does he feel about you trying out for *In the House?*"

"He's cool with it. He's usually really supportive of everything I do," I say. Which is true. Corey *is* usually supportive of everything I do, but Grant and I just found out about the casting call yesterday, so it was kind of spur of the moment. When I mentioned it to Corey, I don't think he really expected me to get out of bed so early. "He's been pretty busy with basketball practice and everything, and this was kind of a last-minute thing."

Mike nods, looking at me with interest. After Grant and another boy tell their most embarrassing moments (having an Internet blind date ditch him after they met in person and tripping in front of everyone at graduation, respectively), Mike thanks us for our time.

As we're getting up to leave, Mike stops me. "Ally," he says, "can I talk to you for a second?"

NOW

They wanted me. But it was all a setup.

THEN

"**Absolutely not!**" **my mom says, slamming the potato** masher into the potatoes for emphasis. To find my mom mashing potatoes when I get home just illustrates the fact that I should never have gotten on the show in the first place. My family life is way too normal.

"Why not?" I say from my seat at the kitchen table. I made the mistake of blurting out my news the second Grant dropped me off, which was obviously not a good idea.

"Because it's ridiculous!" my mom says, adding some milk to the pan and continuing her mashing. "I will not have my daughter broadcasting our lives on national television."

"Not *your* life—my life."

"No, *our* lives," she says. "Those people tape everything. Phone conversations, family visits . . . I've watched that

17

show! All your family secrets get put out for everyone to see!"

"Mom, we don't have any secrets," I say, rolling my eyes. It's true. Our family is completely and totally normal. No affairs, no addictions, no secret crimes. We have a dog, an SUV, and Sunday dinners at my grandmother's house in Chappanga Falls. I figured my parents wouldn't mind I was going on the show, since we have nothing to hide. I should have realized it would have the exact opposite effect—my family didn't have any secrets because they never did stuff like going on reality TV shows. "Why are you making mashed potatoes, anyway?" I ask, in an effort to change the subject. "I thought we were cooking out."

"We are, but you know your father likes his mashed potatoes," she says, rinsing the masher off in the sink and taking a plate of hamburgers out of the refrigerator. "And don't try to change the subject, Alexandra. This is something that really needs to be discussed."

"What's going on?" my brother Brian asks, walking into the kitchen.

"Oh, nothing much, just your sister wanting to expose the whole family on national television," my mom says, throwing her hands up in exasperation. She's acting like I've just told the family I want to scrap this whole college idea and try my luck at the Bunny Ranch.

"You got on the show?" Brian asks, his eyes widening. I nod. "Oh my God, Ally, that's so great!" He hugs me, pulling me out of my chair and swinging me around the kitchen. I scream at him to put me down, but he flips me over and the blood rushes to my head.

"You're happy about this?" my mom asks my brother. "I would have thought you'd have a little more sense than that, Brian." My parents are both convinced that my brother is the more level-headed of their two children. He's the oldest and a boy, so, it's, like, the natural assumption. They're probably right. Brian's going to be a junior at Villanova, where he's majoring in architectural engineering. He's known he wanted to be an architect since he was seven. I, on the other hand, marked all of my college applications "undeclared."

"Oh, come on, Mom," Brian says now, setting me back down. I collapse back into my chair, my head spinning from the blood rush. "This could be a really good experience for Ally." He grabs a tomato out of the salad sitting on the counter and pops it into his mouth.

"Brian, please!" my mom says, and I'm not sure if she's talking about me being on the show, or him sticking his fingers in our salad. She moves the bowl to the other side of the stove. "How could this possibly be a good experience?"

"Well," my brother says, "a lot of times cast members end up getting offered really good jobs because they were on *In the House*." My mom looks at him skeptically. "Plus, this way you can keep an eye on Ally. Make sure she's not doing too much partying at school. You don't think she's going to do anything bad when she knows you and Dad are watching, do you?"

My mom considers this. "Well, we don't have to decide anything this instant," she says slowly, rinsing her hands off in the sink. "There's a lot of things that would have to be figured out. Let's just worry about dinner for right now. Brian, wash your hands, they're filthy!"

The phone rings, and I lunge for it. I see Corey's cell phone number on the caller ID and take the cordless out onto the deck. The last thing I need is my mom over my shoulder making comments about being on the show.

"That's so great, Al," Corey says when I tell him my news. Corey's the only person who calls me Al. I won't answer to it from anyone else. I don't like the way it sounds—like some kind of auto mechanic in a dirty gray jumpsuit who calls people "buddy." But when Corey says it, I dunno, it sounds cute.

"Really?" I ask him, settling down into a lounge chair and taking a sip of my iced tea. "You don't mind the fact that everyone in America is going to know about us? I mean, all our phone calls are going to be recorded, and when you come to visit, you're going to be taped. My parents are flipping out."

"Of course your parents are flipping out. They're from another time. Everyone's been on a reality TV show these days. It's like the Internet. At first, everyone online was a pedophile or a stalker. Now everyone's got a computer and it's the way to meet your soul mate."

I giggle and press the phone closer to my ear. "I miss you," I say, wishing he were here with me so we could take on my parents together.

"I miss you, too," he says. "But we'll be together soon."

"No, we won't," I say, feeling a lump rise in my throat. Fuck. I hate this. It's like I'm fine one second, and then something will remind me of Corey, or I'll want to share something with him and I'll feel like I'm going to start crying hysterically.

"Yes, we will," he says. "I'm going to come up and visit you on Columbus Day, remember?"

"Columbus Day is, like, a month and a half away. That's forever. It's longer than some whole relationships," I say, thinking of Grant's last boyfriend, who he dumped after a mere seventeen days.

"It will go faster than you think," Corey says. "I promise. And until then, I'll watch you on TV every day, so at least I'll get to see your beautiful face."

WHY COREY IS THE
PERFECT BOYFRIEND (A LIST):

1. He always tells me I'm beautiful.
2. He always calls when he says he will, even when he's busy. For example, he's been at school for two weeks, and even though he has practice twice a day *and* his classes, he still calls every night at nine o'clock when he gets his free cell phone minutes, plus whenever he can during the day.
3. He always makes me feel better about stuff, like when Mariah Keats and I showed up at the Senior Ball wearing the same dress. To understand the seriousness of this situation, you would have to know what Mariah Keats looks like. Picture Blake Lively's face with Scarlett Johansson's body and you'll get

the idea. Needless to say, I flipped out when I saw her. I was wearing a Wonderbra and I still couldn't compete with her in the chest department. But Corey told me I was the most beautiful girl there and that he'd heard from Mariah's ex-boyfriend Brad Westcott that Mariah's boobs were fake, a present from some guy at her dad's office she was rumored to be having a scandalous affair with.

4. He always says things like "When we get married" or "Someday when we have kids." How cute is that? Not that Corey and I are talking about marriage or anything. I mean, we're only eighteen. But I know we're going to be together forever.

Corey and I started dating at the beginning of our junior year. He was new—a transfer student from a few towns over. Corey immediately became popular because: a) he's an amazing basketball player, and b) he's totally hot.

By the second week of school, everyone knew who he was and all the girls wanted him. It looked like Mariah Keats (see above-referenced incident starring me as the innocent bystander and Mariah as the skank-ass prom dress poacher) was going to be the one to get him. She was the most popular girl, and it looked like Corey was soon to be the most popular boy, so it was only fitting. Her friends were dating the guys on Corey's team, the ones Corey had been hanging out with since he'd gotten to our school.

But for some reason, after we were paired up on a biology lab project, Corey decided he liked me. I think it was because he was too new to realize that, while far from a dork, I was definitely not as popular as anyone he was hanging around with.

That's the thing about Corey, though—he doesn't really care what anyone else thinks. It's one of the things I love about him. One night around Halloween, Corey and I were at the library writing up our bio lab. We'd had to meet there kind of late, since Corey had a basketball meeting right after school. I had offered to write up the lab myself, but he insisted on doing his share. Later, when he drove me home, one of my favorite slow songs came on the radio as we were pulling into my driveway. I told Corey there was no way I was getting out of the car until it was over. He laughed, put the car in park, and climbed out.

"What are you doing?" I asked him as he opened my door. I thought maybe he was going to escort me nicely but firmly to my porch.

"You said it was your favorite song," Corey said, taking my hand and pulling me out of the car. "You should dance to it."

"You're crazy," I told him, laughing as he wrapped his arms around me.

"Could be worse," he said, pulling me close. As I rested my head on his shoulder, I felt a current of electricity coursing through my body, and when the song was over, Corey pulled back slightly and kissed me softly on the lips. We've been together ever since.

It created a slight stir at school, since all the girls wanted him and we traveled in such different social circles. But we worked it out, and whenever I'd start feeling weird about it, Corey would do something cute and I'd feel better.

"It's not going to go by fast," I tell Corey now. "It's going to be like waiting for Christmas. It's never going to come, ever."

"Well, I'll just have to make you one of those paper chains we always had to make in elementary school. You can take off one link a night, and before you know it, I'll be there."

I giggle, already starting to feel better. By the time we hang up the phone a few minutes later, I feel strong, and I head for the kitchen, ready to convince my parents that going on reality television is going to be the best thing that's ever happened to any of us.

An hour later, they're totally trying to stonewall me.

"Why not?" I ask, struggling to keep my voice calm. Now is not the time to flip out. Must prove to parents that I am responsible, intelligent girl who can be trusted not to reveal family secrets and/or show inappropriate amounts of skin on reality TV show.

My brother conveniently disappeared after dinner, which totally sucks because I was hoping he'd help me sway them. I consider calling him back into the kitchen, but decide this might look too suspicious.

"Because it makes us uncomfortable," my mom says. I glance at my dad, who's finishing up the ice cream he's having for dessert. At the best of times, my dad is clueless, so when my mom says "us" she really means "me."

"Dad?" I try.

"Ally?" he counters.

"Dad, what do you think? Don't you trust me?" I try to make my eyes fill with tears, but not too much. I want to seem like I'm hurt by their obvious lack of trust, but not that I'm throwing some sort of crying temper tantrum.

"I don't know, Ally. Why would you want to even do something like this?" he asks, and they both look at me expectantly.

Um, hello? Because it seems fun? Because Corey is going to be far, far away? Because why wouldn't I? BECAUSE IT'S A MIRACLE I EVEN GOT PICKED?

"I think it's a really good opportunity," I tell them. "It will force me to interact with different people, and with all the press the cast gets after the show, it will help me to make contacts for jobs and stuff."

My mom frowns. "What sort of contacts?"

"In broadcasting," I say, reaching. "Like Tansy McDonald? She got that job for the TV Guide Network because they have a partnership with YTV. And I'm constantly going to be around reporters and stuff after the show's over."

"You want to get into broadcasting?" my dad asks. He takes another spoonful of ice cream.

"I've been thinking about it," I lie.

They look at each other skeptically over the table. I'm losing them. "Look," I say. "I really want to do this. I promise I'm not going to do anything horrible. I won't expose any of your secrets, I won't get naked and dance on some bar." My mom looks shocked at that last statement, like the thought never crossed her mind, but my dad just nods.

"Also," I rush on, realizing it may not have been the best idea to put scenes from *Girls Gone Wild* into my mom's head, "you'll be able to get the housing fee back. Since I won't be living in the dorms anymore."

"Ally!" my mom says, shocked. "We would never sell you out for money!"

Did my mom just say "sell you out"?

"I even have the number for the producer," I say, in a flash of brilliance. "His name is Mike! You can call him directly. I'm sure he'd be happy to answer any questions you might have."

My mom nods. "Okay," she says. "Get me the number."

What? Get her the number? I wasn't serious. I mean, I do have the number, yeah, but not for her to call. It was just to show that I'd be willing for her to do it. Kind of like when you offer to let your boyfriend check your emails to prove you're not cybercheating on him. You don't actually *expect* or *want* him to do it. Having your mom call the producer of a reality TV show is the equivalent of having her call your elementary school to tell on someone who's teasing you.

"Get you the number?" I echo weakly.

"Yes," my mom says. "I'd feel better if I could talk to this Mike person. I have a few questions."

My dad nods and drops his spoon into the empty ice-cream bowl, then leans back in his chair, looking satisfied.

"Like what?" I ask her.

"I'd just like to talk to him," she says, taking a sip of her coffee calmly. "It would make me feel more comfortable."

"Fine," I say. I pull the paper Mike gave me out of my purse and hand it over.

She slips it into her pocket. "We'll think about it," she says calmly.

"Thank you, thank you, thank you!" I say, throwing my arms around her. I run upstairs to call Grant.

NOW

Later I would find out that I was a late addition to the cast, that they already had a girl all picked out who'd backed out at the last moment. The other cast members had gone through extensive and multiple interviews, but by the time they got to the Syracuse casting call, they were getting desperate.

Because of this, Mike and his crew were more than happy to assuage my mom's fears about her daughter's fall into the world of sin and debauchery. She was told about the high-security measures that would be in place, including twenty-four-hour security guards stationed around the house, a state-of-the-art alarm system, and surveillance cameras that are constantly monitored. He made living in the dorms sound like living in squalor compared to the lap of luxury I was going to be in.

But like I said, they set me up. There was a specific

reason they wanted me, and I think in the back of my mind, I knew what it was. I just chose not to think about it. So on the morning of August 29, a day before the rest of the freshman class was supposed to arrive at Syracuse College, I packed up my stuff, said a tearful good-bye to my brother, and climbed into my parents' Explorer to start my first semester at college, and my new role as Ally Cavanaugh, reality TV star.

THEN

Not to sound like a bitch, but these people are freaks. I'm usually not so judgmental, I swear. I definitely lean toward the liberal end of the political spectrum, and am totally open to the beliefs and ideas of others, but I've been here about an hour, and I can already tell I'm going to be spending a lot of time OUT of the house.

MY ROOMMATES, A BREAKDOWN:

JAMES: Dresses kind of like Bow Wow, complete with the gold chains and baggy pants. Talks in ghetto-speak, such as "shorty" and "whaddup." He's like a bad *Saturday Night Live* skit, where the Jonas Brothers play a rap group.

SIMONE: Long red curly hair, flawless pale complexion, and lanky body. She has the softest voice I've ever heard, and you have to strain to figure out what the hell she's saying.

JASMINE: She looks very exotic, like half Asian or something, with dark hair and big boobs. I swear to God, her breasts are huge. She looks like one of those high-maintenance girls who always turns out to be a shallow bitch.

DREW: The token hottie. Dark hair, blue eyes, buff body. Which means he's probably an asshole who will hit on anything that walks.

Somehow, an hour after meeting these characters, I'm in the hot tub with them. It's like some kind of unspoken rule that the first episode of *In the House* involves everyone in the hot tub, in a bonding session before the fights and scandals take over everyone's lives. I really didn't want to wear a bathing suit on national television, but I couldn't exactly say no to getting in the hot tub. I don't want my roommates to think I'm some sort of stuck-up bitch who thinks she's too good for them. Even though I kind of do. Think I'm too good for them, I mean. Ha. Just kidding. Sort of.

Anyway, I opted for a dark blue one-piece, figuring it would serve the dual purpose of being flattering while not giving my mom a heart attack at seeing her only daughter on TV in a thong bikini. Not that I have a thong bikini. But still.

Jasmine apparently doesn't care about the mental health of her immediate family, because she's wearing a red bikini that looks a size too small for her. Which may not be her fault, seeing as how I'm sure it's extremely difficult to find a bikini top in her size.

"So, who's the virgin?" James asks, looking around at us with a shit-eating grin on his face. The steam from the hot tub rises up around his face and, with Jasmine in her tight bikini next to him, he looks like he's in a music video, pimpin' on some hos or something.

"What do you mean?" Drew asks, running his fingers through his hair. The steam from the hot tub makes it stand up in little spikes. He looks very Hollister.

"Come on, playah, you know what I mean. There's always one virgin in the house." He looks at all of us closely. Please don't ask me, please don't ask me, please don't . . . "So how about it, Ally?" Four pairs of eyes and one camera turn to me.

Fuck. What is it about everyone always wanting to know if you're a virgin? It's, like, the worst possible question to have to answer. People always assume that if you *are* a virgin, then there's obviously something wrong with you and/or you're a prude. If you're *not* a virgin, then you're a slut. If you haven't had actual intercourse, but you've had oral, then you're a slut *and* a tease. It's all very complicated and confusing, and the whole system is bullshit. It's like the answer to this one question makes people think of you in a certain way, and it's hardly ever accurate.

"You know I've been with half my high school," I say, tossing my hair flirtatiously. I figure flip and sarcastic will get me out of answering any questions that pertain to anything sexual and/or something my parents really should not be hearing. It's not, like, I'm embarrassed to answer the question or anything. I mean, I can be mature about sex. I just don't really think it's anyone's business.

"It's me," Simone says. "I'm probably the only virgin in the house." She looks almost apologetic.

"There's nothing wrong with that," Drew says to her. "I think it's cool that you're waiting."

"I'm not waiting for marriage or anything like that," she says, pulling the hair tie out of her long red hair and gathering it back up into a ponytail. "I'm just waiting until I find someone I really like, that I'm comfortable with."

"Good idea," Drew says. "I wish I would have waited until I found the right girl." Yeah, right. I wonder how many girls he's been with, and put his total at close to five. I think it probably would have been more, except he seems like the type to be super picky about who he goes out with, limiting himself to the hottest girls in school.

"What is this noise, man?" James says. "I gotta get mine wherever I need to get it, you know what I'm sayin'?"

I catch Jasmine rolling her eyes, and I bite my lip to keep from laughing. When I got to the house about an hour ago, James took one look at me and said, "Damn, girl, your parents put out some good product." I think it was a compliment, but I'm not quite sure. It's hard to decipher James's ghetto-speak when there's a camera in your face. I have to use all my concentration to suck in my stomach and keep the right look on my face.

"So whaddup wit you, Jazzy?" James asks, turning his

attention to Jasmine. "Are you a virgin?" The look on his face says *Yeah, right.*

"First of all, don't call me Jazzy. If you do, expect to be ignored, or for me to start calling you Jimmy. Second, I think if you refrained from asking girls inappropriate questions within an hour of meeting them, you'd 'get yours wherever you need to get it' a lot more than you currently do."

James looks startled.

"That's coo, girl," he says after a moment, starting to chuckle. "Homegirl's got attitude."

"So do any of y'all have boyfriends or girlfriends?" Simone asks softly.

"Nope," Drew says, running his hands through his hair again.

"No boyfriend," Jasmine says. Her boobs bob up and down in the water.

"Puhhleeze," James says, giving Simone an *Are you kidding me* look.

"I'm single too," Simone says, looking at James.

They all look at me. "I have a boyfriend," I admit, feeling like it's some kind of dirty secret. "He goes to the University of Miami."

Drew looks surprised. "Don't look so shocked," I say, taking a cue from Jasmine. "I'm smart, I'm funny, I'm cute. I'm a catch."

"Oh, no, it's not that," he says quickly. "It's just that I would think it would be hard to have a long-distance relationship to begin with, not to mention the fact that now you're on a reality TV show, which definitely can't help the situation."

"It's not hard for us," I say assertively. "We're totally in love."

"How long have you been with your boyfriend?" Simone asks.

"Almost two years," I tell them, sliding my hands through the hot water and watching the ripples from the movement.

"Damn, you know homeboy is gettin' his somewhere else," James says, winking at me.

Ugh. Whatever.

We stay in the hot tub for about an hour, and then we get out because it's starting to get way too hot and James is starting to get way too personal. After we dry off and get dressed, we pick our rooms. The house is ridiculous. As in, ridiculously amazing. Besides the hot tub, we have a pool table, a huge bathroom with floor-to-ceiling mirrors, and a breakfast block with these really cute stools. The house is decorated in shades of navy blue and turquoise and, in keeping with the color scheme, we have a huge aquarium in the living room with all kinds of colorful fish.

There's two bedrooms, one with two double beds and the other with three. To keep it simple, we decide to do the boys in one room and the girls in the other. I think James is a little upset that he's rooming with Drew and not a girl (aka Jasmine), but he tries to act like everything's cool. Or coo. Whatever.

By the time I get a chance to call Corey, it's past ten

o'clock. We talk for about five minutes before I pass out. Who knew being famous could be so exhausting?

"Ally," Jasmine hisses at ten the next morning. "Ally!"

Through my half-open eyes, I see her approaching my bed gingerly, her purple nightgown flapping in back of her. I jump for a second until I realize that the person behind her is a cameraman, following her with a handheld. She better be careful, I think before rolling over. Her breasts are going to fall out of that nightgown and give America a peek.

"Ally, you awake?"

"No," I say, pulling my pillow over my head. "I'm not." I glance at the digital clock on my nightstand. "And I won't be for a few more hours," I add, just in case she's one of those annoying people who tries to wake you up every ten minutes.

"We don't have a few hours," she says, sitting down on my bed. "I want you to come with me."

Come with her? Where could she possibly have to go? We don't have class until tomorrow. Is it possible she's met some new friends already? Friends who get up at the crack of dawn and have breakfast parties? If so, do I want to be involved with said early-rising friends? Is being friendless better than having friends who rouse you out of bed on your last day to sleep in before school starts?

"We don't have classes until tomorrow," I remind Jasmine, in case she's forgotten and thinks I'm going to chaperone her to school.

"I have a job interview," she tells me, shaking me. Jesus. Is it acceptable to shake your roommate awake less than twenty-four hours after you meet her? Maybe she's one of those people who's just really comfortable with touching. Like those girls at school who are always hugging each other every five minutes. I hate people like that.

"I need moral support," Jasmine's saying. "Now come on, I want to leave in an hour." She disappears back out the door. I glance over to where Simone is still sleeping soundly in the bed next to me. I wonder why Jasmine didn't wake *her* up. She seems like the type who's sweet and nice, always willing to help out a friend. I'm obviously selfish and value sleep over a roommate in need.

I sigh and debate whether or not I should go back to sleep. Ten is not ridiculously early, but it's not my preferred wake-up time either. I quickly weigh the pros and cons of getting up. Cons: Will not be able to sleep until noon, will be cranky, will have to deal with cameraman who is standing at the foot of my bed. The cameraman who followed Jasmine into our room has followed her back out, but has been replaced by my own personal cameraman, who has his camera trained on my face. Hmm. I contemplate pretending to go back to sleep to see if he will leave, but then I realize this is a horrible plan. Of course he won't leave. He's going to film me. That's his job.

Pros of waking up: Will make good impression on roommate, will not have to worry about deciphering James's ghetto-speak, as chance of anyone else being up is slim, will convince America that am making an effort to get to know my roommates, and nation and school will think of me as sweet, kind girl.

I sigh and throw the sheets off. Thank God my mom insisted on buying me all sorts of pajamas before I left, because they really weren't kidding when they told us we'd be filmed 24/7. There are cameras everywhere except for in the bathroom, plus cameramen who work the house, chronicling our every move. Whenever we leave, a cameraman shadows us, to pick up on any scandals we might get involved in.

There are floodlights on the ceiling of every room, which I'm hoping will not cause me to sweat, smearing my makeup all over. Although if they do, at least I won't be wearing any white clothes, since we're not allowed to wear white *anything* because it messes with the lighting somehow, making it, like, impossible to see anything on-screen.

There are mikes all over the place, strategically set up to catch everything we say to anyone, ever. We also have to wear a mike pack under our clothes at all times, so that our conversations can be picked up and broadcast to the world. I can already tell the mike pack is going to be a pain in the ass. It has to go across your back and around your waist, making it almost impossible to wear anything low-rise. And who wears stuff that sits on your waist these days? Do they even sell pants like that anymore? The mike pack cuts into your skin, making it hurt whenever you move, and causing me to imagine all sorts of gross welt-type bruises that may appear in the next few days.

The show is broadcast every night at ten o'clock,

starting tomorrow. They call it almost live reality, and they're doing it this way so it will be more relatable to the *In the House* demographic. The producers figure that kids who are going back to school will watch the show and see us going through the same things they are—kind of like running a Christmas TV special around the holidays.

Cast members aren't allowed to watch the show, which is a little freaky. The producers are afraid that if we know what's being shown, it'll affect how we act, so all the TVs in the house have YTV blacked out. Of course, we can always find out from our friends and family what's being aired, so I intend to grill Corey every night and get the lowdown on what America's seeing.

Once I've taken my time showering and blow-drying my hair, I find Jasmine in the living room, flipping through a *People* magazine. Sam—all the cameramen have to wear name tags in order to make us feel less creeped out, the rationale being that as long as we know someone's name, it's all good—follows me dutifully.

"Oh, good, you're ready," she says, standing up from the couch. I look at her and do a double take. For her job interview, Jasmine has selected a tiny denim skirt, frayed at the bottom, and a dark pink tank top with wide straps that pushes her boobs up and out.

She notices me staring and rolls her eyes. "Before you even ask, yes, they're fake." Sam the cameraman's eyes widen.

"No, it's not that," I say, trying to choose my words carefully.

"Ally, don't be embarrassed," she says, grabbing her purse and herding me out the door. "It doesn't mean you're a *lesbian* or anything. You're just curious about my implants—there's nothing wrong with that."

"Curious about your implants?" I repeat dumbly, struggling to keep up with her as she power walks down the sidewalk. Her high black shoes clack on the concrete, and I wonder how the hell she can walk so fast in shoes like that. "Jasmine, no, it's not your implants, it's just that um . . . well, I was thinking that what you have on may not be the best interview outfit."

She stops on the sidewalk, and Sam the cameraman moves to the side so that he can get both of us in the shot. She smiles. "Ally, honey, this is the kind of tryout where dressing a little bit sexy can definitely give you an edge."

"Tryout?" I say, struggling to keep up with her as she starts walking again. "I thought you said it was a job interview."

"It's both."

"Oh." I think about this for a second. "You mean like for an acting job?"

Jasmine throws her head back and laughs. "You crack me up, Al. That's actually a very good comparison. Some people would think of it as an acting job, yes."

THINGS I CAN'T STAND:

1. Anyone but Corey calling me Al.
2. People acting condescending toward me.

"Whatever," I say, turning on my heel and heading back toward the house. She's on her own. My self-respect is definitely much more important than making America love me. I think.

"Ally, no, wait," Jasmine says, grabbing my arm. She slides her sunglasses off her eyes and onto her head. "It's a stripping audition. I didn't want to say anything because I thought it might freak you out." She bites her lip. "But I could really use someone there with me. I mean, it's just safer, and it won't freak me out as much."

"A stripping audition?" Like for furniture or something?

"Yes."

"You're a stripper?"

"Tuition doesn't pay itself, Ally," she says, opening her purse and reapplying her lip gloss. "Sometimes you do what you have to do."

"Oh." I stand there, considering this and feeling like a fool.

"So," she says finally, shifting her weight from one foot to the other. "Are you coming or not?"

I look at Sam, his camera broadcasting my every move to all of America. I think of my mom's prediction that I would fall into the underground world of sex and debauchery all the while embarrassing my whole family and disgracing their good name. I look at Jasmine's hopeful face. "I'm coming," I say, picking up the pace and rushing down the sidewalk so I can keep up with her.

THEN

"I can't believe you went to a strip club!" Grant says that night on the phone.

"Why not?" I ask, settling into the huge tan chair near the phone. There's a little camera perched on the table next to it, so that all our phone conversations will have both audio and video.

"I don't know," Grant says. "It just doesn't seem like something you would normally do, you know?"

"Well, of course it's not something I would normally do," I say, sighing. I pull my legs up underneath me and curl up in the chair. "I mean, why would I?"

"I just mean it's not something that it seems like you would do, ever. Like, even if the opportunity presented itself, you know?"

"Why do you say that?" I ask. "I'm not a prude." I can

go to a strip club if I want. I'm hip and open-minded. I don't have to cringe at the sight of a naked girl. Besides, it wasn't really that skanky in there. I mean, it could have been because it was during the day and there weren't too many people there, but it seemed classy. Almost sexy.

Plus. It's not like I'm a virgin or anything. Corey and I held out until the beginning of our senior year, when his parents went away for Labor Day. We had the whole house to ourselves, and it just kind of happened.

Actually, that's not true. It was totally planned. Corey had been wanting to do it for a while, but I was scared. I always thought that I would wait, if not until I was married, then at least until I was, like, twenty or something. But Corey and I were in love, and we'd been together for a year, so it felt like the right thing to do. Corey wasn't a virgin—he'd been with one other girl at his old school, which actually didn't bother me. I knew he loved me, and I figured it would make it easier—at least one of us would know what they were doing.

The sex itself wasn't that great—it was awkward and kind of painful, and when it was over, I was glad we'd gotten it out of the way. It was like this huge thing that had been hanging over our heads, and now we could just move on. I was totally sick of the whole "when are we gonna do it?" conversation that had been becoming more and more frequent with us.

I'm not ashamed of it. Sleeping with Corey, I mean. Yeah, I know I avoided the question entirely during our little hot tub sex conversation last night, but I just don't think it's anyone else's business. Especially the millions of Americans who are going to be tuning in to my life every night.

Besides, it got better. The sex, I mean.

"I know you're not a prude," Grant says now. "It just doesn't seem like you would put yourself in that position."

"Grant, she didn't want to go alone. She was nervous."

"I know. But you don't usually . . ." He trails off before he can say anything that can totally damage our friendship, but I know what he's thinking. The thing is, I don't have many friends that are girls. Okay, I have none.

I'm not sure why that is, exactly. My best friend from junior high moved away to Nebraska, and I guess I just never met any new female friends. Grant thinks that subconsciously I'm afraid Corey will leave me for another girl, and so I don't hang out with any of them in order to limit their access to him. Which is totally ridiculous.

"Oh my God, am I going to be on TV? I mean, not like me or anything, but a little arrow pointing to the phone with my name on it? Is it going to say 'Grant, Ally's best friend'? You did tell them I was your best friend, right?" Grant says, steering the conversation back to himself.

"Yes," I lie, counting on the fact that production will be able to figure it out.

"So what are your parents going to think about this whole strip club debacle?"

"I don't know," I say, feeling a nervousness starting in my stomach. I try to push the thought of telling my mom I spent the afternoon with naked girls out of my mind.

"What do you think Corey will say about it?"

"Why would Corey even care?" I ask. "I mean, it's not like *I* was stripping or anything."

"I know, but it's just, like, the thought of you being in that kind of environment, you know?"

"I guess," I say, pushing that thought to the back of my mind as well. I don't understand what the big deal is. I mean, who cares if I went to a strip club? When you think about it, it's not any worse than being in the girl's locker room before gym class.

"What are you doing tonight?" I ask Grant in an effort to change the subject.

"My roommate and I are going to a party at Crows," Grant says, naming one of the fraternities on campus. "Wanna go?"

"I do," I tell him. "But I think it would be better if I stay here tonight. You know, bond with the roommates some more." The truth is that Corey's supposed to call me later, and I don't want to miss his phone call.

"Whatever," Grant says. "Listen, I'd better go. I have to call my parents back before it gets too late. They're freaking out."

"About what now?" Grant's parents are in a perpetual state of freaking out. Every little thing sends them into a state of hysterics. Not just about Grant, but about everything. One time, when Grant's little sister Eva was in second grade, her teacher commented to Grant's mom that Eva was a little bit behind the rest of the class in cursive writing, and could she please help her a little at home?

Grant's parents made an appointment for Eva with the school psychologist—they thought she had a learning disability.

"Same old stuff," Grant says, sighing. "They're convinced this whole bisexual thing is just a stage, and they're hoping college will snap me out of it. They're probably going to want to know if I've met any girls yet."

I snort. "We still having lunch tomorrow?"

"Totally."

Grant disconnects, and I stare at the receiver for a second, then pick it back up and dial Corey's cell number. I want to hear his voice, and plus I figure it will give me a chance to warn him about the whole strip club thing before he sees it on TV. I have no delusions that they're NOT going to show it. I mean, why wouldn't they? One of the cast members tries out to be a stripper? That's huge. Especially since Jasmine is hot.

"Hello?" Corey answers the phone, and I hear voices and music in the background.

"Hey," I say. "What's goin' on?"

"Not much," he says, yelling in order to be heard over all the noise.

"Can you talk?"

"Not really," he admits, sounding apologetic. "I'm out with the team."

Out? What is "out"? Out studying? Out having dinner? Out partying and getting crazy with sorority girls? From the sounds of it, the latter seems like the accurate choice. Okay, stay calm. Must not morph into psycho jealous girlfriend.

"That sounds fun," I say brightly, while visions of Florida girls with tanned stomachs and belly rings dancing around Corey flood my head.

"Can I call you back?" he asks.

"Sure," I say, twisting the phone cord around my finger and trying not to sound upset. "When?"

"I'm not sure," Corey says. "Whenever I get home." I debate telling him about the strip club thing now, but figure I have at least until tomorrow night's episode airs to warn him. Plus, on the off chance that he's going to make a big deal about it, I want to make sure he has time to talk.

"Okay," I tell him. "But make sure you do, because I have something important to tell you."

"Of course. I'll call you later tonight."

"Okay."

"Hey, Al?"

"Yeah?"

"I miss you."

"I miss you, too."

"I'll call you later."

But he never does.

Until six the next morning. It's our first day of classes, and so for a second, I think the show has some sort of crazy wake-up-call system. I wonder who set mine for so early. My first class isn't until nine. When I got scheduled during orientation, my advisor was surprised that I didn't pitch a fit about having such an early class—apparently classes that start before eleven are super unpopular. But high school started at 7:19, so classes at nine seem ridiculously late, and I intend to take full advantage of this.

I reach for the phone by my bed, ready to inform whoever it is that they can call me back in two hours, thank you very much.

"Hello?" I say sleepily, trying to keep my voice down so that I don't wake up Jasmine or Simone.

"Ally, what the fuck is going on?" Corey demands, his voice booming through the phone.

"Corey?"

"Why were you at a strip club?"

"What?" I ask, sitting up in bed and trying to push the sleep off my brain long enough to focus on what he's saying.

"Why. Were. You. At. A. Strip. Club," Corey repeats, acting like I'm six years old.

"Cute," I say, rolling my eyes. "Listen, can I call you right back? I'm going to switch phones so that I don't wake up my roommates."

"Answer the question," he says, ignoring my request.

I sigh and lean back on my pillows. I cradle the phone and pull the covers over my head to muffle the sound of my voice. "Because one of the girls I live with was thinking about getting a job there," I say, trying to play it off like it's no big deal. Which it isn't. "How did you even know about that, anyway?"

"I saw it on the preview for tonight's show."

"Really?" I say, interested in spite of myself. "What did it say?"

"It showed you, on the phone with Grant, saying that you went to the strip club. Now are you going to tell me what the fuck is going on?" Corey sounds mad, and I start to get a little annoyed.

"Don't say fuck," I instruct automatically, the reality TV language rules ingrained in my brain.

"You could have at least told me. I thought you'd have enough sense to let me know about important shit before I have to find out along with the rest of the nation."

"I tried to tell you," I say, struggling to keep my voice calm. "But you were out with your friends last night, and you told me you couldn't talk, remember? Besides, it was really no big deal. Jasmine was going for an audition, and she didn't want to go alone."

"Jesus, Ally, you're living with a stripper?"

"She decided not to do it. She got a job at Hooters instead."

"Oh, well, in that case, I feel much better," he says sarcastically.

"What are you doing up at six in the morning, anyway?" I ask him, trying to change the subject. Silence. "You just got in?" I ask incredulously.

"I was out with my team, Ally. It's important for me to bond with them, especially since I'm only a freshman. I have to prove myself." The Florida temptresses and their belly rings pop back into my head. Girls who are on the Zone Diet and wear clothes from bebe. Girls with names like Halle and Brynn. Imaginary girls who are apparently developing personality characteristics in my mind, which means I'm totally losing it.

"Sounds fun," I say breezily, pushing the boyfriend-stealing sluts out of my mind.

"Ally, stop trying to change the subject. This is serious. I don't like thinking about you living with a stripper or going to strip clubs or whatever the hell it is you're doing over there." He sighs, and I picture him running his hand through his dirty blond hair, looking sexy without even trying. "If I knew this was the environment you were going to be in, I would have never let you do this."

Let me do this? *Let* me do this? Has Corey been smoking crack with Halle, Brynn, and his teammates? Since when do I have to ask his permission for anything? We've never been one of those super-controlling couples who have to approve each other's every move.

"Corey, it's really not a big deal. We weren't even in the strip club for that long." I don't mention the fact that after the strip club I spent an hour in Hooters, having lunch and watching Jasmine flirt with the bartender.

"Not a big deal? Are you kidding me?"

I take a deep breath. I don't know how, but at some point I've completely lost control of this situation. I decide I need to regroup.

"Corey, I've been here one day," I say, keeping my voice deliberately even and light. "I haven't been doing anything— I haven't had a *chance* to do anything." I pause for effect. "I think you're really tired, which isn't helping matters, and this situation is getting blown completely out of proportion. Now can we talk about this later? It's six in the morning,

I don't want to wake up my roommates, and I have my first class in three hours."

"Fine." The line goes dead, and I look at the phone in shock. Corey has never, ever hung up on me. On the few occasions that we've disagreed about something, we've always at least said "I love you" before hanging up. I'm about to call him back when I see something move out of the corner of my eye. I jump as Sam moves into my field of vision, the red light on his camera blinking merrily. Lovely. America will now be treated to my fight with Corey.

I sigh and place the receiver back on the hook. Maybe it's best if we both have time to cool off a little.

There's no way I'm going to be able to get back to sleep, so I head to the kitchen for some coffee. I usually don't drink coffee, but isn't that what college students are supposed to do? Live on coffee to make up for their drunken nights of partying and their sleepless nights of studying? Not that I'm really planning on doing either. I mean, I don't really drink all that much, and what sort of work could they give you that you would possibly have to stay up all night studying? There's, like, fourteen hours of awake time during the day. If I can't finish all my work then, I might as well just throw in the towel now.

I turn on the coffeepot, trying to ignore Sam, who's behind me, the camera capturing my every move. The worst part of having the cameras around is when they're filming me doing something like this—something totally normal by myself, like making coffee. It feels weird. We're supposed to ignore the cameras and not converse with the cameramen at all. It's this huge rule. The production people can even get fired if they "line-cross." I think it's because of Corrine, who was on *In the House: Las Vegas.* She gave one of the cameramen a blow job in the bathroom of a casino one night, and it was this huge fiasco.

The door to the house opens as I'm pouring coffee into a Syracuse College mug with a blue handle.

"Let me guess," Drew says, walking into the kitchen. He's wearing mesh shorts and a gray tank top. His biceps are huge and defined. "You're a morning person too?"

"No, not at all," I tell him, grateful someone else is here to share the spotlight. "Sorry."

"It's okay. I should have known better than to assume you were." He winks. What's that supposed to mean? I look lazy? I stand up straighter.

"Where were ya, coming in at six in the morning, looking out of breath and flustered?" I ask, sitting down at one of the stools at the breakfast bar. I dump about six spoonfuls of sugar into my coffee, figuring it will make it drinkable and aid in keeping me awake.

"The gym." The gym? At six in the morning on the first day of class? Figures. He looks like the type who would get up early and work on his body. Vain bastard.

"Bor-ing," I say, adding cream and giving the coffee a good stir. "I was hoping it would be something a bit more scandalous, something having to do with, say, a blond girl who lives in Gradner Hall and possibly her roommate."

"The treadmill and the bench press are sadly the only

things I've had contact with this morning." He sighs, heading to the refrigerator and taking out a bottle of water. He takes a long drink.

"That's okay," I tell him seriously. "The semester is young. You have plenty of time to create scandals that will keep America hating you."

Drew shuts the refrigerator door and sits down on the stool across from me. "Why does America have to hate me?"

"Isn't that your role?"

"My role?" He frowns and takes another swig of his water. I sigh. Is he really that naive to think that none of us have roles? I mean, it's so obvious. *In the House* is just, like, a bunch of personality stereotypes that rotate on a show-by-show basis.

"Yeah, you know . . . we're all supposed to have roles, aren't we? The slutty one, the gangsta, the innocent shy one, the hot player guy who uses girls for sex, throwing them away when he's done, like some kind of used tissue."

"The hot girl with the long-distance college-basketball-playing boyfriend, navigating the temptations of college while her boyfriend does the same, thousands of miles away."

I frown. Is that my role? The girl with the long-distance boyfriend? I feel a twinge of uneasiness start to rise up inside me, and I push it back down.

"Coffee?" I ask, taking another sip of the warm liquid.

"No thanks." He slides his chair closer to the counter and twirls the cap to his water bottle between his fingers.

"So, Alexandra, if you're not a morning person, then what are you doing up so early? Don't tell me you're one of those girls who has to be up three hours before she goes somewhere just so she can look good."

"How do you know my full name?" I ask. No one calls me Alexandra except my parents when they're pissed. Or my brother Brian, when he wants to annoy me.

"It's on your registration form," he says, looking down at the paper on the counter, where I must have left it last night.

"You shouldn't look at things that don't belong to you," I say, picking up the form and folding it in half.

"Maybe," he agrees.

"And no," I say. "I'm not high maintenance." Well, not really. "I had a fight with my boyfriend."

"Oh." He suddenly looks slightly uncomfortable. "You want to talk about it?"

"Not really." Like I'm really going to discuss my problems with him. I know a ton of guys like Drew, guys who know nothing about what it means to actually be in love. Not to mention the fact that I'm sure Corey would be less than thrilled to hear me talking about him to a complete stranger. "It's actually nothing," I say, thinking about Drew's perception of my role in the house. "Everyone has fights, you know?"

"Sure," Drew says, smiling reassuringly.

"I should get in the shower," I say, getting up and dumping the rest of my coffee in the sink. "I'll see ya later."

"Later, Ally," Drew says, and takes another sip of his water.

* * * * * *

Going to class is like being Lindsay Lohan in the movie *Mean Girls*, only a thousand times worse. Over the past couple of days the rest of the students have arrived on campus, transforming it from an empty place to one that's filled with energy and bodies. As soon as I walk out the door, I'm accosted by people. Kids walking to class, professors with briefcases, people who seem in no way connected to the school and are on campus for no apparent reason but to walk their dogs. The best part? They're all staring at me.

Not that I can blame them. I mean, I have a cameraman following me with a huge handheld. Today my cameraman is Frank, which just adds to the unfortunateness of the situation, since Frank is a huge black man who favors gold jewelry and flannel shirts. The circumference of Frank's neck is roughly that of Fenway Park, so Frank is forced to leave the top of his shirt unbuttoned, exposing an inch of curly black chest hair.

I am now officially A Spectacle. As I walk to the psychology building, where my first class is, people gape at me openly. One girl in a pink skirt says, "Hi, Ally," as I pass by, as if we're old friends. I smile and say hello, even though, for some inexplicable reason, I feel like pulling her hair. Hard. But I can't have America thinking I'm a stuck-up bitch, so I do my best to look happy and approachable.

Thankfully, cameras aren't allowed inside the classrooms, so Frank has to wait outside for me while I'm in class. As I'm walking into the psychology building, I realize the show has totally overshadowed the fact that this is my first day of college. This is serious shit. These grades are going to determine my future. Yeah, I was pretty smart in high school, but what if it was *all a fluke*?

I've heard of things like that happening. People who are smart in high school, then rush off to college with no study skills and no self-control, causing them to be kicked out and scrambling to find somewhere that will take them as a transfer student.

I smooth my hair and pick a seat toward the front of the classroom so that I can absorb everything the professor says, but not *in* the front row, because I've seen *Legally Blonde* and I know how such a move can backfire.

The fact that I've left Frank the cameraman in the hallway happily munching on a glazed doughnut does nothing to diminish the stares. My classmates watch me as I make my way to my seat. Apparently they all know who I am.

At least I look cute. I'm wearing my only pair of Seven jeans (I got them for my birthday from Corey, yay!), and a light blue tank top. My usually wavy dirty blond hair is blown straight, then curled with a big-barreled curling iron so that it falls in soft waves around my shoulders. My brown sandals have a high heel, and are open-toed, showing off my pink toenail polish and my silver toe ring.

I look effortlessly put together. Well, I hope I look effortlessly put together. Knowing what to wear is so freaking hard because I don't want to look like I'm trying too hard, but I'm on TV, for fuck's sake. So I have to look at least *presentable*.

I open my notebook to the first blank page and pretend to write something in an effort to ignore the stares. *Ally Cavanaugh*, I write in bubble letters. *THIS SUCKS*, I write next to it. It starts to make me feel better until I realize the kid behind me is looking over my shoulder, trying to see what I'm writing. Freak. I close my notebook and stare straight ahead until the professor walks into the room.

"Good morning," he says, walking to the lectern, and the class finally shifts their focus. Well, most of them do. There are still a few who continue to stare at me, and I'm reminded of that scene in the movie *First Daughter* starring Katie Holmes. Katie is the president's college-aged daughter, and when she goes to her classes, everyone stares at her. She has to have the Secret Service with her in class and everything, so she's kind of on display.

Anyway, Katie handles the pressure really well and even manages to meet the love of her life, though, unbeknownst to her, he's actually an UNDERCOVER SECRET SERVICE AGENT who's been sent to protect her. This, as one can imagine, becomes quite the situation and serves to raise tons of questions and problems, not the least of which involves whether or not he was pretending to be in love with her the whole time. And is he going to get fired for his improper dealings with the president's daughter? Through the whole thing Katie manages to exude an air of confidence and ambivalence toward the scrutiny she is under, and refuses to be rattled by the revelation that her new love may be a sham.

Well. Except for a small transgression where she skanks

around a little bit, in an effort to make the ex-boyfriend jealous, since for some strange reason, he's still guarding her safety after the truth comes out.

Anyway, the point is, Katie (well, Katie's character—I don't want to get into that whole weird Tom Cruise situation) will be my role model. I can be regal. I can hold my head high. I will look straight ahead, concentrate on the professor, and ignore my nosey classmates.

"Excuse me," the boy sitting behind me says, poking me on the shoulder. He is apparently oblivious to the fact that the professor is talking. When I turn around to look at him, he grins. "Are you going to be a stripper too?"

"Come on, Ally," Grant says, taking a bite of his cheeseburger. Ketchup squirts out of the bun and lands on his plate. "It's not that bad."

"Are you kidding me?" I ask, wondering if it's possible that Grant has recently developed an eye condition that compromises his ability to see. "Look at them! Seriously, it's like one of those dreams where you're walking around naked. Only it's worse, because it's not a dream, and because IT'S ON NATIONAL TELEVISION."

Grant looks around the student union, where we're having lunch. People are staring but pretending not to, except for the ones who are gaping openly. Frank the cameraman sits at the table across from us, the handheld capturing our every move. Once every few minutes he scratches his chest where his necklace rests against his skin.

"Do you think this will be on the show?" Grant asks,

lowering his voice and leaning toward me. "Because I think maybe I should have worn something a little, uh, dressier." He looks down at his button-up navy Banana Republic shirt and khaki pants. Most people around here are dressed like slobs and look like the walking dead. I give Grant a mean look for obsessing over his own clothes when I'm the one with the cameraman recording her every move.

"Sorry," he says, taking a sip of his iced tea and leaning back in his chair. "So tell me about your roommates. Are they all nuts?"

"A stripper, a gangster, a virgin, and a player. Oh, and this morning the player told me that I got on the show so that America could watch my relationship fall apart."

"Are you serious? What an asshole! Is the player hot?" Grant harbors this illusion that every hot guy who sleeps with tons of girls is secretly gay and compensating for their in-the-closetness with their sexual conquests.

"Well, he didn't say that exactly," I admit, spearing a forkful of salad and trying to ignore the two blond girls in the corner who are trying to pretend they're not paying attention to what Grant and I are saying. "He said my role was 'the hot girl in the long-distance relationship who has to watch out for temptation.' Or something. And yeah, I guess he's hot, in one of those preppy jock kind of ways."

"Sweet," Grant says. "So wait, he called you hot?"

"Grant, please! This is serious. Focus."

"Sorry," he mumbles, shoving another fry into his mouth.

"That's not true, Grant, is it?" I ask him. "I'm not on the show just because of Corey, am I?" I lower my voice, mindful of the girls in the corner hanging on my every word.

"Well," Grant says slowly, chewing on his fry, "I don't think that's the *only* reason you're on the show, no. But I'd be lying if I said I don't think it has something to do with it."

Corey and Grant have a love/hate relationship. Actually, Grant has a love/hate relationship with Corey. He likes Corey as a person, but can't fathom the fact that people who meet in high school may just be together forever.

Grant hoards statistical information that's really very depressing, like the fact that the divorce rate for people who get married when they're twenty is a bazillion times higher than that of those who get married in their thirties. I keep trying to tell him that statistics don't mean anything when it comes to true love (and slipping human interest stories about high school sweethearts into his backpack), but he won't listen.

I sigh.

"Ally, come on, you're not that stupid. Think about how many relationships end because of distance, or going off to college." I shoot him another look. "I'm not saying that's going to happen to you," he adds quickly. "But you have to admit it does make for an interesting story."

"Great," I say. "Everyone wants me to end up broken-hearted and miserable so that America can be entertained." I have visions of people across the nation popping popcorn and celebrating the fact that Corey and I are broken up. They'll have, like, office polls or something to pick the date of the big breakup, just like they do for the score of the Super Bowl.

"It's not like that, Ally," Grant says. "You got picked for certain reasons, and your relationship was probably one of them. But who cares? Just because that *might* have had something to do with you getting on the show doesn't mean anything bad is going to happen."

"You're right," I say, staring down the girls in the corner determinedly. "It's not."

NOW

Walking home from lunch with Grant, I started to feel for the first time that maybe coming on the show hadn't been the best idea. I was beginning to realize that blending in was going to be impossible. How was I supposed to meet any cool, new college friends with those stupid cameras following me? Would they even allow cameras at frat parties?

Plus, it was a bit disconcerting to think that my relationship with Corey was the reason I got cast. I mean, it's not like it never crossed my mind that it may have had something to do with it. Mike the producer's eyes had lit up when I mentioned the fact that Corey and I had been together for two years, and he practically had an orgasm when I told him Corey was a college basketball player. But I never thought that could be the *only* reason they would cast me. I mean, how stupid was that? We were strong, we loved each other, and a little distance wasn't going to change that. I was convinced we could outlast this, and whatever else was put in our way. But then Corey met Jen, and everything changed.

THEN

Two weeks later, I'm lying on my bed doing some reading for my psych class when Simone walks slowly into our room, a weird look on her face.

"Something horrible is happening," she says, sitting down on the edge of my bed. She's wearing a light blue hooded sweatshirt and a pair of dark jeans. Her cheeks are red, like she's been out in the cold, even though it's seventy degrees out.

"Wow," I say. "Like what?"

"Yeah," Jasmine echoes from the other side of the room where she's sprawled on her own bed, reading the latest issue of *US Weekly*. "Like what?"

I start imagining all sorts of horrible things. An STD? No, she's a virgin. She wants to leave? That would be such drama, a cast member leaving. I think we'd have to have a house meeting and everything.

"I think I have a crush on James," she says, sounding apologetic.

For a minute, I'm sure I misheard her. On James? Simone? Is she blind and deaf? She's so, I dunno, whimsical and sweet. He's so . . . crazy and kind of ghetto.

Jasmine throws her magazine down and leaps up. "Oh my God! You do not!" She bounds across the room and plops herself down on my bed. My psychology book bounces off and onto the floor, totally forgotten in light of this latest development.

"Wait, hold on," I say. "James? You mean, as in our housemate James?" Is it possible she's talking about another James, someone she's met on campus? And if so, how is she making non–cast member friends so quickly? We've been here almost three weeks, and not one person has made an effort to be friends with me.

"Yeah," she says, looking down at her hands.

"Why?" Jasmine asks gleefully.

"Jasmine!" I say.

"What? Like you're not thinking it?"

I don't say anything, and she gives me a satisfied look.

"I don't know, it's like . . ." She trails off and stares into space for a minute, then plays with her hands nervously. "Last night we ran into each other in the dining hall, and he was just being really sweet, you know? Asking me if I wanted him to get me anything."

Jasmine raises her eyebrows and shoots me a disbelieving look. I can tell we're both thinking the same thing. Getting someone a soda does not a crush make.

"And," Simone says quickly. "He's really smart. Did you know that he's premed?"

James is premed? Wow. I still can't figure out what I want to do with my life and *James* is premed? Note to self: Figure out life plan immediately. "Plus I think he's really hot," she says. It sounds kind of off coming from her, like she shouldn't be using the word "hot." And definitely not while describing James. Although I suppose he is kind of cute, if you're into that whole ghetto fabulous thing.

"Well, whatever," Jasmine says, waving off Simone's explanations. "This is so exciting! Are you going to tell him?"

"Tell him?" Simone looks appalled. "Absolutely not."

"Why not?" Jasmine asks. "We can set up a whole seduction thing. Candles, wine . . . ooh, I have this amazing red skirt you can borrow." She tilts her head to the side and studies Simone thoughtfully. "How do you feel about fishnets?"

Simone looks like she's going to throw up.

"What's wrong?" I ask.

"It's just that I've never really done anything like that before."

"Like what?" Jasmine asks.

"Told a guy I liked him."

"Never?" I ask incredulously. Is she Amish or something? She's from Texas. Do they have Amish people in Texas? Maybe her family moved from Pennsylvania to Texas, and now she's having trouble assimilating to, like, normal society or something. Not that I'm always declaring my love for boys or anything. But I've at least *tried.*

Admittedly, sometimes the results were disastrous, like the time freshman year of high school when I gave Grant permission to tell Luke Sampson I liked him. Grant marched over to Luke's table at lunch and tapped him on the shoulder. I was sitting a few tables away, and although I couldn't hear what was being said, I could see the scene unfolding, which was really just as good, since if someone is telling a boy that you like them, body language speaks volumes.

Grant tapped Luke on the shoulder and whispered something in his ear and I just sat there, acting like I didn't really care, that it was just a little crush, when really Luke was all I'd been able to think about for the past four months. Luke looked at Grant, confused, and Grant pointed at me. Which, as one can probably infer, means that the conversation went something like this:

Grant: Hi, Luke? Ally Cavanaugh wants to go
     out with you.
Luke: Who?
Grant: Ally Cavanaugh.
Luke: Who's Ally Cavanaugh?
Grant: Her, over there. (Points to me.)

Luke Sampson then opened his mouth and stuck his finger down his throat, like he was gagging at the thought of me being his girlfriend. So, yeah, not all putting-yourself-out-there stories have a happy ending, but you have to at least try.

"I haven't really liked that many guys," Simone says, shrugging. "I went to a really small all-girls school, and so I wasn't really exposed to boys."

Geez. Poor girl.

"You should totally tell him," Jasmine says. "I mean, what's the worst that can happen?"

"He doesn't like me?" Simone asks.

"So what?" Jasmine asks. "You've only known him for a few weeks. Besides, you're young, you're cute. If not him, then someone else. That's my motto."

"I don't know," Simone says doubtfully. "I just don't think it's a good idea."

"Suit yourself," Jasmine says, shrugging. She tilts her head and looks at Simone thoughtfully. "But if you change your mind, seriously, black fishnets would be fab."

"Do *not* tell anyone about this," Simone says. She grabs my hand and gives me a pleading look. "Promise me."

"I won't," I vow. We look at Jasmine.

"I won't," she says. "I'm killer at keeping secrets. But you're on a reality TV show, honey." She gestures toward the cameraman in the corner. "There *are* no secrets."

"But we're not allowed to watch the show!" Simone wails.

"But his friends are," Jasmine says, standing up. She stretches her arms behind her and flips her long brown hair over her shoulder.

"You think they'll tell him?" Simone asks, looking more and more like she's going to cry.

Jasmine shrugs. "I don't know," she says. "Now if you'll excuse me, I have a lunch date."

"A lunch date?" I ask. "With who?"

"That guy Dale I met at Hooters," she says, opening her closet and riffling through the contents. She pulls out a long-sleeved black shirt and throws it on her bed.

"The bartender?" I ask. My mind rustles up a vague picture of a guy with dark hair, but I really can't recall much more than that. We went to Hooters right after the whole strip club debacle, and I was more worried about my parents' reaction than I was about Jasmine's potential hookups.

"He's not just a bartender," she says, sounding defensive. "He's a grad student. Philosophy."

"Philosophy?" I ask, frowning. How can someone major in philosophy? Are there copious amounts of jobs out there for philosophers?

"I know. Hot, right? Anyway, we're going to lunch." She's back in her closet flipping through the rows of skirts and halter tops.

"Um, hello?" Simone says softly. "What do I do?"

"I thought you didn't want to do anything!" Jasmine says, sounding exasperated. "You either have to tell him or forget about it."

"I don't know what I want to do!" Simone says. Whoa. She totally needs to calm down.

"Honey, it's okay," I say. "Not a big deal." I glance at the clock near my bed. "I have to go to photography, but we'll formulate a plan when I get back."

"Totally," Jasmine agrees. "I'll be back in an hour, and we'll come up with some sort of totally great idea. Great ideas are my specialty."

Simone and I glance at each other uncertainly.

Jasmine surveys herself in the mirror and holds a pink halter top up to her body. "Do you think showing stomach on a lunch date is too much?"

"Your first assignment will be to take five pictures of love," Professor Lutkiss says, looking at us seriously. It's an hour later, and I'm sitting in photography, trying to keep my eyes open. Professor Lutkiss has this completely monotonous voice that tends to make me sleepy. He also has this really weird gray beard that he's always stroking. It's a little freaky.

I open up my pink planner and write "photo assignment number one: five pictures of love." I seem to have misplaced the syllabus he gave us, so writing assignments down is a plus.

"Do you mean love in the generic sense of the word, or love as a concept?" a boy near the front says. I roll my eyes.

"Well," Professor Lutkiss says. "You could do either, I suppose, as long as the pictures convey love as an idea."

"Convey love as an idea," I write. The only reason I'm taking photography in the first place is because we need a studio art credit to graduate, and it was on the list of courses that qualified. My advisor tried to talk me into ceramics, enticing me with stories of throwing vases and pots on the wheel. He made it seem glamorous and fun, but there was no way I was buying into his scam. I worked with clay sophomore year, when we had to make little statues of wizards. My wizard blew up in the kiln, as did my coil vase, my thrown pot, and a sculpture of a ship that was supposed to represent dreams and their journey.

"You should incorporate the techniques we've been studying so far into your pictures," Professor Lutkiss drones on. "Of course, since this is your first assignment, I'm not expecting you to get everything right, but you should accompany your photos with a brief write-up on why you chose the angles and settings you did."

Yeah, turns out photography is not as easy as just taking pictures. There's aperture, angle, and a bunch of other things to remember while setting up your shot. Plus, we're not allowed to take pictures of whatever we want. We're given assignments. Which doesn't seem very creative to me. Isn't art supposed to be about expressing yourself? How can I express myself when I have to take pictures of what Professor Lutkiss wants us to?

"What about other techniques?" the boy in the front asks. He's wearing the blue parka they gave us all in orientation that says SYRACUSE COLLEGE across the front. "Stuff that we may not have necessarily learned in class, but that we've experimented with in other classes or possibly on our own?"

"You can certainly use other techniques," Professor Lutkiss says, "but don't expect to get extra credit for them."

The boy looks pissed.

"Now," Professor Lutkiss says. "You've all been practicing

loading film into the reels. Today we're going to practice doing it in the blackroom. The blackroom, as you know, is a special room, separate from the darkroom, used only to take your film out of the reels. It is completely dark. Not one speck of light is allowed in. This is particularly important, because if your film is exposed to even one IOTA of light, it will be RUINED. Now, everyone line up."

What a minute, what? Did he say we're going into the blackroom to load film into reels?! This is a disaster. Practicing on old film in the light is fine, because it's fairly easy. But now he wants to usher us into this special little room that is all sealed up with tape to let NO LIGHT IN AT ALL?

I can't even sleep without some sort of night-light, and until about the eighth grade, I slept with the lights in my room on. Like, completely on. Full-blown brightness. I don't like not being able to see what's going on around me. I mean, what if there's a man in there with a knife who wants to brain me? Or what if I'm going blind and I don't know it BECAUSE IT'S TOTALLY DARK?

I slowly take my place in line, hoping the class period will be over before I get a chance to take my turn. No such luck.

Apparently none of my classmates share my fear, because they hop into the room, shutting the door behind them, super happy. They're in and out of the room in about two minutes, ruining my chance at postponing what is certain to be horrible.

When it's my turn, I take a deep breath, walk into the blackroom, and leave the door open just a tad, letting a small beam of light shine onto the floor. No one will notice, right? I start to load the film onto the reel, concentrating on doing it quickly so that—the door shuts. Hard. SOMEONE ON THE OTHER SIDE HAS SHUT THE DOOR. I'm so surprised that I drop the film in my hand. Shit.

Okay, don't panic. I fall to the floor and run my hands around desperately, trying to find the strip of film. I'm in there for so long that someone knocks on the door, asking me if I'm all right. I hear someone else say, "I think she fell."

"I'm okay," I yell back, thanking God the cameras are not allowed in class. "I just, um, dropped my film. But don't worry." I slide my hands over the floor faster, groping desperately for the film. All I can feel is the grit and grime of the floor. I'm about to start having a panic attack when the door to the blackroom opens.

"Oh my God, she's fainted!" a blond girl at the front of the throng screeches when she sees me.

"No, I didn't," I say, spotting the length of film. I scoop it off the floor and stand up, brushing my hands against each other in an attempt to dislodge some of the filth that's transferred itself onto my skin.

"Now this," Professor Lutkiss says, sweeping his hand toward me—I'm assuming that by "this" he means me and my current situation, which, as anyone would agree, can only be characterized as unfortunate—"is why people need to be very, very careful about loading their film onto their reels properly. Young lady, what is your name?"

The whole class stares. "Ally," I mumble, looking at the floor.

"If Ally had been loading real film, pictures she had spent *hours* taking and creating, she would have done all that work for nothing. Dropping her film on the floor could have made scratches on the prints, or distorted the images. Opening the door would have ruined the film altogether." I look down at the strip of film in my hand, which is covered in dirt and has several creases running through it. Thank God it wasn't real pictures. Although I can't imagine spending *hours* taking a few snapshots. I mean, point, click, there's your picture. Even with picking your angles and all that, why would it take hours? I think Professor Lutkiss might be acting a tad over-dramatic.

By the time he dismisses us, I can't wait to get back to the house, change into comfy clothes, and watch Lifetime movies or something equally mindless. I've been totally scandalized by this whole experience—he really didn't have to single me out in front of the whole class. I mean, how embarrassing and unnecessary. Teachers are supposed to *build* your self-esteem, aren't they? Maybe once they become professors that's not, like, a rule anymore. Because in *Legally Blonde,* those teachers could be a real pain in the ass.

I'm sliding my photography notebook into my bag (I don't know why I bother to take notes—as soon as the lights go off, I just get all fucked up) when one of the girls in my class approaches me.

"Hey," she says. "You're Ally, right?" She's wearing a

red sleeveless shirt and low-rise jeans. She shifts the books in her arms, and her shirt rises up, revealing a silver belly button ring.

"Yeah," I say warily, and slide my messenger bag over my shoulder. I'm not sure if she knows my name because of the show, or because I was just made a fool of. Either way, we're not off to a good start.

"I just wanted to tell you that I wouldn't worry about what just happened in there." She smiles and pushes her light brown hair off her face. "My friend had Professor Lutkiss last semester, and that's just the way he is. He's not, like, trying to be a dick or anything."

"Well, that's good to know. I mean, I'd hate to think that my grade was already screwed. I'd like to earn my D myself."

She laughs, one of those cute little-girl laughs. "So you're a sophomore, then?" I ask her, shifting my bag on my shoulder.

"Yeah. I'm sorry, I should have introduced myself. I'm Kelly. Kelly Crisp." She smiles again and starts to walk out of the classroom. "Come on," she says, looking over her shoulder. "I'll walk with you."

"Oh," I say, taken aback that someone is actually being nice to me. Over the past few weeks, as the initial novelty of seeing me wore off, people pretty much just started ignoring me. I'm not sure what's worse, having people stare, or having people not even look at me. I mean, I would at least like to make *some* friends besides Grant. "Um, okay."

Fuck. Now what? Frank the cameraman is waiting for me right outside the door. Even if this girl knows I'm on the show, what am I supposed to say? 'Oh sorry, don't mind him, that's just my cameraman who follows me everywhere. By the way, if they decide to air this, you're going to have to sign a release.' I look around wildly for a back door or something that we can slip out of. Of course there's nothing. This is college, not some spy movie. Damn. How do those *Real World* kids do it? They're always ditching their cameras and messing around behind their producers' backs.

"You coming?" Kelly asks, stopping.

"Sure," I say warily, following her out the door. Frank's sitting on a bench outside. He quickly extinguishes the cigarette he's smoking and throws it into a nearby trash can. He hoists the handheld back onto his shoulder and falls into step behind me and Kelly.

"So where do you live?" I ask Kelly, walking fast and hoping that Frank will get the message. He doesn't, and just walks faster. After a few seconds, his breath starts coming in great gasps, like it's hard for him to keep up. Reluctantly, I slow down, imagining the chaos that will ensue if my cameraman has a heart attack in the middle of the quad.

"Ontario Hall. In a suite, which is cool. And I also got to pick my roommate." She pushes her hair behind her ears. "You should have seen the freak I had to live with last year. But I guess you probably know all about that," she says, smiling and tilting her head toward Frank.

"Yeah," I say, not sure if this is a dig or not.

"Does that ever get annoying?" she asks.

"Kind of, at first," I admit. "But the weird thing now is that I don't even really notice it. It's like he's just become a part of me."

"That's cool," she says, slowing down as we come up on her residence hall. "Hey, listen, if you ever need any help with your photography, I'm all about it. I mean, not that you're bad or anything," she adds quickly. "It's just that I know getting used to college classes can be hard."

"That'd be great," I say honestly.

"So I'll see you next class," she says. "Maybe we can get lunch or something. Meeting people sucks when you're a freshman, and it's probably even harder with . . . you know." She rolls her eyes to show it doesn't bother her.

Kelly smiles, and I smile back. Yay! My first out-of-the-house, non-Grant friend! And to think it all happened because my professor humiliated me.

When I walk into the house, Simone and Jasmine are in the kitchen. Simone's stirring something in a huge tainless-steel bowl, and Jasmine's looking over her shoulder. The counter is strewn with mixing bowls, flour, vanilla, sugar, and other baking necessities.

"Good," she says, watching Simone stir. "Make sure you get all of it, even the flour that's on the side of the pan."

"Whatcha guys doin'?" I ask, sitting down at the counter and looking at the recipe book that's open to a picture of chocolate peanut butter cookies.

"Making cookies," Simone says, and then flushes. She uses her wrist to push a stray auburn curl off her forehead.

"Mmm," I say, inhaling the scent of the cookie dough. "What's the occasion?" I think I've made cookies maybe, like, once in my life. It was last year when the basketball team had a bake sale and this girl Katie who was going out with Corey's best friend Rob said she was going to make three hundred pecan somethings and then Rob said, "Oh, Katie, you're the best girlfriend." Corey gave me this pointed look, so I felt like I had to contribute something. I made the Tollhouse chocolate chip cookies from the recipe on the chocolate chip bag. Being domestic is so overrated. Nobody needs a girl that can cook anymore. That's why there are so many good takeout places.

"She's making them for James," Jasmine reports. She's wearing a light yellow apron with pink and purple butterflies splashed all over it. Her hair is tied back messily, and she's barefoot. She looks effortlessly beautiful, and I wonder how it is that she doesn't have a boyfriend and how she can be wasting her time working at Hooters. She could be a real model.

"How sweet," I say, not sure if baking cookies for James is going to work. Since we've been here, James has hardly ever been home, preferring to stay out partying and using his fake ID to get into bars. During the little time he *is* at the house, I've seen him with no less than three different girls.

It doesn't seem like his stomach would be the way to his heart. Some marijuana might work. Or a new set of rims.

Unless they're pot brownies. I sniff the air experimentally and scan the counter for empty Baggies. Nothing.

Jasmine wipes her hands on her apron and starts to grease a cookie sheet. "Now, the secret to a good cookie is in the way you flour the cookie sheet," she says. "It's all in the flour."

"Is that your apron?" I ask her.

She looks down at it. "Well, I'm wearing it, so . . . yeah, I guess it would be mine."

"No, I mean, did you bring it from home?"

"Of course I brought it from home. What did you think, the show just provides butterflied aprons for us to use at our leisure?"

I giggle. "How was your lunch?" I ask her.

"Good," she says, grabbing a paper towel and wiping up some flour that spilled onto the counter. "He had to get back to work, though, so we're having dinner later."

"Oooh, twice in one day," I say. "Interesting." I reach over the mixing bowls and grab a handful of chocolate chips out of the bag.

"Yeah," Simone says. "What happened to 'if not him then someone else.'"

"Yeah," I say, raising my eyebrows. I settle into one of the stools near the counter and kick off my shoes. "What happened to that?"

"Knock it off!" Jasmine says. "It's not like that. It's more like, if not lunch, then why not dinner? And he just happened to be offering. Like I'm going to say no to a free meal."

"So lame," I say, rolling my eyes. I reach for another

handful of chocolate chips. "What if some disgusting fat guy wanted to buy you a free meal? You're only going because he's hot."

"And because you like him," Simone adds helpfully.

"*Anyway,*" Jasmine says, changing the subject. "Are you going to tell James that you made these for him? Or are you going to act like you have no idea they're his favorites?" She slides two of the cookie sheets into the oven, the back of her shirt sliding up under her apron to reveal a strip of tan skin under her mike pack.

"I don't know," Simone says, biting her lip. "I hadn't thought about it." She looks fearfully at the cookies as if they're snakes.

"Sweetie, you need to loosen up a little bit," I tell her. "Calm down a little." I pop some more chocolate chips into my mouth. I offer her one, but she shakes her head.

"You can't tell him you *knew*," I say, jumping off my stool and heading to the refrigerator for a glass of milk. "It will make it seem more like you're the one for him if you just *happened* to make his favorite cookies. I mean, what are the chances? It's like destiny."

"Yeah, but if she tells him she made them since she knew they were his favorite, she seems thoughtful and sweet. And it gives him the idea that she might be interested in more than a friendship," Jasmine says.

"How did you know they were his favorites?" I ask Simone. I sit back down at the counter and take a sip of my milk. "Did he tell you? Or did you overhear it?"

"Neither," Simone says, looking like this whole debate

is too much for her to take. She pulls out her hair tie and shakes her long red hair so that it cascades over her shoulders. "I read it on his casting application."

"How'd you get to see his casting application?" I ask.

"It's online."

"It is? Are all our casting applications online?" I furiously rack my brain trying to remember if I wrote anything completely ridiculous on mine. I feel somewhat relieved when I remember my phone sex story and the fact that I offered to sleep with a director were confined to verbal exchanges.

"Sure," Jasmine says, pulling off her apron and tossing it on the counter. "Along with our pictures, bios, message boards, fan sites—you name it."

"Message boards?"

"Yeah."

"What are they saying about me?" I ask, suddenly curious. I can't believe that the thought of people talking about me online hasn't crossed my mind. It's probably because we're not allowed to use instant messenger while we're here, since production doesn't want any secret IM convos covering up something that may be interesting to the viewers and make for good ratings. With no instant messenger access, I haven't really had too much interest in the computer.

But now I start to imagine all these fan sites and message boards dedicated to me, sites done in pink and aqua (since I put those down as my favorite colors on my application) that say things like "Welcome to the fan site of Ally Cavanaugh, *In the House: Freshman Year.*" Then they'll have all these nice things about me, like about how it was so generous of me to go to the strip club with Jasmine on our first day even though I knew my family probably wouldn't approve. They'll also express their displeasure for the student body of Syracuse College for being so mean to me and not making an effort to get to know my wonderful, fabulous self. These sites will be run by the girl fans, but a few guy fans will have them too. On these sites I'll be called a "hottie with a body," and boys will bemoan the fact that I have a boyfriend and call Corey mean names.

"I don't know, Ally," Jasmine says, sounding a little annoyed. "Get online if you want to read about yourself. But I'm warning you, it's not all nice." It isn't?

"How do you know?"

"Because I read the stuff about me." Oh. Well, of course they're going to say bad things about Jasmine. She's a stripper. Well, a stripper turned Hooters girl. I mean, hello. People hear "stripper" and make a snap judgment about her sluttiness, whether or not it's true. Not to mention the fact that Jasmine's beautiful, and so people are going to hate her just on principle.

"Um, hello, guys?" Simone asks softly, reminding us that the conversation was originally about her.

"Oh, right." I consider pointing out the fact that Sam the cameraman is recording this whole conversation, so it's very likely James will hear about it from one of his friends that watches the show, making all this obsessing obsolete. I don't want to scare Simone, though, so I keep my mouth shut. "Well, the fact that you found out online settles it. He will inevitably ask you how you knew they were his favorite, and then you will have to tell him, and he'll think you're a stalker."

I look to Jasmine for confirmation. She nods her head. "Agreed."

That settled, I grab one last handful of chocolate chips, grab my milk, and head to the computer to find out what the world is saying about me.

NOW

Ignorance is bliss. That's all I'm saying.

THEN

I settle into the computer chair in the living room, thankful no one's using it. We have one computer for everyone in the house to use and we weren't allowed to bring our own computers from home. Just another way the show controls every single aspect of our lives.

I decide to check my email before stalking myself online. Two new emails! Yay! Oh. Busty sluts stripping and a Viagra advertisement. Great. I was hoping I'd have an email from Corey, but I should have known better. Corey doesn't believe in emailing. He thinks that if you have time to sit down and write an email, you might as well just call the person. I guess it makes some sense. But it would have been nice.

I type Google.com into the Internet address bar and then do a search for "In the House message boards." The first link site that pops up is the official YTV site, where apparently there's cast bios, applications, photos, links to fan sites, and message boards.

I click on the link to the message board, which prompts me to create a screen name and enter a valid email address. Great. Now I have to think up an alias. I chose Natalie19, since I've always wanted my name to be Natalie. I was going to be Natalie18, since that's my age, but I figured 19 would throw people off the track. You know, like, this can definitely not be Ally pretending to be Natalie, because Ally is eighteen and Natalie is obviously nineteen. Whatever, it makes sense.

The message boards are divided into topics. Each of us has our own thread, labeled with our first name. Fun! I click on the one that says "Ally." My thread is divided even further into subtopics, like "Appearance," "Her Boyfriend," "The Strip Club."

I click on the one that says "Appearance." It starts off well, but soon takes a drastic turn for the worse.

I think Ally looked so cute on her first day of school. She is my favorite member of In the House.

—princessval1020

I love princessval! I wish she went to my school.

Ally's pathetic. She should stop whining so much and get to the gym. She looks like she could tone up her ass a little.

—turbo1

What? Get to the gym? Tone up a little? I'm a size seven! A size seven is NOT fat. Is it? The camera adds ten pounds. At least. Maybe "Appearance" isn't the best thread for me to start with.

I click on the thread marked "Her Boyfriend."

Ally and Corey are so cute! I wish I had a boyfriend!
—princessval1020

Seriously, who is this girl? I want to buy her a present.

Ally should get together with Drew. I think they would be so cool together. He's a major hottie! I know she has a boyfriend, but she needs to be with a sweetie, and Drew is so sweet!
—JanaGirl99

Is she stupid? Drew is not sweet.

I go to school with Ally's boyfriend Corey at the University of Miami. And just so everyone knows, Corey is NOT all that sweet. He's kind of a jerk. He thinks he's so cool just because he plays basketball. And besides, everyone knows he's cheating on Ally with this girl named Jen who lives on his floor.
—cheerlead23

My heart stops. It is not beating. I can't breathe for

what seems like six hours. Blood is probably backing up in my lungs. I take a deep breath. It's okay, I tell myself. There's no way it's true. This girl probably doesn't even *go* to Miami, and she's making it up to start drama on the message boards. I mean, it's *obviously* not true. Yeah, Corey was a little sketched about the whole strip club thing, but he's fine now. I promised to give him advance warning on any other scandals that might pop up, and now everything's cool. This has obviously been posted by some sort of psycho attention whore who has nothing better to do. I keep reading.

> Oh, yeah, that one blond girl Jen he's always with. She's in my lit class and he's always waiting for her afterward. She's a hot piece of ass. I don't blame him for getting a little extra on the side, LOL.
>
> —MiamiHurricanezRule

Oh my God. This is not happening. My stomach starts churning, and I close out the Web site, not wanting to read anymore. I feel like I'm going to throw up, and I lean back in the computer chair, taking deep breaths and trying to calm my heart, which has apparently decided to start beating again, only this time at an absurdly fast rate. When I open my eyes, I see Frank the cameraman standing in the corner, the handheld focused on my face.

God. Can he leave me alone for, like, one freaking minute? Whatever. This can be taken care of in, like, two seconds. I'll just call Corey, he'll tell me that he knows no such Jen slut, and I can forget about it. It's stupid to even be *thinking* about it, because Corey would never, ever cheat on me. Obviously the losers on the message boards have nothing better to do than start rumors and try to create scandal. But I'm not going to fall for it. I will hold my head high and ignore them. If Paris Hilton can get through that whole sex tape thing, I can surely handle some stupid losers on the Internet.

I try Corey on his dorm phone, but he doesn't answer. His cell goes to voice mail, and I leave him a message telling him to call me back as soon as he gets it, that I'm having a bit of an emergency.

I disconnect, then pick back up and dial Grant.

"Grant!" I practically scream when he answers. "You're never going to believe it!" I'm hysterical. Somewhere over the last five minutes I have become hysterical.

"Me first!" Grant shrieks back. "I met a guy! His name is Brett!"

"Grant, please, no time for your little anecdotes starring you as the hot stud. This is serious."

"Oh my, God, Ally, what's wrong?" Grant asks, obviously alarmed that I'm cutting him off while he's talking about himself. A huge staple of our friendship is the fact that I'm usually perfectly content for him to rattle on about anything and everything for hours on end.

"I think Corey is cheating on me," I say. Something about saying the word "cheat" out loud makes me feel sick, and I wonder if I should put my head down between my legs so that I don't faint.

"No!" Grant gasps, probably more surprised by the fact that I'm willing to even entertain this possibility than the fact that Corey might possibly be cheating. "What happened? How do you know?"

I give him the lowdown, all the while getting more panicky.

"Oh," Grant says when I'm done, sounding slightly disappointed. "Is that all?"

"Is that all? IS THAT ALL?" I scream. "I'm having my first experience with infidelity and you say 'Is that all?'" Why am I friends with Grant again?

"No, no, that's not what I meant," he says, his tone softening. "I just mean I wouldn't worry too much about it. It's an Internet message board, Ally. There's no, um, censorship on those things. No filters. I mean, you were on it pretending to be some chick named Natalie."

Hmm.

"True," I say, forgiving him for freaking me out.

"It's probably just someone looking to cause trouble."

"That's what I thought too!"

"You're probably going to start getting a lot of that stuff now, Ally. It's like celebrities in tabloids. You can't let it affect you. Now go try Corey again."

"Okay," I say, sighing. "Hey, Grant? Thanks."

"No problem," he says.

Over the next six hours, I call Corey eleven times, leave three more messages, eat twenty-seven cookies, and read over those two posts on the message boards sixteen times. At around nine o'clock, I make a cup of tea, figuring I'll watch Lifetime movies while I wait for Corey to call me back. But Jasmine's watching something on the TV in our room for a class, and when I wander into the living room, Drew's watching ESPN.

"Um, Drew? How long is this going to be on?" I say slowly, being careful not to let an edge creep into my voice. Must remain calm. Do not take bad day out on innocent roommate, causing America to think you are psycho, temperamental bitch.

"How long is it going to be on? Or how long am I going to be watching it?" he says, smiling. He's wearing a navy blue Abercrombie shirt, and his hair is wet, like he just got out of the shower.

"How long are you going to be watching it?" I sit down on the couch next to him and pull the blanket that's hanging over the back of the couch down over my legs. It's seventy degrees outside, but for some reason the air conditioning in this house is always cranked up. Jasmine says it's because they want to get us cold so that we'll all get into the hot tub and create some scandals.

"I was going to be watching it until you arrived and gave us something much more entertaining to watch," he says, leaning back into the cushions and tossing me the remote. What does he mean, *us*? How can I watch Lifetime movies with Drew sitting next to me? Movies with titles like *Her Violent Secret* and *The Doctor's Baby* do not make for good viewing pleasure with a guy. That's why it's television for *women*.

"Uh, thanks," I say, taking the remote and turning to the guide channel.

"No problem." There's an awkward silence while we watch the TV listings slide up the screen. "You okay? You seem kind of quiet."

"Bad day," I tell him, squirming under the blanket.

"Ya wanna talk about it?" he asks, turning his body toward me on the couch. What is up with this kid and wanting to talk about shit? Is he Dr. Phil?

"Oh, it's no big deal, really. I'm going to fail photography because I'm afraid of the dark, my boyfriend is probably cheating on me with some slut named Jen, and I can't even ask him about it because he has his cell phone off. Oh, and I'm never going to make any friends here because I'm a freak with a camera following her all the time. But besides that, I'm great," I say brightly.

Drew laughs, revealing even, white teeth.

"I wasn't trying to be witty," I say grumpily, pulling a pillow from behind my back and placing it behind my head.

"I know, I'm sorry, I wasn't laughing at you," Drew says, continuing to laugh. I raise my eyebrows. "I mean, I wasn't laughing at your problems. It's just funny how you said that." He turns serious. "Okay, one thing at a time. Let's start with the photography issue, because that seems like it would be the easiest to fix. What exactly is the problem?"

"We have to load our film into these little black

canisters. I forget what they're called. Reels or something? You know, to develop them? Only we have to do it in complete darkness, and I'm scared of the dark. Everyone else in the class can do it in, like, five seconds. I end up exposing the fake film and getting yelled at."

Drew laughs again.

"It's not funny!" I say again, starting to get exasperated. Like I said before, if there's one thing I hate, it's being laughed at. I take the couch pillow from behind my head and throw it at him, only half joking.

"Okay, okay, I'm sorry," he says, throwing up his hands in mock surrender. "I'm not laughing at you, I swear. It's just that I used to have the same problem. I took photography freshman year of high school, and I was always exposing my film by accident. All my pictures always came out black or with a big white smear through them or something. I had to take it pass/fail."

I look at him skeptically.

"Why are you looking at me like that?'

"Because it just seems weird that you would have the exact same problem I do," I tell him. "I mean, what are the chances?"

"Probably pretty good," he says, shifting on the couch. "I mean, people's problems aren't really all that unique, when you think about it. It just seems that way when you're going through them." He runs his hand through his hair and looks at me. He has a small scar on his chin, which, for some reason, makes him look hotter than he already is.

"I guess," I say. "But I don't know many guys that are afraid of the dark."

"Ahh, but that's the thing," he says. "I'm not afraid of the dark. I just had trouble loading the film into the reel."

"So what'd you do?"

"I told you, I took it pass/fail. And my dad taught me a trick that helped a lot."

"Lucky," I say. "Is your dad a photographer?"

"He used to be," he said. "He died in a car accident when I was fifteen."

His voice changes when he says it, and I swallow hard. "Oh," I say. "I'm sorry." It sounds corny, even to me, but I don't know what else to say. "Were you guys close? Oh, my God," I rush on, "I'm so sorry, that sounds so stupid."

"Nah, it's okay," he says. "We were close. He was a great guy."

"Did you guys look alike?" I ask.

He smiles. "We did, actually," he says. "No one's ever asked me that before." There's a pause as I try to rack my brain for something else to say.

"So, what's the deal with the boy?" Drew says, changing the subject. He leans back against the couch and drapes his arm over the top of it. I try not to show my relief. "Trouble in paradise?"

"Just something stupid," I say. "I read something about him and some other girl on one of the message boards."

"Message boards?" he asks.

"Yeah, online. They have message boards about the cast members."

"Really? So people we don't even know are talking about us?" he asks, sounding amused at the obvious absurdity of this. I smile. Now that I think about it, it IS kind of ridiculous.

"I know. Hot, right?"

"Totally. So you read something about your boy that you didn't like?" He frowns and looks at me seriously. His eyes are really blue. I wonder if he wears contacts.

"Yeah, about how he's hooking up with another girl."

"Wow," he says. "That's rough. But I'm sure it's nothing. You guys have been together for a while, right?"

"Yeah."

"And you trust him?"

"Completely."

"So then don't worry about it, right?" He reaches over and takes the remote out of my hand. "Now that your crises have been taken care of, you've lost the right to have control of the remote." When his hand touches mine, an electric current passes through my body. Great. Not only is my boyfriend cheating on me, I'm compensating for it by going completely insane.

"Yo, Ally!" James yells from the other room before I can decide if it would be appropriate to ask Drew about the Lifetime movies. "Your man's on the phone!"

Oh, thank God. I jump up from the couch and race to the phone.

"Yo, chill, girl," James says as I snatch the phone out

of his hand. "Where's the fire, baby?" He's wearing a shirt that says "outta my way or you're gonna get played." I roll my eyes and wait for him to move past me, back to his room. Mental note: Ask Simone what she sees in James, in order to learn some of his good qualities and therefore not be so judgmental.

"Corey?" I say, once James has left the immediate area.

"Why did that guy just call you 'baby'?" he demands.

"'Cause he calls everyone that. Listen, I need to talk to you about something," I say, the nausea coming on full force. I collapse into the chair by the phone and take a deep breath. Now that Corey's finally on the line, I have no idea what to say to him. I mean, how do you ask your boyfriend if he's cheating on you? Frank moves around in front of my face, the red light on the camera blinking at me steadily.

"What is it?" Corey asks.

"What?"

"What do you have to talk to me about?" Corey asks, sounding impatient.

"It's about something that I heard today," I say, the words coming out slowly, like I'm talking through a mouthful of peanut butter. I take a deep breath and decide to just go for it. "Corey, who's Jen?"

Silence. At this point, I expected Corey to say something like, "Jen? I don't know. Jen who?" or "Jen? I have a cousin named Jen, I think, who goes to Georgia Tech," or "Jen? Like Jen Aniston?" or something that basically shows he has no clue what I'm talking about. But silence is not good. Silence is almost as good as saying, "Oh, Jen. She's just one of those tanned strumpets you've been imagining that I'm out clubbing with every night. Only she's not imaginary after all. The only part you got wrong was her name."

"She's a girl who lives on my floor. A friend," he says, emphasizing the word "friend," which immediately sends up red flags. Nobody goes out of their way to say someone's a "friend" unless they're really not.

"Oh," I say carefully. "A friend."

"Yeah," Corey says, his voice becoming more solid. "She lives on my floor. A friend." Can he stop saying the fucking word friend? "How do you know about her, anyway?"

"I read about her. Online."

"You read about her online?"

"Yeah. On the *In the House* message boards. They said you and some Jen girl were hanging out a lot."

"I would hardly call it a lot," he says, laughing like it's totally ridiculous. "She just lives in my dorm, that's all. Actually, I think she hooked up with one of the guys on my team last night." He lowers his voice like he's letting me in on a secret. "If you want to know the truth, I think she might be kind of a headcase."

"A headcase?" I ask. A stalker headcase? Or just, like, one of those people that you can tell isn't all there? The gyrating tanned goddess gets replaced by a vision of a girl writhing around on a bed in a straight-jacket. "What sort of a headcase?"

"Just, like, a basketball groupie. You know," he says, "one

of those girls who wants to sleep with anyone that's on the team, or make friends with anyone who can get them closer to the team." The evil strumpet pops back into my mind, only this time she's holding a sign that says GO HURRICANES! #11 and her skanky clothes are replaced with Corey's orange and green basketball jersey.

"Is that supposed to be comforting?" I ask. "That this girl wants to have sex with anything on the team?"

"It is if you know the kind of person I am," Corey says. "Come on, Ally, what's wrong with you? You know I would never go for a basketball groupie."

"Oh, gee, thanks," I say, rolling my eyes even though I know he can't see me. "You wouldn't go for her because she's a basketball groupie and not because you're in love with me."

"God, Ally, what is your problem? Why are you acting so insecure all of a sudden? You never used to be like this. Ever." I wrap the phone cord around my finger and consider the question. The thing is, Corey's right. I've never been one of those girls who has to know where her boyfriend is at all times and freaks out if he's a few minutes late calling. But maybe that was because Corey and I were always together. I never had to worry about what he was doing, because I knew. I was with him.

"I know," I say, feeling my eyes fill up with tears. "I just miss you, that's all. This isn't easy for me. Being away from you, you know?"

"I know," Corey says, his voice softening. "It's not easy

for me, either. But I'm going to be there next month. Just hang in there, okay, Al? Everything's going to be okay, I promise."

And even though I want to believe him, I still cry myself to sleep that night.

THEN

Later that week, in an effort to become more social, and also to get my mind off the whole Corey thing, I invite Kelly from photography over to the house to hang out. I give her the tour, and she makes the requisite "this house is so amazing" remarks without sounding jealous, which I think is really cool.

When we get back to the living room, Jasmine and Simone are already there, watching TV and eating Oreos.

"Hey," Jasmine says. "We're just getting ready to watch a movie off On Demand." She's sprawled out on the couch, her dark hair in ringlets. She's wearing a pair of tight black pants with a wide silver belt, and a button-up black shirt that shows off her cleavage. She looks like she's going to a party.

"You guys have On Demand?" Kelly asks, plopping

down on the couch next to her. "I'm Kelly," she says, smiling. "You're Jasmine, right? I think you're in my bio lab."

"Oh, I'm sorry. I'm such a spazz," I say. "Kelly, this is Jasmine and Simone. Jasmine and Simone, this is my friend Kelly."

"Hey," Simone says softly from the corner.

"Yes, we have On Demand *and* Pay-Per-View," Jasmine says, shooting Kelly a look. Jasmine gets really cranky when anyone who's not a cast member comes over. Mainly because James had some sort of hot tub party the other night that got pretty loud. Jasmine had a big test the next day, and she couldn't sleep, so they had this huge blowout fight at, like, two in the morning. She called his friends dirty (which they kind of were—like, they looked like their jaunt in the hot tub was the first contact with water they'd had in a while). James told her to chill out, that it was his house, too, and he could have friends over if he wanted. The next day Jasmine spent an hour cleaning out the tub with disinfectant.

"You're so lucky," Kelly says, not noticing the look Jasmine's giving her. She grabs an Oreo off the plate on the table. "We don't get On Demand in the dorms." She breaks her cookie apart and licks the icing off one half. Jasmine rolls her eyes behind Kelly's back.

"Let's pick something to watch," I say quickly, grabbing the remote and scanning through the On Demand movie choices. "We'll vote. Simone?"

Silence.

"Simone?" I look over to where she's sitting, in one of

the plush armchairs. She has it in recline mode, her red hair making a curly halo down the back of the chair.

"Yeah?" she asks, looking up. She blinks, like the light is hurting her eyes.

"Were you sleeping?" I giggle.

"Oh no, sorry, I was, um, thinking about something," she mumbles, a flush lighting up her cheeks. When is this girl *not* blushing?

"James." Jasmine rolls her eyes again.

"No way. You have a crush on James?" Kelly asks, looking intrigued. She leans forward, eager for details.

"Yeah," Simone admits, blushing. "Just a small one."

"She made him cookies," I report.

"He said he loved them," Jasmine says.

"She wants to marry him," I say.

"And have all his babies." Jasmine.

"At least five." Me.

"So what's the deal?" Kelly asks. She bites into the outside part of the cookie and chews thoughtfully.

"What do you mean?" Simone asks.

"Are you going to ask him out?"

"I don't know," she says.

"Ooh," I say, lying back on the couch and letting my hair fall over the side. "Before, it was a 'definitely not.' Now we've upgraded to an 'I don't know.'"

"What about you?" Kelly asks Jasmine. "Any hot prospects?"

"No," Jasmine says. "I make it my policy not to get involved with just one guy. It's bad for my emotional state." She pushes her hair back from her face and looks haughty.

"Oh my God, you are such a liar!" I say, rolling my eyes at her for once, instead of the other way around. "You had two dates in one day with the same guy last week." I turn to Kelly. "She's lying. She's, like, in love with this guy named Dale."

"I am not!" Jasmine protests. "We only hung out a couple of times."

"Whateeever," I sing, knowing full well that she's seen him at least three times since then.

"Whateeever is right," she says, picking one of the throw pillows off the sofa and throwing it at me. "I'm not looking for a relationship right now." She looks satisfied.

"Really?" Simone says innocently. "That's funny, because hanging out with someone all the time certainly sounds like a relationship to me."

Kelly and I giggle.

"How did we start talking about me, anyway?" Jasmine says. "Simone's the one slaving away in the kitchen for true love, and Ally's the one who's practically married."

"Oooh, yeah, how *are* things with Corey?" Kelly asks, turning her attention toward me. Whoa. It's weird, hearing her ask me about Corey when I've never mentioned him to her. But, duh, I mean, I'm sure she watches the show.

"Oh," Kelly says quickly, noticing the look on my face. "I'm sorry, I didn't mean to—"

"No, it's fine," I say, ignoring the look Jasmine shoots me

from across the living room. "Things with Corey are great." I don't mention the whole Jen/message board debacle. I'm not sure if they've shown that yet, and it's really the last thing I want to talk about. Besides, for the most part, things with Corey *are* fine. There *is* a little part of me that feels like something isn't right. A tiny part. Miniscule, even. But I'm sure that's just because he's not here with me.

"Are you still worried about the Jen thing?" Kelly asks. So much for them not showing it yet. I'm trying to forget about the whole Jen thing. I'm sure it was just one of those crazy misunderstandings. Besides, what choice do I have? Thinking about it is just going to drive me crazy. Plus, what if I cause some sort of self-fulfilling prophecy, where Corey isn't really cheating on me, but if I start *thinking* he is, that will somehow make him do it?

Don't get me wrong, it's not *easy* to forget about it or anything—I spent a few days last week harboring a couple of borderline psychotic fantasies, including one where I somehow befriend a Miami University student who then becomes my personal undercover spy and reports back to me on all of Corey's activities. But I'm getting better.

Besides, Corey will be visiting in a few weeks, and then everything will be back to normal.

The four of us order pizza and spend the rest of the night watching movies on the flat-screen TV. I end up falling asleep on the couch at a little after midnight, and I'm still there when Drew comes in from the gym at around seven the next morning. The sound of the door opening wakes me, and I look around groggily.

Drew takes in my messed-up hair, my wrinkled clothes, and my weary expression.

"You drunk?" he asks, moving closer and peering at my face carefully.

"No, I'm not *drunk*," I say, rolling over.

"Rough night?" he asks. He unzips his gym bag and pulls out a bottle of water.

"Not really," I admit, laying my head back down. "Just too lazy to move into my bed."

"I hear ya," he says. He takes a swig of his water and sits down on the couch by my feet.

"Do you mind?" I ask. "Some people are sleeping. Besides, you're all sweaty." I wrinkle my nose at him to convey my disgust. In reality, he's not all that sweaty. He's wearing mesh shorts and a gray T-shirt with the Nike symbol on the front. His hair's glistening a little bit, but other than that, he seems clean. Well, as clean as you can be after you've just worked out.

"I don't mind," Drew says, grinning. "And it's seven o'clock. Time to get up and face the day," he says, grabbing one of my toes under the blanket. A wave of heat starts in my toe and moves its way up my body.

"Quit it," I say, moving my foot away. "Besides, I don't want to get up and face the day. I have to work on my photography project and so I'd prefer the start of this day be put off as long as possible." I bury my head in my pillow and try to ignore my stomach, which for some reason has decided this would be a great time to develop butterflies.

"Ahh, that's right. The whole *Creature of the Black*

Lagoon thing," he says easily, taking another drink of water. There's condensation on the outside of the bottle, and he looks like he belongs in one of those sports drink commercials, where the buff hottie scales some ridiculously high mountain or makes the winning shot in the hockey game and then rehydrates himself with a huge gulp of electrolytes. I look away so that he doesn't think I'm staring.

"What *Creature of the Black Lagoon* thing?" I ask, trying to sound disgruntled.

"Isn't that what you're afraid of? That the Creature of the Black Lagoon is going to get you in the blackroom?"

"Very funny." Why did I ever tell him I was afraid of the dark? Must have been a major moment of weakness. "And it's not the Creature from the Black Lagoon, FYI. It's more like that guy with the mask from Halloween."

"Right," Drew says. "So you want some help?"

"No." Yes.

"Oh, come on," he says, screwing the top back on his water and standing up. "What time are you going?"

"Going where?"

"To the photo lab," he says. He stretches his arms behind him.

"I'm not," I say. "I haven't even taken the pictures yet."

"You haven't taken the pictures yet?" he says incredulously, sitting back down on the couch.

"No," I say. "Why? How long can it possibly take?"

"I'm not sure," he says, biting his lip. "It depends on a lot of different things."

"Well, it doesn't matter," I say breezily, trying not to show my panic. What if I fail? What if I flunk out of school? Oh my God. That would be horrible. And everyone would know about it. They'd see it on TV. And when I went for job interviews and tried to lie about my GPA, potential employers would be all, "Aren't you that girl from *In the House*? The one who flunked out?"

"It doesn't matter?" he asks, looking confused.

"Yeah. I mean, once I take the pictures, I'm not actually going to be able to develop any of them, so it's kind of pointless."

"What time is the photo lab open tonight?" he asks me.

"Six," I tell him.

"Meet me here at five forty-five," he says. "We'll walk over together."

"Why?" I ask, "I don't even have any pictures taken."

"So work on them today," he says. "And tonight I'll show you a trick so that you don't have to worry about the dark again."

"Fine," I say, in an effort to shut him up so that I can fall back asleep.

"Cool," he says, "I'll see ya then."

He heads to his room, and I roll over and try to fall back asleep. But I never do.

"I don't understand why we have to walk around in the cold for this," Grant complains a couple of hours later. I've dragged him out of bed at eleven in the morning to help me work on taking the pictures. "I mean, the assignment is love, right? So why are we outside? Love can be found inside, too, you know."

"True," I say. "But I don't think we should limit ourselves to love that can only be found inside. I mean, love can be found anywhere."

Grant rolls his eyes.

"It's not even that cold out," I tell him.

"It is," Grant complains. "I'm freezing. And right now, Brett is probably sitting at home, waiting for my call."

"Remind me who Brett is again?" I ask, spotting a dog running across campus a few feet away. I wonder if a dog and his master count as love. People love their pets, right? Not that I would know. I've never had one. A pet, I mean. My mom's allergic to, like, everything.

"Why would I want to remind you who Brett is when you're obviously not listening to me?" Grant asks as I get down on one knee, trying to set up a shot of the dog. So far, I've taken almost a whole roll of film, and I have no idea if I'm doing it right. I'm trying to remember to use the techniques we've learned in class, but I just don't know if I'm doing it right. I'm having fun, though. Taking the pictures, I mean. Even if Grant *is* being a pain in the ass.

I adjust the aperture settings and snap a picture of the dog as he runs toward his master. I remember Professor Lutkiss saying something about how to take a picture of a moving image, but I can't remember exactly what it was. Shit.

"Um, hello? Remember me?" Grant says. He plunges

his hands into the pockets of the fleece he's wearing in an effort to make it seem like he's freezing.

"What?" I ask. "No, I'm listening, I swear." I get up off the ground and dust the dirt off my jeans.

"Brett," Grant declares. "is only the hottest guy in school. I met him the other night at the Crows party."

"Oh, right," I say, vaguely remembering him mentioning something about it the other day when I was hysterical over the Jen thing. "That's great," I add, not really sure if it is or not. I love Grant—but he tends to go a little over the top with his relationships, scaring off any potential hookups before they even happen. "So what's the deal?"

"This camera is totally freaking me out, Ally," Grant says, staring at Frank distastefully.

"Frank is freaking you out?" I ask, surprised. "He doesn't even do anything. All he does is stand there." I get down on the ground again to take another shot of the dog.

"I know," Grant says. "That's why he's freaking me out." He frowns. "Do I look okay?"

"Will you stop asking me that?" I say. "Seriously, America doesn't care. Now are you going to tell me what the deal is with Brett or not?" I pick up the pace a little bit, scanning the campus as we walk toward the library.

"Ally, he's amazing," Grant's saying. "So smart and so sweet. The only problem is my parents found out about him, and now they're completely freaked out."

"When are they not freaked out?" I ask, rolling my eyes. "And how did your parents find out?"

"When they came to visit last weekend," he says. "He was in my room when they got here."

"Oh my God, Grant!" I say. "Did your parents catch you guys messing around?" Visions of Grant and some faceless guy tumbling around his bed flash through my mind, and I quickly try to push them out. Not a mental picture that I need.

"No," Grant says, rolling his eyes. "But you know my mom. She was all, 'Why was there a boy in your room?' and I was all, 'Mom, because I am bisexual. I told you.'" He stamps his red and white K-Swiss sneakers on the sidewalk. "Ally, can we please go in the library for a second? Just to warm up?"

"Fine," I say, sighing. Grant is always about the drama.

"So, anyway," he says as we walk through the automatic doors into the library. The warm air does feel good, I must admit. "They were totally rude to him."

"To who?"

"To Brett! Hello, are you new?" He pushes his way through the turnstile, and I follow him dutifully.

"Oh, right, sorry," I say. "That sucks. Maybe you could just start introducing guys to your parents as friends? And then they might be more accepting later on, when you tell them you're dating?"

"But they're not just my friends!" Grant says. He plops down at one of the long wooden tables that take up most of the space on the first floor of the library. "And it doesn't matter—they get wicked suspicious of any guy I hang around with."

"I'm sorry, Grant," I say. "That totally sucks. They'll come around, though. You just have to give it time."

He frowns and looks down at the table.

"Hey, at least they haven't totally disowned you."

"True," he says.

"They love you, Grant." I finger the camera strap around my neck, wishing I knew what to say to make him feel better. "They're just kind of freaked out by the whole thing. Like I said, you have to give it time."

"Yeah," he says. "Maybe." He sighs and looks down at the floor. After a second, he picks his gaze up and looks at me across the table. "Hey, Ally, no, but seriously, do I look okay?"

NOW

I spent five hours that day taking pictures. The weird thing was, even though it was hard work, the time flew by. I should have realized the fact that I was actually excited about doing schoolwork meant something.

Actually, maybe it wasn't as obvious then as it is now. I mean, I had tons of stuff to keep me distracted: classes, my new friend Kelly, the fact that my life was being broadcast to America. Oh yeah, and the fact that for some ridiculous reason, I started getting hot and weak everytime I was around Drew.

THEN

Things That Are Fucked Up:

1. That Vanessa Hudgens had naked pics of her leaked on the Internet not once, but twice.
2. The fact that there are people out there who think it's totally acceptable that Brad picked Angelina over Jen.
3. That I've spent two hours getting ready to go develop my pictures with Drew.

What is wrong with me? I mean, it's just developing pictures. I look at myself critically in the mirror. I'm wearing a pair of dark flare jeans that I borrowed from Kelly and a blue-and-white striped sweater that shows off my chest. I blow-dried my hair until it was wicked straight, then used the curling iron to create loose waves around my shoulders. I borrowed a pair of huge silver hoop earrings from Jasmine, and high black shoes from Simone. What the girl was doing with a pair of hooker shoes like these, I don't know. Ever since she started liking James, she's been dressing decidedly more slutty.

I check my reflection one more time before heading to the living room, where Drew's waiting for me.

"Ready?" he asks.

"Not really," I say.

"Got your camera?" I hold it up hesitantly. I grab my coat off the stand by the door and follow him outside.

"Are you scared yet?" he asks as we walk to the photo lab.

"No, of course not," I tell him, trying to sound flippant. I bury my hands further into my puffy red jacket. Grant was right—it *is* a little chilly out today, even more so now that the sun has gone down. It seems like overnight the weather got cooler, even though it's barely October. Figures that I'm in Syracuse, which has some of the highest snowfalls in the country, while Corey's in Florida.

"That's good," Drew says. He glances at me out of the corner of his eye.

"What?" I say. "Why are you looking at me like that? I'm not scared." The truth is, I'm terrified. I want to run back to the house screaming. I look down at my camera and wonder if it's too late to drop the course. It's easy to drop courses, isn't it? People do it all the time. You just get a slip and have the professor sign it. If you do it before the add/drop deadline, it doesn't even appear on your record.

"I know you're not scared," Drew says, trying to hide his smile. "You already said that."

"I know," I say. "It's because I'm not. So I don't know why we're still talking about it."

"Me neither," Drew says, opening the door to the art building and following me up the stairs to the photo lab. He's wearing a navy blue Syracuse College baseball hat, and his face is a little scruffy, like he hasn't shaved today. The door starts to shut behind us, and Jim, Drew's personal cameraman and the one who's been assigned to shadow us, grabs it right before it hits him in the face. Drew and I giggle.

"Sorry, man," Drew says to Jim. "I forgot you were there." Jim says nothing, but looks a little perturbed.

I follow Drew into the classroom, where he takes his coat off and sets it on one of the chairs. The gray striped sweater he's wearing underneath slides up a little bit, revealing a strip of his flat stomach. I quickly look away, and throw my own coat on one of the nearby tables.

"So did you get any good shots?" he asks. He sits down at one of the long tables while I grab a reel from one of the cupboards against the wall. We're the only ones in the photo lab, which scares me. I was counting on having to wait at least an hour to use the equipment, which would give me time to slow my beating heart and maybe put my head between my legs to keep from fainting. Although I'm not sure how I was planning on putting my head between my legs with lots of people around. I mean, it's one thing to have your personal problems exploited to the world, it's quite another to look like a crazy person.

"Um, shouldn't we just chill for a little while?" I ask Drew, setting the reel on the table and sitting down across from him. "I mean, you know, talk, relax. You must be tired."

"Tired? From what?" Drew asks, looking confused.

"Class?" I try desperately. "The gym? The emotional exhaustion of having your every move taped?"

Drew laughs. "Nah, I'm cool."

"Okay," I say, sighing.

"Now," Drew says, setting the reel and a practice piece of film on the table in front of me. "The trick to getting your film loaded into a reel is twofold. First, you need to practice doing it with your eyes closed, and second, you need to find the place where the film enters the reel *before* you go into the darkroom, so that you don't have to fumble for it in the dark."

"Okay," I say doubtfully. Drew hands me the reel.

"Find the place where the film goes in," he instructs. "And keep your fingers on it. Hold the roll of film in your other hand. Then close your eyes and load it." I practice doing this a few times until I have the hang of it.

"Wow," I tell him. "That really makes a difference. Keeping your hand on the place where it's supposed to go in, so that you don't have to find it. Your dad taught you that?"

"Yeah," Drew says, his voice softening.

"Oh," I say, swallowing. "You must miss him a lot."

"Yeah," he says. "I do."

"So, um . . . how did . . . I mean, was it like a drunk

driver or something?" I ask, wondering if it's appropriate to ask someone how their father died.

"No, actually, it was a tractor-trailer," Drew says, looking down at his hands. He plays with a string that's popped out of the sleeve of his sweater. "It was February, in the middle of a really bad snowstorm. The guy's brakes failed, and my dad tried to swerve, but he couldn't get out of the way in time."

"I'm so sorry," I say. "It's really none of my business, seriously." What is wrong with me? You don't just ask people things like that. Private, personal things. Especially not when they're on a reality TV show. Like he's going to want to talk about it in front of the whole nation.

"Nah," he says. "It's not a big deal. That you asked, I mean. Most people are afraid to talk about it or something." He smiles, and my eyes start to get a little wet. I concentrate on the surface of the table so that Drew doesn't notice, blinking fast in an effort to keep my eyes from spilling over.

"Anyway," Drew says. "He taught me a lot. And now I can teach you." He smiles. "Ready?"

"Not really."

"Come on."

I follow him obediently to the back of the room and down the hall to where the blackroom is located. I look at the door fearfully.

"Do you want me to go in with you?" Drew asks.

"I don't know," I say honestly. I do, but I'm not sure if it's the best idea. I mean, do I really want to have Drew with me every single time I need to load film onto a reel? I should be able to do it myself at some point. On the other hand, I don't want to wreck this roll of film, because I don't have time to take the pictures over again, and I'll end up failing the assignment.

"It's up to you," Drew says easily. "I think you can do it on your own, but if it will make you feel better, I'm happy to go in there with you."

"You'd better come in," I say. "Just so that I don't end up wrecking everything. But I have to warn you, I might faint. Oh, and you might have to physically restrain me from opening the door after I become convinced that I'm blind, or that there's some sort of crazed loon in there, just waiting to gouge our eyeballs out with a knife. Or a nail clipper."

Drew turns his baseball hat around so that it's on backward and laughs. "Ally, you're a riot," he says, and I flush. He makes it sound like it's the ultimate compliment. I wonder if that's how Corey describes me to his new friends at college. "My girlfriend's a riot." Somehow I doubt it.

Drew holds the door to the blackroom open and peers inside. "Nobody in there," he says. "Empty."

"Check behind the door," I say, only half joking. He obliges.

"All clear."

I follow him into the room, the reel in the one hand, the roll of film in the other.

"Ready?" Drew asks. I take a deep breath and nod. He shuts the door, plunging the room into complete darkness. I start to feel the familiar panic rising up in me immediately, but then I hear Drew's voice. "Do you have the reel ready?"

"Yes," I say, taking the tip of the film and sliding it carefully into the reel. For a second, my hands start to shake and I almost drop the reel and the film on the floor, but suddenly Drew's hand is on mine, steadying it.

"Thanks," I say gratefully, wondering how he knew.

"You got it," he says softly, and I start to slide the film onto the track, moving quickly as it falls into place. I close my eyes while I do it and pretend I'm out in the bright classroom, just practicing with my eyes closed.

"Okay," I say, "I'm done."

"I'm going to turn the light on, okay?" Drew asks.

"Wait! Will you check it? To see if it feels right?"

"Sure." I try to hand him the reel with the film in it, but I can't see anything. My hand brushes against his cheek. I feel the scruffiness of his face, and a wave of heat flows through my body.

He moves my hand down and takes the reel from me. "Feels great. Ready to turn the light on?"

"Are you kidding?"

The room becomes flooded with light, and I fan myself, pretending to be hot, in case I'm flushing from when I touched his face. What is wrong with me? Am I really such a loser that being away from my boyfriend for six weeks makes me want to jump on any guy I'm the least bit close to? Ugh.

Drew squints and looks down at the reel. "Good job,"

he says, squeezing my arm. I take a step back. "You all right?" he asks, opening the door to the blackroom.

"Of course!" I say, my voice and my step a little shaky. I glance down at the reel in my hand. It looks like it's loaded properly, with no film sticking out or anything. "Oh my God!" I say, delighted. "It totally worked!" I throw my arms around him in a moment of bad judgment and unmitigated happiness over the fact that I just might possibly not fail this assignment.

"No sweat," Drew says, once he's detangled himself from me.

"Thanks so much," I say. "Really, this was huge." My head is reeling from his closeness, but I'm trying not to show it.

"No prob," Drew says. "So do you want to develop them?"

"Yeah, I think I will," I say, "but you don't have to stay, really." Please stay, please, please, please. "You've done enough."

"I don't mind staying," Drew says. "Besides, I'm kind of interested to see what Ally Cavanaugh, amateur photographer, has come up with."

I smile. "You sure?"

"Absolutely."

We spend the next hour or so making negatives and moving my prints around the trays of chemicals in the dim light of the darkroom. Being in the darkroom doesn't bother me. Once the film is loaded into the reel, it's protected from the light, and so the darkroom isn't completely dark—just sort of dim and murky, with the sound of water running out of the hose in the corner. It reminds me of a rainy day.

When the pictures are hanging up, drying off, Drew looks at me. I look at Drew. We both look at the photos.

"Wow," Drew says softly, and I have to agree.

THEN

"Corey," I announce the next day on the phone. "I've found my passion."

"You've found your passing?" Corey asks, sounding confused.

"No," I sigh. "My passion. I found my passion. You know, what I want to do. Like you and basketball."

"Oh," Corey says, sounding uncertain. Pause. "And what is this newfound passion?"

"Photography!" I announce with a flourish, and lean back in my chair. Somehow I expect this announcement to be accompanied by the sound of trumpets and other woodwind instruments. Are trumpets even woodwind instruments? They might be brass. I only took clarinet for six months in the fifth grade, so I don't really remember. "That's right," I say, mistaking Corey's silence for sudden awe and admiration for the fact that I've figured out what I want to do with my life. "I'm going to be a photographer."

"But you hate photography," Corey says.

"No, I don't."

"Yes, you do."

"No, I don't."

"Yes, you do. The professor is mean to you, and it's not as easy as just taking pictures," Corey recites. Ugh. Does he have to remember my exact words?

"Whatever," I say, rolling my eyes. "I don't hate it anymore. Something happened, Corey, when I started taking pictures. It was like, I didn't think about the angle and the lighting and all that kind of stuff. Somehow I just knew what the picture should look like. And they're really good."

"What's really good?"

"My pictures!" I say, throwing up my hands in exasperation, even though he can't see me. "Are you even listening to anything I'm saying?" How is it he remembers exactly what I said about photography weeks ago, yet he can't focus on what I'm saying now?

"Of course I am," he says. "It's just that it's hard to take you seriously, that's all."

"Why is it hard to take me seriously?" I ask, frowning.

"Because last week you hated photography, and now it's suddenly your passion," he says. He sounds like he can't believe how obviously fickle I am. Okay, granted, I did hate photography, but now I like it. Would it kill him to act a little supportive?

"I didn't like it because I was scared of it, and because I'd never really done it," I tell him. "But now I think it's what I want to do with my life."

"Think? I'd make sure before you decide to major in it, Ally. Your parents aren't paying thousands of dollars in tuition so that you can get some art degree." Some art degree? *Some art degree?* This from a boy who's convinced that his broadcast journalism degree is a necessary but ultimately useless step to getting him into a Lakers uniform. "What did the professor say?"

"Well, nothing," I admit. "I haven't turned them in yet. But I think they're really good. And so did my roommate," I finish lamely.

"Your roommate? The stripper?" He sounds amused.

"How many times do I have to tell you? She's. Not. A. Stripper. She works at Hooters." Is he deaf? Has he acquired some sort of Floridian disease that affects his auditory powers?

"Same difference," he says. "But, anyway, what did the stripper say about the pictures?"

"Her name's Jasmine, not 'the stripper.' And it wasn't her. It was my roommate Drew." There. That will show him. Now he'll have no choice but to listen to me. Some other guy, a guy I *live with,* told me that my photos are good. Now Corey will turn all jealous and rush to out-compliment him. "He helped me develop them," I add for good measure. "In the *dark*room."

"Well, I wouldn't start counting chickens until the professor sees the pictures," Corey says. What? Did he not hear me? Is he not concerned with the fact that some other guy is telling me I'm good at something? Sure, it was only my pictures he was complimenting, but doesn't Corey realize that's really only one step away from worshiping my body, my face, my kissing abilities? Maybe he didn't hear me.

"*Drew* knows a lot about photography because his dad was a photographer," I tell him. "But you'll probably hear all about it on the show." I try to sound breezy, all the while hoping Corey will fly into a jealous rage and book a flight to Syracuse immediately, demanding that I marry him.

"I don't watch the show anymore," Corey says.

"What?" I say, almost choking on the iced tea I'm drinking.

"I don't watch the show anymore," he says, sounding like it's no big deal.

He doesn't watch the show anymore? Is he nuts? How can he not want to know what's going on in my life? "Why not?" I say.

"I dunno," he replies, again sounding like it's no big deal. "Just figure it's not worth driving myself nuts over." Oh. My. God. That is the most ridiculous thing I've ever heard in my life. Driving yourself crazy over your relationship is, like, the basis of civilization.

"Well, whatever," I say, not knowing how to respond. "The point is, *Drew* knows a lot about photography. So he helped me."

"Okay." I hear the sound of keystrokes in the background.

Is he typing something while he's on the phone with me? Is it possible he thinks Drew is a girl's name?

"What are you doing?" I ask suspiciously.

"Just sending my coach an email about tomorrow's practice," he says. Type, type, type.

"Oh, cool. Good to know that you're paying such close attention," I say. "Would it kill you to listen to me about this? It's not always about you, you know."

"Excuse me?" Corey says. The typing stops.

"Look, I'm sorry, but can you be at least a little bit supportive? I'm always supportive of you and your basketball," I say.

"I *am* being supportive, Ally, I'm just saying not to get your hopes up, that's all. Look, I didn't call to get in another fight with you. I called to talk about booking my flight to see you." Another fight? *Another* fight? We don't always fight. We don't talk enough to always be in a fight.

"What about it?" I ask. I cradle the phone between my shoulder and my neck and rub my temples with my fingers. I'm way too young to be getting stress headaches.

"I know I'm supposed to get in on Friday night," he says. "But if I book a flight on Saturday morning, I can save fifty bucks. Is that cool?"

No, it's not cool.

"Fine, whatever," I tell him. The typing noises start back up. How long is this freaking email anyway? Shouldn't he be done writing it by now? He *hates* email.

"We wouldn't be doing much Friday night, anyway, I'm sure," Corey says. Wouldn't be doing much? How about sleeping in the same bed, spending time together, having sex?

"That's fine," I say again, clearly implying it's not.

"All right, well, I'm out. I'll give you a call tonight or tomorrow."

"You're *what?*"

"I'm out. It means, good-bye, I'm hanging up, I'm leaving . . ."

"I know what it means. I've just never heard you say it before."

"Really? I say it all the time. Must be a Miami thang," he says, laughing.

"Yeah, must be." Did my boyfriend just say "I'm out" and "thang" within the space of thirty seconds and not while imitating Jay-Z?

"Love you," Corey says.

"I love you, too." I hang up the phone and close my eyes. The throb behind my temples has now progressed into an ache.

I sit there for a second, staring at the phone, and then head to the bathroom in search of pain relievers. I'm a big fan of over-the-counter remedies. I'm not a druggie or anything. I just don't understand people who won't take something when they get sick. My brother, like, absolutely refuses to take an aspirin. One time he broke his leg playing lacrosse and hardly touched the pain relievers his doctor prescribed for him. His friend David—who everyone called "Skunk," for some reason—ended up stealing them from Brian's room and selling them to people for twenty bucks a pop.

Jasmine's in the bathroom, in front of the mirror, getting ready for work, but the door's open, so I walk in and sit down on the closed toilet.

"Feel free," Jasmine says sarcastically. She's wearing her Hooters uniform: tight orange shorts and a white tank top with the Hooters logo. It doesn't appear as if she's wearing a bra. But that's impossible. Isn't it? I mean, how can she go to work and be on national television with no bra on? She catches me staring and frowns.

"What's with you?" She dips a makeup brush into her foundation and starts applying it to her face.

"I have a headache," I say, rubbing my temples.

Jasmine opens the cabinet over the sink and throws me the bottle of Advil. I down two of them, not moving from my spot on the toilet.

"Anything else?" she asks, moving on to a gray sparkly eye shadow.

"Something weird is going on," I tell her, looking at the floor. I concentrate on the swirling pattern of the tiles, wondering how much I should reveal.

"Besides the fact that James and Simone are going to the movies tonight?" she asks. "Do tell."

"James and Simone are going to the movies?" I ask. Lately Simone's been trying to think of a way to get the two of them alone together off campus, the rationale being that once she gets him out of the house, it qualifies as a real date, and therefore hooking up can ensue.

"I guess," Jasmine says, shrugging

"Did she ask him, or did he ask her?"

"Dunno," she says. "So what's up with you?"

"It's, um . . . it's . . ." I look back down at the floor and trail off.

"I'm leaving in fifteen minutes, so spit it out. I have to go work a half-shift 'cause someone called in sick." She lines her eyes carefully with a sharp black eyeliner. When she's done, her eyes look smoky and sexy. If I tried to do that, I'd look like a raccoon.

"It's this whole Corey thing," I say slowly, trying to figure out exactly what I want to say and how I should say it. There are no cameras allowed in the bathroom, so it's not like anyone's going to see this. Not that I have to worry, since Corey apparently doesn't watch the show anymore.

"Are you still stressing about that slut Jen?" Jasmine's asking. She makes a pouty face in the mirror and studies her reflection. "Listen, sweetie, forget about her. I know a million girls like that—I work with them, I go to school with them, I've even been *friends* with some of them. They find some guy or group of guys and stalk them until someone finally breaks down and sleeps with them, and then the girl becomes a complete joke." She studies herself critically in the mirror, pulling her shirt down tighter over her breasts. She is definitely not wearing a bra.

"It's not Jen," I tell her. "It's Drew."

Jasmine puts her eyeliner down on the sink and turns to me. "Drew?" she says, her eyes widening. "What about him? Did you . . . did you *fuck* him?"

"No!" I say, shocked. "I didn't have sex with him. God,

what kind of a whore do you think I am?" Why would she think this? Does she know something I don't?

"Oh." She turns back to the mirror, disappointed. "I just heard Drew and automatically thought sex."

"Why?" I ask, fighting down a sudden wave of jealousy. Does Jasmine like Drew? If that's the case, then really, there's no issue. Even if I *do* like Drew, I would never have a chance with him if Jasmine likes him, too. But I don't. Like Drew, I mean. I'm just feeling weird for some reason.

"Because he's hot," she says. "In one of those Abercrombie ways. Totally not my type."

"You like guys with an edge?" I ask hopefully.

"Yeah. Tattoos, a piercing, an addiction . . ." She trails off. "So what's the deal? If you haven't hooked up with him, then why are we having this conversation?"

"I don't know," I say, frowning.

"Do you *want* to hook up with him?"

"No." Yes.

"Oh my God, you do! You total slut!" She abandons her mascara and turns to me once more. "You want to have sex with him!"

"I have a boyfriend!"

"So?"

"So I can't just cheat on him! I love him."

"So again, then why are we having this conversation?" She throws her mascara into her makeup bag and turns back to the mirror, lining her lips with a shiny red lipstick.

"I just . . . I'm just . . ." I take a deep breath and decide to change tactics. "What was your longest relationship?"

"You mean, like, hooking up or actual boyfriend?"

"Actual boyfriend."

"Six weeks." She considers. "No, wait. A month."

I sigh. It'll have to do. "And while you were with your boyfriend, did you ever, like, look at other guys?"

"You DO want to sleep with him!" Jasmine shrieks. "I knew it!"

"Jasmine! Focus!"

"Okay, okay, I'm sorry. Go on."

I sigh and run my fingers through my hair, thanking God once again that cameras aren't allowed in the bathroom. I consider the idea of nightly chats in this safe, camera-free zone, and make a mental note to run this idea past Jasmine and Simone later. I take a deep breath. "It's just that lately, I've sort of kind of been finding myself wanting to, like, kiss Drew or be close to Drew. And I don't know what's going on with that." I feel the tears start to well up behind my eyes and I blink quickly, trying to push them back, but it's too late. A tear slides down my cheek. "I love Corey. He's everything to me. I'm a horrible person and a horrible girlfriend."

"Oh, Ally." Jasmine sighs. She abandons her makeup and sits down on the side of the tub. She looks at me seriously. "Sweetie, it's normal for you to be attracted to other guys. That doesn't stop just because you have a boyfriend. I mean, even people who are *married* can appreciate when someone's good looking." I look down at my hands, unable to speak. The tears are falling freely now. Jasmine pulls a wad of toilet paper off of the roll and hands it to me. I wipe my eyes.

"I just don't know why I would even feel like that. It really makes me feel like I'm an awful person," I sniff.

"You're *not* an awful person," Jasmine says. "You're just far away from your boyfriend right now, that's all. When you're used to seeing someone every day, it makes it really hard."

"I don't know," I say, wiping my nose. "I've never looked at another guy since I've been with Corey. Ever."

"This whole Drew thing is completely physical," she says. "It's a *normal* physical reaction to being far away from your boyfriend. Drew's hot, no one's denying that, but you don't even like him that much. Didn't you say when you first got here that you thought he was kind of cocky?"

"Yes," I say, not mentioning how nice he's been to me lately.

"Well, there you go," she says, standing up and returning to the mirror. She flips her head over and starts to fluff her hair. "You love Corey. You're just hormonal." She flips back over, her hair forming a cascading wave around her shoulders.

"Things will be much better once Corey gets here," I say, blowing my nose.

"Exactly," Jasmine says. "You just have to see him, that's all. I'm sure everything will be fine."

"You're right," I say. I wipe my eyes and blow my nose, then throw the tissue into the trash can forcefully. What am I getting so upset about? Everything's fine. So what if I think a guy's cute? Jasmine's right—it's completely normal. It doesn't mean anything *bad's* going to happen. I push it out of my mind and go to the kitchen to find something to eat.

I have a psychology test in the morning that's a pretty big deal, and I haven't even started studying for it, since most of this week was consumed with my photography stuff. I grab some Diet Coke and a bag of hickory barbecue chips and head to my room, figuring I'll watch whatever's on the CW and eat snacks while I immerse myself in my studying.

A few hours later, I'm watching TV and simultaneously learning about Freud's conception of the human psyche (it's totally possible to watch teen dramas and learn psychology at the same time, I swear) when Simone rushes into the room, looking flushed.

"Hey," I say, "What's going on?"

"Oh my God, Ally, I think I'm in love," she says, spinning around the room like some kind of weird stereotypical romantic comedy heroine.

"So you had a good time?" I say, slamming my book shut and turning off the TV. Who says I'm not a good friend? I'm totally letting Simone's date trump the drama of Orange County.

"What's going on?" Jasmine asks, coming into the room. She's still in her work uniform, and I see the light on Sam's camera start blinking, which means he's probably zooming in on her cleavage.

"Simone just got back from her date," I report.

"Oooh," Jasmine says, pulling her Hooters tank top over her head and throwing it on the bed. She has no problem with public nudity. Like, at all. I refuse to change anywhere but the bathrooms, but she just whips it around no matter where she is. I guess when you've been on a stripping audition, you're not all that concerned with America seeing you in your underwear. "Give us the details."

"It was great," she says. "We went to the movies and to dinner. He paid for everything."

"Kiss?" I say, wanting to get to the good stuff immediately.

"Yes," she says.

"No way!" Jasmine says from across the room. She pulls a lowcut red shirt over her head. "Way to go, Simone. I didn't think you had it in ya."

"So where is he now?" I ask, not really sure how it works when you're dating someone you live with. Like, how can they drop you off at home if they live there too?

"He's at his friend's house," Simone says. "They're having a few people over there." Jasmine and I shoot a look at each other.

"He went to a party after a date?" Jasmine asks incredulously.

"I'm meeting him there!" Simone protests. "I just wanted to come home and change first."

"Good thinking," Jasmine says, looking at Simone's jeans and pink hooded sweatshirt.

"You guys want to go?" Simone asks, heading toward the closet.

"Can't," I say, holding up my psychology book. "I gotta study."

"Oh, come on," Simone says. "We'll only go for an hour."

"But what about Locke's property theory?"

"It'll be there when you get back."

"Fine," I say, jumping out of bed and heading to my dresser to find suitable hanging-out-off-campus attire. "I'm in."

"Jasmine?"

"I can't," Jasmine says from inside her closet. She emerges holding a pair of strappy red shoes. "I'm going out with Dale."

"Oooh," Simone and I chorus.

"Shut up!" she says. "It's not anything!"

"What happened to having fun and not being tied down?" I ask.

"I'm not tied down," she protests, sliding into the shoes and fastening the buckles. "I'm just bored. I mean, have you seen the guys around here? So immature." She rolls her eyes.

"Wow, you must be bored a lot," I say. "With the amount of time you guys have been spending together."

"Do you want to borrow something to wear?" she asks Simone, ignoring me.

The party turns out to be a house party at one of James's friend's places. It's pretty lame, as parties go, but it takes my mind off the whole Drew thing for a while.

I don't drink, mostly because James's friends are kind of shady, and I'm totally afraid one of them might slip something sketchy into my drink. Even without the aid of chemicals, the party serves the purpose of keeping my mind off Drew. But later that night, after I've spent two hours studying psychology, when it's three in the morning and I'm about to fall asleep, all I can think about is Drew's face against my fingers in the darkroom.

The phone rings at eight the next morning, jolting me out of a dream about Derek Jeter just five hours after I got to sleep.

"Hello?" I croak into the phone by my bed, having trouble verbalizing.

"Alexandra?" my mom says on the other line. She's talking way too loud for this hour.

"Hi, Mom," I say, sitting up and looking around to see who else may have been disturbed by my mom's call. Jasmine's bed is empty, which means she probably spent the night at Dale's. Casual thing, my ass.

Simone's bed is empty, too, which means she probably got up early and went to the library. She thinks studying early in the morning keeps her focused. What is up with my roommates and their crazy sleep schedules? Jasmine out all night, Simone up studying, James out partying, Drew up for the gym. Thinking about Drew floods me with guilt, and I push him out of my mind.

"What's up?" I ask my mom, sliding back under the covers and closing my eyes. They feel like someone has put two huge weights on the lids, and they're closing, closing . . .

"Why didn't you tell me you and Corey were having problems?" my mom asks, and my eyes spring back open.

"What are you talking about? Corey and I aren't having

problems." Oh my God. What is she talking about? Maybe someone at home found out something about Corey and Jen? Or maybe it's not Jen at all, but another evil strumpet, one of the Brynn/Halle/insert cool and trendy name here variety. What if Jen was just a *decoy*, a red herring designed to throw me off the track? And now someone's found out about Corey and the *real* girl, and they've told my mom. My mom! Instead of coming to me first, like any sane person would do. Unless it's one of my mom's friends, who heard something from their kid. I'll bet it's Kristi McConnell's mom. She has a big mouth, just like her daughter. "Who told you we were having problems?"

"I heard it on TV."

"On TV?" I ask dumbly.

"Yes, Ally, on TV. I heard your voice saying that you and that kid Drew you live with are going to start hooking up." Did my mom just say "hooking up"?

"Wait a minute. When did this happen?"

"Just now. I saw it on a preview." What is up with these previews? I mean, really. I just said that to Jasmine *last night*. "Almost live reality" is right. Jesus. Plus, don't people realize that a preview is taken out of context, engineered to make things look more scandalous than they really are? And why is my mom watching YTV at seven in the morning?

Wait. How could my mom have heard me say I wanted to hook up with Drew? I never said that, except for when I was in the bathroom, and there are no cameras. Shit. I was wearing my mike pack. So they got everything I said. Shit, shit, shit. Which means if my mom saw it, Corey may hear about it, too. And Drew. Drew might hear about it. Deep breath.

"Mom, I told you not to take everything on the show so seriously. You know everything's edited." Ever since my parents saw the strip club episode, I'm constantly trying to convince them everything they see is not really happening, that it's all designed to look way more dramatic than it really is. Sleeping in because I was up too late watching DVDs with Simone and Jasmine? I tell her it's an edited shot of the clock to make it look like I'm skipping class. Me wearing a red bikini in the hot tub while drinking a fruity rum drink that James made for us? The only bathing suit I had clean, fruit punch, and a backache that forced me into the hot tub in an effort to soothe my muscles.

"Oh, I know," my mom says. I hear dishes clanging in the background. "It's just that I would hope if you and Corey were having problems, you would come to me and talk about it."

"Of course I would," I tell her, not really meaning it. "But we're not having problems, Mom. Everything's fine."

"Okay," my mom says, not sounding completely sure. "I just want you to understand that you're young, Ally. You don't have to decide anything right now. But long-distance relationships are tough, even in the best of circumstances." Oh my God, she sounds like one of those really cheesy shows on ABC Family.

"It's fine, Mom, really," I say, looking at the clock and mentally calculating how much sleep I've lost.

"Corey's coming here in a few weeks, anyway, so . . ."

"Well, that's good," my mom says, sounding satisfied. "How's everything else? How are your classes?"

"Good and good," I say.

"Okay," she says, sounding hesitant. "I miss you, Ally. Be careful."

"I will," I say.

I lay in bed for a few minutes after we hang up, staring at the ceiling. Not being completely honest with my mom feels weird. I mean, I didn't *lie* to her or anything, but things with Corey and I are definitely not completely normal. If I were at home, it would be impossible to keep this from her—I would be seeing her every day.

I take a deep breath and bury my face in my pillow. No big deal. The best thing to do is just stay away from Drew, that's all. I mean, Jasmine's totally right. It's just a physical thing that serves no other purpose than to confuse me and make me feel weird. Plus, if he does hear about what I said from one of his friends who watch the show, it will be much easier if I'm just not talking about him. Maybe I could do damage control and tell him I was drunk.

IMAGINED CONVERSATION:

ME: Hey, Drew, just so you know, the other day I got drunk and accidentally said I had a crush on you, so if you hear about it from any of your friends, it's totally not true, okay?

DREW: Sure, no problem.

It shouldn't even be that *hard,* when you think about it. Staying away from him, I mean. Except for the fact that we live together. Maybe I can just start being really mean to him. Or maybe I can do something to make him hate me.

"Oh, great, you're awake!" Drew says brightly, knocking on my open door and peeking his head around the corner. Ugh.

I close my eyes and pretend to be asleep. "Ally, I saw your eyes open," he says, coming into my room and sitting down on my bed.

I try to fake snore. He laughs. Fuck.

"I'm sleeping," I tell him, rolling over. The back of my pajama pants rides down as I twist, exposing the top of my underwear to both America and Drew. I hike them up, hoping he didn't see. And hoping he did.

"Well, I'm leaving for class now, anyway," he says. "I just wanted to wish you good luck in photography today. You're turning your pictures in, right?"

"Yeah." I roll back over and face him. He's wearing a long-sleeved gray T-shirt under a navy blue puffy vest. His hair's gelled, and his face, as usual, is a little scruffy. He smells amazing.

"Well, good luck. Not that you'll need it."

"Thanks," I manage, trying not to breathe through my nose. His cologne is turning me on. When he leaves, for the second day this week, I can't fall back asleep.

Photography, two o'clock that afternoon. Something bad is happening. Instead of just handing in our pictures like one would do in a *normal* class, Professor Lutkiss has decided to show one picture from each person's assignment and tell us WHAT HE THINKS OF THEM. Like, in front of the whole class. I think this is a terrible idea, but I don't say so for fear of him using it against me.

IMAGINED HUMILIATION:

ME: Please don't show my pictures, I'm embarrassed.
PROFESSOR LUTKISS: Let's start with Ally, shall we?

I wouldn't put it past him. After he made a spectacle of me that day, I'm suspicious of his motives and aspirations. The only thing that makes this somewhat bearable is the fact that he's not giving our names with the pictures. So at least if mine suck, they'll suck anonymously.

Kelly sits next to me at one of the long tables. She seems unconcerned about the teacher's announcement and is checking her reflection in a compact. She smears some lip gloss on her lips and smiles at me. I return the smile nervously, feeling as if I'm going to throw up.

"This," Professor Lutkiss says at the front of the room, holding up a picture of a couple holding hands. "Who can tell me what is wrong with THIS?"

Hands shoot up around the room. For some reason, the class is eager to offer their opinions on what is wrong with the work of their classmates.

"The lighting."

"The angle."

"It's out of focus."

"You're all wrong," the professor says. "This photo is technically perfect."

The class looks confused.

"But," the professor says, "being technically perfect doesn't always make a picture successful."

Oh, great. So basically we can do everything right and end up failing, anyway. Lovely. I say a silent thanks that I didn't tell my mom this morning that I wanted to be a photography major. No use getting her all worked up for nothing, especially with her already on edge about this whole Drew thing.

"The subject is boring," Professor Lutkiss says. "We've seen picture after picture of couples holding hands. What makes this one special? What makes this one any different from the others? Nothing."

I look nervously at Kelly. She's doodling in her notebook and looks bored.

"Hey," she whispers to me. "You want to go to a party this weekend?"

"A party?" I repeat, still trying not to throw up.

"Yeah. At DK," she says.

"DK?"

She giggles. "It's a frat."

"I'm not sure," I say, watching Professor Lutkiss as he shuffles through the manila folders he's holding, looking for his next victim.

"Come on," Kelly says. "It'll be fun. You haven't been to one frat party since you've been here. That's insane."

"Um, hello? Do they let huge, middle-aged men holding cameras into frat parties?"

"Sure. Why not? James goes out all the time, and he's in the same situation you are."

"I guess," I say reluctantly. I'm having trouble focusing because Professor Lutkiss has opened the manila folder holding my pictures. I can tell it's mine because I wrote my name on the side in purple pen, and I can see the purple ink from where I'm sitting.

He pulls out the picture of a man playing chess with his son. I saw them in the library that day with Grant, and took their picture because I liked how content they both looked. Professor Lutkiss studies the picture carefully, and I grip the edge of the table until my knuckles turn white. He flips through the rest of my folder. In addition to the picture of the man and his son playing chess, I've taken a picture of Simone on the phone with her mom, the look on her face betraying just how much she misses her, a picture of a toddler on a slide with a look of glee on his face, two dogs playing in the quad, and a picture of a mom crying as she watches her son head back to the dorms after dropping him off from a weekend at home.

I had several shots of each, but Drew helped me pick out the final prints.

"Would the person who took this picture," Professor Lutkiss announces, holding up the print, "please see me after class?"

I'm so fucked.

NOW

He loved them. He told me I had a knack for seeing outside the obvious and he thought I had potential. I told him I was thinking about making photography my major. He told me that once you came in undeclared, you had to be invited to apply for the photography program, but that if this was any indication of the work to come, he would be more than happy to extend the invitation. He told me I had some technical things to work on, and that some of the explanations in my writeup about the techniques I used were off, but he could see the raw talent that was there. I left class feeling better about myself than I had in a long time. Maybe ever.

Something was happening. It wasn't just the photography thing or the Corey thing, although those were major aspects of it. Looking back, it's so easy to see. Watching tapes of the show, it's even more apparent, since the production staff did an excellent job of editing out all the boring, insignificant parts of my life. At the time, though, I had no idea.

Now it seems almost insane that I couldn't see the changes that were taking place. But maybe that's the problem with changes—you never notice the signs until it's too late, until all these little things add up to become one extreme event, one that changes your life and makes you take notice.

THEN

REACTION TO THE ANNOUNCEMENT THAT I WANT
TO MAJOR IN PHOTOGRAPHY (A SUMMARY):

MY MOM: Oh, sweetie, photography? That sounds like
it could be . . . fun. Do they allow any kind of dual
major? You could major in photography and something
else. That way, you'd have a fallback plan.
GRANT: You mean, like, one of those photographers that
go around and takes pics of celebs? And, like, stalks
them? Oh my God, Ally, that would be, like, so cool!
Did I tell you Brett and I finally had sex?
MY DAD: Didn't you say something about majoring in
broadcast journalism? I could have my friend Hugh
email you some information. That's what he majored in,
you know. Now he makes six figures.

BRIAN: Learn how to take pictures? Ally, you got a 1980 on your SATs. You could do *anything*.

My family and friends obviously think I'm playing Russian roulette with my future. The only person I can see being remotely excited for me would be Drew, but since I'm avoiding him, this doesn't help. Maybe everyone's right. Maybe it *is* stupid. I mean, I *did* hate photography in the beginning. And until I got to school, I had never even shown an interest in photography, much less considered devoting my life to it.

I'm so distraught by all these negative reactions (and the fact that I got them all within the span of an hour—my brother was home for the weekend, and when I called my parents, they all passed the phone around like some kind of horrible triple play on that Debbie Downer skit from *Saturday Night Live*), that I somehow let Kelly talk me into meeting her at the DK party on Saturday night.

The party turns out to be nothing like I expected. The frat house is dirty and bare, with no furniture to speak of except for a tan couch that may or may not have been tan when it was brought into the house, since there are numerous unidentifiable stains covering its upholstery. It's best not to think about what these stains may consist of. There is a bar set up in the corner, and a long table where kids are playing some sort of drinking game. Other than that, there is no furniture.

Where do the frat brothers sit? I wonder. I mean, they must hang out here, right? It's *their* house. Certainly not on the floor, which I can tell, even through my shoes, is slightly sticky and very dirty. Who knows what kind of disgusting germs could be lurking on this floor, causing them to get sick or die. Like this special I saw on TV once about this guy who caught a flesh-eating bacteria somewhere. It destroyed his whole face. The bacteria actually *ate* his face. By the time it was finished with him, he had, like, no eyes and half a nose. How gross is that? I think he caught it from old bread or something. If you can catch a flesh-eating disease from old bread, think about what you could catch from a floor like this.

"Where do the frat brothers sit?" I ask Jasmine, figuring she might know since she has more life experience than I do. I made Jasmine come to the party with me. I knew Kelly was already coming with a group of her friends, and I didn't want to end up feeling awkward. Plus, I figured instead of being the freak with the camera, I would be part of a pair of freaks with a camera, which is definitely better. Frank the cameraman isn't around tonight for some reason, so we have Sam, who looks decidedly cranky since we've only been here five minutes and already someone (accidentally) spilled beer on him.

"Beats me," Jasmine says, shrugging her bare shoulders. She's wearing a sparkly black halter top that shows the bottom of her stomach. Tight black pants and a pair of high black boots complete the ensemble. Her long dark hair falls in waves down her back, and she's dusted her exposed skin with body glitter.

Before we left the house we had this huge debate over

what to wear. I took her advice and wore a short white skirt with a tight red shirt that belongs to Kelly. I almost froze to death on the walk over here, since Jasmine also refused to let me wear a coat, saying there would be nowhere to put it when I got to the party.

"Hey, ladies. You girls need cups?" a curly-haired frat brother says, approaching us. He's holding a stack of clear plastic cups in one hand and a stack of dollar bills in the other. I look at him blankly.

"We'll take two," Jasmine says, smiling. She pulls two five-dollar bills out of her strapless bra, and hands them to the kid. He pulls two cups off the stack and gives them to us.

"Uh, Jas," I tell her once he's out of earshot. "You just paid ten dollars for two plastic cups." Is this some sort of bizarre ritual? I've heard of fraternities having, like, secret underground activities and stuff, but I thought they were for frat brothers only. And I think, but I'm not exactly positive, that they involve secret insignias and the occasional wild animal.

Jasmine rolls her eyes. She does this a lot. Not in a mean way, but in a can-you-believe-she's-so-sheltered kind of way. My only comfort is that she rolls her eyes at Simone more than she rolls them at me. And I think she secretly finds our cluelessness endearing.

"It's for the beer," Jasmine says. "So that we can get some."

Oh. Right. I guess it makes sense. I mean, we didn't expect to come here and just drink for free, did we? Frat brothers are, after all, just broke college students. They can't just *buy* beer for everyone and let us come over and drink it for *nothing*.

"Hey, guys," Kelly says, pushing her way through the throng of people. "I was starting to think you weren't going to show."

"Of course we were," I say, rolling my eyes to convey that I wouldn't miss it for the world, even though I didn't decide until the last minute that I wanted to go.

"Let's get you some beer," she says. She's wearing tan flared pants and a blue gauzy shirt. Her hair's in pigtails. "Come on." She grabs my hand and starts leading me through the crowd.

"I'll catch you later," Jasmine says to me. I look at her, confused, but she gestures toward Kelly's back and rolls her eyes.

"You sure?" I say, feeling bad for ditching her.

"Yes," she says, "positive. I got my eye on something a little better over there, anyway." She looks to the side of the room, where a guy with spiked hair and a nose ring is leaning against the wall, looking bored.

I smile and follow Kelly to the keg. A hot frat boy fills up my cup and hands it to me. I take a sip. It's warm.

"You wanna dance?" Kelly asks.

"Um, not right now," I say, looking around the room at the gyrating bodies. Whoever's in charge of the music is leaning toward a pop/dance feel with lots of remixes. I spot Drew on the other side of the room talking to a short, blond girl in a pair of expensive-looking jeans and a stomach-revealing brown shirt. He sees me looking and waves. I wave back, and then quickly look away. I didn't know he was going to be here. Oh my God. What if he heard what I said in the bathroom the other day, and now he thinks I'm stalking him? What if he's saying to that girl, "I can't believe Ally's here—can she leave me alone for two seconds?"

"Hey, do you know her?" I ask Kelly, tilting my head in the general direction of Drew and the mysterious belly-shirt wearer. The keg is right next to the stereo speakers, so I have to scream to be heard over the music.

"Who?" she asks, leaning in close to my ear.

"The one that's with Drew."

"That's Andrea Goldstein. You know, the one he works out with?"

"The one he *what?*" Did she just say MAKES OUT WITH?

"Works out with. At the gym, you know?"

"How do you know that?" I ask.

"I've seen it on the show," she says. Oh. I want to ask her more, but I'm super aware of Sam and his camera bearing down on us. People are dancing in groups around us, and suddenly I start to feel really hot.

"Bottom's up!" Kelly says, raising her cup. And when she downs her beer, I do too.

That's the last thing I clearly remember from the actual party. The rest of it is kind of like a bunch of fuzzy snapshots in a flip book, or a memory from when you were a kid.

I can remember Jasmine telling me she's leaving with Jason, the guy with the piercing. I remember feeling like the room was vibrating almost immediately after finishing my first drink. I remember Drew in the corner, talking to Andrea for most of the night, and I remember Kelly asking me what I thought of this guy named Rick she had been hooking up with.

I remember filling my cup, then losing my cup, then finding a random cup on the bar, which I then drank out of. I remember dancing to an Alicia Keys remix and thinking I may quite possibly be the best dancer ever to live. I remember laughing. A lot.

Then, all of a sudden, Kelly's telling me it's time to leave. I look around, and people are starting to clear out of the frat house. How can this be? There's no way it can be one in the morning. We just got here. Someone has obviously set everyone's watches and all the clocks in the place a few hours ahead. I'll bet it's one of those fraternity pranks that they're always doing in movies.

"What time is it?" I ask Sam the cameraman, figuring if there's someone in the room who's been spared the prank, it's Sam. He's been stoic all night, standing in the corner with his camera trained on me. He ignores my request for the time.

"You know," I say, putting my hand on my hip. "Would it kill you to be helpful just this ONE time? You follow me around as much as you PLEASE and I don't say anything."

"Come on, Ally," Kelly says, giggling. "You gotta go home. You're wasted."

"I'm not wasted," I say. But by the time Kelly drops me

off outside the house, I start to think I am. I lie on my bed and the room is spinning. My head feels like it's expanding, and like it's really fuzzy. I want to call Corey. I need to call Corey. I reach for the phone by my bed and dial his number. I get it right on the third try.

"What's wrong?" Corey asks immediately.

"I'm fine," I slur, my bed spinning under me. I put my foot on the ground to steady myself, but I feel like that's spinning too. I suddenly have a thought. What if I'm the one that's spinning? *And every time my body touches something, that thing begins to spin too?* I place my hand on the end table next to my bed experimentally. It starts to spin.

"No, you're not," Corey says. "Ally, you're drunk. Where were you tonight?"

"At a party," I say, pleased that I can remember this. It obviously proves that I'm not drunk, since drunk people have a hard time remembering stuff. And I most definitely was at the party. I had a cup and everything.

"Well that's just great," Corey says. "You went to a party and got drunk, and now everyone's going to see it on TV. Way to be classy, Ally."

"Wait, you're pissed? A'cause I went to a party?"

"I'm not *pissed,*" he says. "I just think you need to understand that there's a certain way you need to be conducting yourself. And going to strip clubs and getting wasted is not the way to do that." Jesus. Who does he think he is? He's always out partying and drinking with his friends. I do it once and all of a sudden I'm a candidate for AA.

"You go out with your friends all the time," I tell him,

suddenly feeling like I'm going to cry. "All the time." I say it again, to make sure he heard. I take my hand off the end table and put it on my head, which seems to be spinning at a faster rate than the rest of my body. I wish I would stop spinning. It would be ever so much better.

"Ally, I'm not going to have this discussion with you right now," Corey says firmly. "I have practice at eight in the morning." He sounds mad, and I feel a panic rising up in my throat, like when you get the feeling that something bad is happening and everyone knows but you. Actually, I don't know that I've had that feeling until right now. Is this what drinking does to you? Make you paranoid? Or is that pot? I think it's pot. Definitely pot. Drinking is supposed to make you mellow.

"Corey, wait. You're still coming for Columbus Day, right? To visit?" I start to feel sick to my stomach, and now my body feels like it's spinning in compartments. My stomach, head, and legs are all spinning at different rates and in different directions.

"We'll talk about it tomorrow," Corey says, sounding exasperated.

"Please don't hang up," I say, the panic and spinning starting to accelerate. "I need to talk to you. I'm scared. I don't feel good."

"Go to bed, Ally," Corey says. "I'll call you in the morning." The line goes dead.

I place the phone back on the table by my bed and all of a sudden I know I'm going to throw up.

"Bob," I tell the night-shift cameraman who's filming me.

154

"I'm going to throw up, I think." Bob doesn't say anything, just stands there with the handheld. I wish for Frank, with his hairy chest and comforting presence. Frank would help me. Frank would tell me it was going to be okay. Frank would not ignore me when I obviously have alcohol poisoning.

I muster up the strength to get out of bed and head to the bathroom. I make it there, barely, and throw up most of what I've had to eat that day, along with a clear spill of I don't know what. When it's done, I lean my head against the wall, wondering what would happen if I just fell asleep here. I must have dozed off a little bit, because the next thing I know, Drew is shaking me awake gently.

I force my eyes open, and his face comes slowly into focus. "Ally?" He looks worried, which instantly makes me scared. "Are you okay?"

"I don't think so," I tell him. "I think I might be dying. I think I have alcohol poisoning. We should probably call the ambulance."

"How much did you have to drink tonight?"

"I dunno. Like four beers, I think." I struggle to remember how much was in each cup, and how many times I had my cup refilled, but the memory of what happened earlier seems to be receding farther and farther away, and I can't quite remember exactly what went on.

"You don't have alcohol poisoning," Drew says, smiling. "You're just drunk. Can you make it back to your room?"

"Yes." No.

Drew lifts me up from the floor and I wrap my arms

around his neck. "You're strong," I tell him, admiring the way his arms bulge under the navy blue sweater he's wearing. "It's because you work out with Andrea. Every morning you go to see her."

"Andrea?" He looks confused.

I sigh and lean my head against his shoulder and force my feet forward. "Whoa, whoa, whoa," I say as the room begins to sway. "I don't think I can make it."

"Okay," Drew says simply, "do you want to sit down and rest for a minute?"

"I need to lie down," I say. "I need to lie down!" I say again, more forcefully. If I don't lie down, I'm going to die, I just know it. "If I don't lie down, I'm going to die," I explain.

"Can you make it to my room?" Drew asks.

"I think so," I say, moving my legs toward the boys' room, which is closer to the bathroom than mine. "Don't let go of me." I wrap my arms tighter around him.

"I won't."

"Promise?"

"Promise."

Drew lays me down in his bed and perches on the side, watching me and waiting for me to get my shit together. "I just need a second," I say, staring up at the ceiling. The spinning has slowed down a little, leaving me with a drowsy, sluggish feeling. My eyelids start to feel like someone's pulling them down, and I try to push them open.

"Do you want to sleep in my bed tonight?" Drew asks me. "I can sleep in James's. He's not here."

"Thank you," I say gratefully.

"No problem," Drew says, standing up and heading to his dresser. He comes back with a sloppily folded T-shirt and a pair of shorts. "You might want to change," he says, handing them to me. "I'll be in the bathroom."

He leaves, and I get changed without getting out of his bed. His clothes smell clean and fresh, and when I'm finished I climb under the covers, the panicky feeling starting to be replaced by total exhaustion. When Drew comes back a few minutes later, I'm already half asleep, and when he goes to turn the light by his bed off, I stop him. "Can you leave it on?" I ask. "I'm sorry, I'm just . . . I'm scared."

"Sure, I'll leave it on," Drew says. "If you need to shut it off in the middle of the night, go ahead, okay?"

"Okay," I say. He turns toward James's bed, but I grab his arm. "Stay with me," I say, pulling him down on the bed with me. And that's the last thing I remember.

NOW

We didn't have sex. I didn't even kiss him. There was a moment, right before I fell completely asleep, where his lips were so close that I think I wanted to, but I stopped myself. Of course, there is a definite possibility that was a dream.

The message boards would go crazy after that episode aired, saying that I was using Drew to get back at Corey for the whole Jen debacle. They figured that since nothing really happened, Corey wouldn't have a right to get mad. The truth is, I was drunk, I was scared, and I didn't want to be alone. I was practically convinced I was going to die in my sleep due to some alcohol-related vital-organ shutdown. But people saw it the way they wanted to, and settled on the jealousy theory.

So nothing happened. We slept in the same bed, and that was it. The light stayed on all night. On some level, I had to know, even drunk, that there was a chance Corey would find out about it. Even though he said he wasn't going to watch the show anymore, one of his friends could have seen it or someone from home could have asked him about it. What never crossed my mind was that Corey might not even care.

THEN

Head. Pounding. Not a normal headache, but a weird, heavy feeling that makes my body feel like a fuzzy brick. My eyes are crusted over, and my mouth is so dry, it hurts. I think I might be dead. The clock on the nightstand says 2:07 p.m. But that can't be right, because my clock doesn't show a.m. or p.m., it just has . . . that is not my clock. Oh my God. I've been kidnapped. Someone has kidnapped me! Someone has drugged me, slipped something into my drink, and TAKEN ME TO AN UNDISCLOSED LOCATION. I move my arms experimentally to see if I've been tied up or restrained in any way.

It all comes rushing back to me. The party. Throwing up. Falling asleep in the bathroom. Drew coming in to help me. Pulling him down onto the bed with me. *Pulling him down onto the bed with me.* I turn over slowly. Please don't be next to me, please don't be next to me, please don't be—he's gone. I'm alone.

My eyes fall on my clothes in a pile on the floor where I threw them last night. I look under the cover curiously, wondering if I'm dressed. Fully clothed. In Drew's stuff. Better than being naked, I suppose.

Frank the cameraman enters the room and starts filming, obviously alerted to the fact that I'm awake by the production staff who is monitoring my every move on the overhead cameras. *Now* he shows up. Where was he last night when I was busy almost dying and making a fool of myself? Typical.

I spring out of Drew's bed quickly, hoping to minimize the amount of tape available that shows me in it. I need a shower and a drink. A nonalcoholic drink. And I need to get out of these clothes. I pour myself a huge glass of orange juice in the kitchen, and am on my way back to my own room to grab some clothes and shower stuff when the phone rings. It's Kelly.

"So you're finally awake, eh, party girl? I've been trying you all morning." All morning?

"Barely," I say, collapsing into the chair in the phone alcove and sipping my juice. I stop myself from chugging the whole glass, realizing this may not be a good idea, since my stomach is still probably a little sketchy. "Don't ever let me drink like that again."

"Drink like what?" Kelly asks, laughing. "You had, like, three beers or something. We couldn't believe you were so out of it."

We? Who's we? Everyone at the party? Random people I can't remember talking to? Kelly and people she told? It's not my fault that I have no alcohol tolerance. I never really drank that much in high school. I heard it's pretty easy to build one up, though. An alcohol tolerance, I mean. Although if it makes you feel like this, who could be bothered?

"I threw up when I got home," I confess.

"Really? You totally need to get out more. Anyway, I was going to ask if you wanted to go to the mall and catch a movie, but it sounds like you're really hungover."

"I am," I say, resting my head against the back of the chair. The thought of picking it up ever again definitely doesn't appeal to me. Neither does the thought of taking a shower or getting dressed, even though I stink. My hair is stringy and smells like smoke, and I didn't wash my face last night, so my makeup has congealed into a gritty film. I don't even want to look in the mirror.

Oh, and I'm wearing Drew's clothes, which need to be taken off, washed, and promptly returned.

"I'd invite you over here to watch a movie or something, but my roommate has this huge paper due and I'm supposed to be keeping quiet," Kelly says.

"You wanna come over here? We could order a Pay-Per-View or something and just hang out."

"Cool," she says. "Is anyone around?"

"Um, I'm not sure," I say, not sure why it matters. "I just woke up and I haven't seen anyone."

"Like half an hour, okay?"

"I have to warn you that I'm probably still going to be in my pajamas," I tell her.

"That's cool," she says, giggling. "Maybe I'll wear mine. See you in a few."

I put the phone back on the cradle, and then consider picking it back up to call my house. I figure I should warn my parents about last night. If I tell them, it may make it seem like it's not that big of a deal. If I *don't* tell them, it's like I kept it a secret because I thought it was bad.

It's like Jasmine and the whole Hooters thing. Jasmine says she doesn't give a shit who knows she's a Hooters girl, since she doesn't think anything's wrong with it. If she meets a guy and he asks what she does, she tells him. She says keeping it a secret makes it seem like she's ashamed of it, which she most certainly isn't.

The thought of dealing with my parents right now is definitely not appealing, and so I leave the phone where it is and drag myself to the shower.

When Kelly arrives forty-five minutes later, I'm clean and dressed—and NOT in Drew's clothes. I'm wearing a pair of pink pajama pants and a long-sleeved gray shirt made out of a soft fleece material. My hair is in two pigtails. I feel, if not completely normal, then at least much better. Physically, I mean. The thought of having to face Drew is definitely not good for my mental state. I don't know where he is or when he's coming back, which makes it even worse.

"I still can't believe how amazing this house is," Kelly says. We're hanging in the living room, trying to decide on a movie. Two bags of chips are on the table in front of us, along with two huge glasses of diet soda. I almost went with the regular, full-sugar soda, figuring I needed it as a reward for making it through the night, but then I remembered turbo's remark about my ass, so I decided on the diet. I feel kind of stupid for letting someone I've never met dictate my dietary habits, but I figure being healthy is never a bad thing. Besides, I don't want to end up like Carrie Mahaney, this girl who graduated two years before me. When she came back for the summer after her fresh-man year at Salem State, no one could believe how huge she'd gotten. Of course, there was a rumor that she had developed an alcohol problem, so it could have been all the extra calories from the beer.

"The house is amazing, you're right," I say, "and in exchange for living here, I get to have the whole world see me drunk, my mom know that I went to a strip club, and sleep in a room with TWO other girls." I roll my eyes, even though the house is definitely the best part of being on the show. "You're really good with the cameras, by the way." I pick up a chip and take a bite. Full-fat chips are obviously not the same as full-sugar soda. Besides, it's all about baby steps. "Whenever I'm with my friend Grant, he, like, can't take his eyes off of them." I swallow the chip experimentally, seeing how it feels in my stomach.

"Oh. I guess I'm just not bothered by them." She shrugs her shoulders and twirls a strand of hair around her finger slowly. She's wearing white flannel pajama pants with red and yellow M&M's all over them and a blue hoodie. "So what happened last night? After we left you outside, I didn't know if you were going to make it, you were so out of it." She laughs, and I look at her blankly. If I was so out of it, why didn't she offer to help me?

"I got in fine," I say breezily. "And just passed out."

"Where?"

"Where?" I ask, studying her face closely. If she tells me she saw me in Drew's bed on a fucking preview, I swear to God . . .

"Yeah, I mean, did you make it to your bed?"

"Why wouldn't I have made it to my bed?" I ask, phrasing the question carefully. I don't want to admit I slept in Drew's bed, but I don't want to lie to her either. If I lie, chances are she'll see it on the show, figure out I'm being deceptive, and get pissed. Then I'll be stuck in this house for the rest of my time here. Actually, stuck in my *room,* since I most certainly won't be able to venture out for fear of running into Drew.

"Hello! Because you were so drunk," she says, exasperated.

Fuck it. "Actually," I say, "I ended up sleeping in Drew's bed."

Her eyes widen. "Drew's bed?" she asks. "What happened?"

"Nothing," I say, shrugging. I swing my legs up onto the couch and lie down, my head resting against one of the pillows. "I kind of ended up crashing there."

"Oh," she says, sounding disappointed. What is up with all my friends thinking I'm going to hook up with Drew?

Don't they understand that I have a boyfriend?

"So did you start your next photo project yet?" I ask her, anxious to change the subject. All this talk of Drew and beds is making me nervous.

"Yeah. Did you?"

"Not really," I say. Our next project is supposed to be three photos that depict where we are in our lives.

"You really should start thinking about it," Kelly says, taking a sip of her drink. "We only have two projects and a final in that class, so it's a really big part of your grade. Plus, you're probably not that sure how you did on the first one, so . . ."

"Yeah," I say, deciding not to tell Kelly about my talk with Professor Lutkiss and the fact that I'm considering majoring in photography. The last thing I need right now is another person telling me I'm crazy. Although after getting drunk and sleeping in another guy's bed, I'm starting to have serious doubts about my mental health myself.

I pick up the remote and turn on the TV.

"What do you want to watch?" I ask Kelly, but the front door opens before she can answer. My heart leaps into my chest.

POSSIBLE OPENERS AFTER YOU'VE
GOTTEN DRUNK AND SLEPT IN YOUR
GUY ROOMMATE'S BED (A LIST):

1. Hey, Drew, thanks for letting me sleep in your bed. I hope I didn't puke all over your sheets.

2. What do you mean? I slept in your bed? Really? I don't remember any of it, I was so wasted.

3. Thanks for not trying to molest me.

It's only Simone. I breathe a sigh of relief, thankful I'm saved from coming up with anything witty just yet.

"Good afternoon!" she sings, her voice louder than I've ever heard it. She flings her book bag onto a nearby chair and plops down next to it. Her normally curly red hair is blown completely straight, and she's wearing lip gloss.

I raise my eyebrows. "What's with you?"

"I'm just in a good mood, that's all. Can't someone be in a good mood?" She blushes. Hard.

"Of course," Kelly says. She smiles at Simone. "But usually there's a reason."

"Oh my God. Did you . . . ?" I ask. Simone puts a finger to her lips and pulls a piece of paper out of her bag. She scrawls on it quickly with a pink pen, then hands the paper to me.

Kelly and I huddle around it.

"Last night, James and I ditched the cameras and went back to his friend's apartment. WE HAD SEX. I know it seems kind of sudden, but it just felt right. DO NOT SAY ANYTHING OUT LOUD. My parents would totally flip if they knew. Besides, I think we're going to try to keep our relationship under wraps for a little while. Avoid all the publicity and stuff. But I'm very VERY VERY happy." She's drawn a little smiley face after the last word.

Kelly and I look at her, our mouths open. "Wow," I

say. I make a mental note to ask her later how she ditched the cameras. It might come in handy when Corey comes to visit, and I most certainly could have used it last night.

She nods. "I got back early this morning, took a shower, and went to the library." She looks at her hands. "It's weird, because it's like everything's the same, but completely different at the same time," she says softly, then looks up. "Does that make any sense?"

Everything being the same and totally different at the same time? Tell me about it.

Drew still hasn't shown up by the time Kelly, Simone, and I finish watching the movie. After we grab some dinner, I spend the rest of the night in the library studying for my midterms and then outside, taking pictures in the dark. It's one of the warmest nights we've had in a while, and I sign out three rolls of film from the photo lab and start taking pictures not only for my photo project, but just for fun. Something about taking pictures in the dark is mysterious, and I walk around campus for a while, enjoying the freedom of being out of the house, and the fact that I'm alone. Well, except for Frank, who I think gets slightly annoyed that I'm making him walk so much.

By the time I get home, it's after midnight and the house is quiet. Everyone's either out or sleeping. I grab a bottle of water out of the refrigerator and check the messages by the phone. "Ally, Corey called at 7:30," Jasmine's handwriting says. "Where are you?" 7:30? Nice to know he was in such a rush to make sure I was okay. I consider calling him back, but I really don't want to listen to his bullshit about how I'm such a bad person for drinking at a frat party. I'm just too tired to deal with it.

I make my way to my room, which is empty. I think Jasmine's still at work, and I have no idea where Simone is. In James's bed, maybe? I turn the light on and am about to head to the bathroom to brush my teeth and wash my face when I notice the note on my bed.

Dear Ally,
I had to go to a seminar this morning for my anthropology class, so I'm sorry if I disappeared. Anyway, you haven't been around, so I'm hoping you're okay and that your hangover isn't too bad. I was at the mall this afternoon, saw this, and thought of you. It seems pretty interesting, and I remember seeing something like this around my dad's studio, so hopefully you'll get something useful out of it. I'll talk to ya tomorrow, I'm sure.
—D

Underneath the note is a copy of *Photographer's Market*, a book that lists all the magazines and other publications that buy pictures from freelance photographers. Along with who's buying what and how much they pay, there's tons of articles about how to break into freelance photography. It's, like, a thirty-dollar book. I can't believe he did this. Everyone in my own *family* thinks I'm ridiculous, and Drew, who I haven't even known that long, believes in me enough to buy me a book like this.

It doesn't mean *anything*, I think, stroking the shiny cover and flipping through the fresh pages. That he gave me a present, I mean. It's just something a friend would do for another friend. Although. It *is* a really nice book. He wouldn't have done it unless he liked me a little bit, right? Not that I care. I have a boyfriend. But still. What if he does? Like me, I mean. I don't *care* if he does, it doesn't really *matter* either way. . . . But he wouldn't have given me the book if he didn't, right?

I'm getting ready to leave for class on Monday morning when Grant knocks on the front door of the house.

"Hey," I say, opening the door. "What's up?" I grab him in a tight hug.

"Hi," Grant says, pulling away and looking serious. "How long have you been up?"

"Um, I don't know, forty-five minutes? Why?" He pushes past me into the house.

"Okkaayyy, come on in," I say, closing the door behind him. "How'd you get by security, anyway?"

"I can be very charming when I have to," he says, taking a seat at the breakfast bar. "Listen, there's something I have to tell you, and I don't think you're going to like it."

"Okay," I say, settling in on the stool next to him. "But I have psychology in twenty minutes, so I can't talk long." I'm expecting normal Grant drama—he's fooled around with one of his professors, a sex tape of him has somehow ended up on the Internet, he's cheated on Brett, etc. So giving him a time limit up front is definitely beneficial.

"First, before I tell you this, I want you to promise me that you're not going to flip out."

"I won't flip out."

"Promise?"

"I promise."

"Okay, because it's really not that big of a deal, in the grand *scheme* of things. I mean, people have been through lots worse than this, Ally. Some people have cancer, or are paralyzed, or have had their spouses leave them with two kids and a mortgage or . . ."

"Grant!"

"Right. Okay." He looks sad as he hands me a newspaper.

"Oh, God, Grant, what did you do?" I ask, wondering what sort of scrape he's gotten into that would actually be news to anyone but him. "Did you . . . did you get *arrested*?" I know for a fact they announce all the arrests in the newspaper. Grant's not a thief, and he doesn't do drugs, so I have no idea what this could be about. Grant's parents are not going to be pleased. This on top of the whole Brett thing—it's just going to make it worse.

"Grant, um, we might not want to talk about this here," I say, tilting my head toward the cameras. I mean, someday he'll want to find a real job, and this definitely will not look good.

"Ally"—Grant grabs my shoulders—"just read it."

I look down at a copy of the school paper and relax slightly. If it's only the school paper, then it can't be that big of a deal. Hopefully we can keep it from leaking to the bigger presses.

The headline on the front page reads, "Confessions of a Pseudo-Friend: What's Really Going on *In the House*," by Kelly Crisp. This headline is accompanied by a small picture of Kelly, smiling brightly for the camera. My jaw drops as I continue to read:

As most of you know, this semester, Syracuse College was chosen as the setting for the reality TV show *In the House*. Recently, this reporter had the opportunity to get close to the cast through my friendship with cast member Ally Cavanaugh. What I soon learned is that what you're seeing on the show is only half of what's actually going on.

The producers have painted a cute little picture of what the cast is like, but as someone with the inside scoop, I can tell you this portrait is not accurate. The only one who's remotely like the way he's portrayed on the show is James. He really is an ebonics-speaking player. And while you may not like James's womanizing ways, you have to admire him for being real, which is more than I can say for the rest of the cast.

Simone, who is made to look like a softspoken Southern girl, spent this weekend ditching the cameras and losing her virginity in a random apartment. Who did she experience this milestone with, you ask? Why, none other than Rico Suave himself, her roommate James.

Jasmine is not the beautiful, intelligent bombshell forced into stripping in order to pay her tuition. That girl knows exactly what she's doing, and isn't afraid to use her sexuality to get whatever she wants. She told me she thinks one guy just isn't enough for her, and she doesn't intend to have a relationship anytime soon—although that definitely doesn't stop her from hooking up.

Ally, while endearingly naive, is sometimes so over-the-top clueless that it's hard not to get annoyed. All she talks about is how much she loves her boyfriend Corey, while secretly lusting after her roommate Drew. While I've never had the opportunity to meet Drew, I know for a fact Ally spent the night in his bed this weekend after getting drunk off half a beer at DK. When she told me this, she was so obviously flustered that it was hard not to call her out on it. I didn't want to push, though, so as not to blow my cover. She complains about having to live in the lap of luxury while everyone else is stuck in the dorms, and has trouble handling the pressures of college classes. The girl almost fainted when our photography professor critiqued our first project.

"Grant." I toss the paper away and grab his shirt. I can't breathe. This is not happening.

"Ally, it's okay," he says, prying my fingers loose from the fabric. "Like I said, it's not that big of a deal, in the grand scheme of things. And remember how you promised not to flip out?"

"That little bitch," I say, my shock turning to anger. "How could she? *Why* would she? What was she *thinking*?"

"Um, that it would make a good story?" Grant offers

helpfully. "Oh, and I heard she's hoping it'll be picked up by some other newspapers."

"Other newspapers? It's not even that well-written! She's all over the place with her pronouns!" I say, not sure if it's true.

"I heard she already has interest from a few Internet publications," Grant reports. I glare at him.

"This is what I get for being friends with a girl," I say. "This is exactly what I get. Backstabbing and bitchiness."

"Oh, come on, Ally," Grant says, hopping off his chair and opening the refrigerator. He starts to root through the contents. "That's not fair to say. It's not girls. It's people in general. Most of them are shits." He pulls out a container of leftover Chinese food, grabs a fork, and starts to eat right out of the carton.

"Help yourself to whatever you want, "I say, rolling my eyes. I drop my head into my hands.

THE PAST FEW DAYS (AN EVALUATION):

1. Slept in the same bed with another guy, one who happens to be hot, my roommate, and who for some inexplicable reason I want to kiss.
2. Got drunk on national television.
3. Have been backstabbed by the only non-roommate, non-Grant friend I have here.

Again, right on track.

"Hey," Grant says, rubbing my back. "It's okay. So

she wrote some shit in the school paper. You'll be fine."

"I know," I say, and I can feel the tears welling up behind my eyes. I will NOT cry. "I just thought she was my friend, you know?"

"Yeah," Grant says softly, and we sit in silence for a few seconds, considering. My eyes keep drifting to the newspaper lying on the counter, focusing on the words "secretly in love with Drew." I still haven't seen him. I spent the whole day yesterday in the library, studying and poring over the book he got me.

The front door opens and slams. Simone walks into the kitchen, a copy of the paper clutched in her hand, her face streaked with tears.

"Simone," I say, rushing over to her. "I'm so, so sorry." I throw my arms around her, and she hugs me back. "It's all my fault," I say. "I should have never let her in the house."

"It's not your fault, Ally," she says, pulling back. She wipes her tears on her sleeve. "You couldn't have known what she was going to do. Besides, I was the one that told her."

"I know, but . . ."

"I'm not upset about that, anyway."

"You're not? Why are you crying?"

"I'm crying because James broke up with me," she says, looking down at the ground. "Well, actually, if you ask him, he didn't break up with me, because we were never really together." She gives me a wry smile. "It was just a one-night thing to him."

"Simone!" I say, shocked. I can't believe she's talking about sleeping with James in front of the cameras.

"It doesn't matter," she says quietly. "It's in the school paper—he already dumped me. Who cares if my parents find out?"

"I'm so sorry," I say, looking at her tear-stained face and starting to get upset all over again.

"Guys are such dicks," Grant says, spearing a piece of chicken out of the Chinese food carton and popping it into his mouth. We stare at him. "What?" he says. "They are. Honey, I could tell you story upon story, couldn't I, Ally? Like that one substitute teacher who gave me head and then totally denied it the next day? It's such bullshit." He stabs another piece of chicken forcefully.

"Uh, I'm sorry. Simone, have you met Grant?"

"I don't think so," she says, staring at him. Grant's wearing a salmon-colored button-up shirt and a pair of black dress pants. He's wearing shiny black shoes and is eating our Chinese food.

"Nice to meet you," Grant says, holding his hand out. Simone accepts it uncertainly. "Sorry about the grease," he says, pulling his hand back and grabbing a napkin. "Chicken and broccoli." He holds up the carton in explanation.

We ignore him. "How could I have been so stupid?" I ask, plopping back down in one of the stools on the breakfast bar.

"You're not stupid," Simone says, looking at her hands.

"I'm the one who's a joke. I saved my virginity for eighteen years, and then in a matter of six weeks . . ." she trails off. I reach over and squeeze her hand.

"You got any more of this?" Grant asks, brandishing the empty carton. We look at him, disbelieving. "What?" he asks, heading back to the fridge.

NOW

This is going to sound kind of ridiculous, and it's horrible to even admit, but I think I was more upset by the fact that Drew might read I had a secret crush on him than I was about Kelly's betrayal. I didn't realize it at the time, but Kelly hadn't really taken away anything I would miss. Yeah, she let me borrow her clothes and gave me someone to hang with outside of the house, but that was about it. She couldn't understand the things I was going through the way Jasmine and Simone could, and she certainly didn't know about the problems I was having with Corey.

But I hated the fact that she could see the feelings I had for Drew. It was humiliating to think that something I was trying so hard to deny to myself was so transparent to someone else. So at the time, I convinced myself that it wasn't about Drew, it was about Kelly. And the more I told myself this, the easier it was to believe.

THEN

"I'm going to kick that bitch's ass," Jasmine says, grabbing her coat off the rack by the door and sliding her arms into it.

"It's one in the morning," Simone says nervously, her eyes moving back and forth between Jasmine and me.

"So?" Jasmine says, pushing her hair out from under the back of her black leather jacket. "That's good. She won't be expecting me to kick the shit out of her this late at night, so I'll have an advantage." Jasmine just got home from work and finished listening carefully while Simone and I filled her in on the Kelly debacle. She read the article and then promptly announced she was going to find Kelly and fight her.

"But you're in your Hooters uniform," I point out. I'm lying on the couch, my legs up in the air and my head hanging over the side, seeing how long it will take for all the blood to rush to my head. For some reason, I see this as a fun game. I'm obviously a loser.

"So?" Jasmine asks again, sounding exasperated.

"So that's not the best outfit to get in a fight with," I say. "A lot of your skin's exposed, so she'll be able to, like, scratch you and stuff. You should wear track pants. And a hoodie. Black ones. To blend in with the night." She looks down, considering. "Plus," I add, "your muscles might cramp up since it's so cold out. Because of all the exposed skin. And if you go to jail, you most certainly don't want to be dressed like that. You'll be in big trouble, for a lot of reasons."

"Y'all aren't serious," Simone says. "You're not going to really hurt her."

"Why not?" Jasmine says. "She messed with my girls. And me."

"But you'll get kicked off the show," Simone says. "It was in the contract we signed: 'I will not cause bodily harm to others or myself.'"

"Good point," I say, still upside down.

"Besides, she's not worth it," Simone says from the chair where she's sitting.

"Fine," Jasmine says, taking her coat back off. "For now. But I reserve the right to go after her at a later time, if I so choose."

She sits down next to me and surveys the spread of ice cream, brownies, chips, and drinks that's laid out before us. Calories I've consumed within the last two hours: 20,317.

"What is this?" Jasmine asks, picking up a glass and taking a sip.

"Diet Coke with Lime," Simone says.

"You just lost your virginity, then got dumped and

outted in the school paper, and you guys are drinking soda?" She looks disgusted. "I have so much to teach you two."

"Alcohol is part of the reason I'm in this mess to begin with," I say, sitting up. The blood drains from my head, and I close my eyes, enjoying the rush.

"Drinking made Kelly write bad things in the school paper?" Jasmine asks.

"No," I say, "but it did make me sleep in the same bed with Drew, which gave her more material to write about. Pass me a brownie."

Simone picks up the plate and hands it to me.

"How many of those have you had?" Jasmine asks, looking at my disheveled hair and pajama'd body.

"I dunno," I say, taking a huge bite. "Four? Five? I figure if I get really fat, no boys will want me, anyway, so all my problems will be solved." I look at her. "So what happened to you the other night?"

"What do you mean?" Jasmine asks.

"With what's-his-face. That guy from the party you left with."

"Oh my God," Simone says. "You left with some guy from the party? How did I not know this?"

"Nothing happened," Jasmine says, looking uncomfortable. "He walked me home because I was a little tipsy, and that was it."

"But you weren't home when I got here," I say, frowning. "Because no one was. I ended up on the bathroom floor, alone. Not that I'm blaming," I quickly add.

"Lightweight," Jasmine snorts.

"So where were ya?" I ask, not willing to let it go.

Jasmine reaches down and pulls at the leg of her tight black shorts. "I, um, spent the night at Dale's."

"Oh my God!" I shriek. "You gave up some random hookup for him!"

"No, I didn't!" she protests. "That guy at the party was a total loser, and so—"

"We know, we know, you got bored," Simone says.

Silence.

"He's totally your boyfriend!" I declare gleefully. I pick up another brownie off the plate and take a bite.

"He is not!" Jasmine says.

"Is." Simone.

"Isn't." Jasmine.

"Yes." Me.

"No." Jasmine.

Silence.

"Fine!" Jasmine says, throwing her hands up in disgust. "He's my boyfriend. Whatever."

"Oooh," I chorus. "Jasmine and Dale, sittin' in a tree."

"Oh my God, you are so corny," she says, rolling her eyes, but I can tell she secretly likes it. "*Anyway*, Simone, how are you doing with this whole thing?"

"I don't know," Simone says, looking at her hands. "I'm okay until I think about it. And then I can't stop crying." Her face flushes a deep red, and I look at her, feeling selfish for getting so upset over the stupid Drew thing. Simone definitely got the worst of this.

"Sweetie, he's not worth it," Jasmine says. "Any guy who has a sticker on his bedroom door that says 'smack my bitch up' is not someone you want to be involved with."

"I don't know what you saw in him in the first place," I say, finishing my sixth brownie and washing it down with a swig of soda. I wipe my mouth with a napkin. No sense in being fat *and* dirty.

"He was different when we were alone," Simone says. "He was sweet."

"Trying to get into your pants," Jasmine reports. "Oldest trick in the book."

Simone looks at the floor. A tear slides down her cheek and lands on her jeans, making a dark circle of wetness. I pass her a tissue wordlessly.

"It's okay," Jasmine says, rubbing her back. "The good news is, no one ever ends up with the person who takes their virginity. So you're no different from anyone else."

Except me, I think, wondering for the first time if Corey and I are doomed simply because he was the first guy I've ever been with. Are there people who've only been with one person their entire lives? There must be. I mean, all those articles I gave Grant about high school sweethearts alone.

"But not everyone is dumb enough to think that they're actually in a relationship with someone just because they had sex with them." Simone sniffs, wiping her nose. "I just feel really stupid. And now, because of that article, every-one's going to know."

"Don't feel stupid," I tell her. "James is the one to blame, not you. He's an asshole."

Jasmine nods.

"But I'm a slut," Simone says so softly, we have trouble hearing her.

"You're what?"

"I'm a slut," she repeats, now sobbing hard.

"You are definitely not a slut," Jasmine says, putting her arms around her. "Having sex with a guy you like does not make you a slut. Now if you start having sex with *every* guy you like, then we'll reclassify you according to level of skankiness."

"I shouldn't have slept with him," Simone says softly.

"Maybe," I say. "But you can't let yourself get caught up in that. Besides, he didn't dump you because you had sex with him—he dumped you because he's an asshole."

Simone smiles. "He *is* kind of an asshole," she says, trying to laugh through her tears. "I mean, his 'outta my way or you're gonna get played' shirt? What is that about?"

"A warning?" I offer.

"A desperate plea for attention?"

"The last shirt left at the dollar store?"

They look at me.

"What? They have shirts at the dollar store," I say. "Besides, it was a joke."

There's a moment of silence, and then we all start laughing.

"So was it good?" Jasmine asks Simone. She grabs a cookie off the plate and takes a bite. She manages to look sexy and put together even while eating junk food.

"What?" Simone asks, looking up.

"She means the sex," I clarify. "How was it?"

"Well, I don't really have anything to compare it to," Simone says slowly.

"So it was bad," Jasmine says, finishing the cookie.

She giggles. "No, it wasn't bad, it was just . . . is it supposed to be so bumpy?"

Jasmine and I look at each other and burst out laughing. "All right," Jasmine says, sighing. "I'm going to change. Someone pour me a, what is it? Diet Coke with Lime? I have a feeling we're going to be here awhile."

She stands up and starts to head to her room, but Simone starts to talk. "This is probably going to sound pathetic," she says slowly. "But I've had a crush on him since I've been here, and now . . . I don't know, now it feels like I have nothing." Her eyes start to fill up with tears, and Jasmine puts her arms around her.

"You have us," she says, and we let Simone cry.

Over the next week, my life becomes an exercise in avoidance. I avoid Kelly in photography, and she avoids me. I wish I could be a badass, but really, what would I say? "Hi, thanks for pretending to be my friend so you could write some half-assed article that you hoped would be picked up by the *New York Times*?" Besides, it wouldn't do any good. I can't change the fact that she wrote it.

I'm still avoiding Drew, because, hello, I slept in his bed. And wore his clothes. I SLEPT IN HIS BED WHILE WEARING HIS CLOTHES. And then, instead of being all sketched out about it like a normal person would, he pretended like it was totally okay and even bought me a present. What the hell is that about? I was going to thank him for the book, I swear to God, I was. But then Kelly's article came out, and I'm sure he read it. And what if, when he read the part about how I was secretly in love with him, he started to think it was true? The whole situation is completely fucked up.

I'm avoiding long phone conversations with Corey, since he's supposed to be coming to visit next Saturday, and I don't want him canceling or changing the plans again. Plus, I'm afraid someone may have told him about the episode in which I slept in Drew's bed. He hasn't said anything about it, which makes me ridiculously relieved. I can't believe I was ever insulted that he wasn't watching the show. Now I'm definitely grateful.

I have a ton of work to do, so I lie low and keep my head buried in my books. When I'm not at the library, I'm working on my pictures. I have some really amazing nature shots that I'm excited to send out to magazines, and of course, my next photography project.

I keep up my life of avoidance for almost a week. Which is a pretty amazing feat when you think about it. It isn't until Friday night at around one a.m. that the jig's finally up. I'm in my room getting into my pajamas when Drew knocks on my door. Jasmine's at work, and Simone's still at the library, where I left her studying for her American history midterm.

I freeze in the middle of tying my hair back. Fuck. It has to be one of the boys, and seeing how it's one in the morning on a Friday night, it's a pretty safe bet to assume James is out, looking for the next victim's virginity.

I ignore the knock and stay very still.

"Ally?" Drew says, knocking again.

"Who is it?" I ask, trying to sound like I'm sleeping and hoping he'll go away. Then I realize this is a terrible plan, since he probably heard me come in two seconds ago, and even though the door's shut, I'm sure he can tell my light is on from the crack under the door. Ugh.

"It's Drew," he says. I imagine him standing in the hall, using one hand to knock on the door, the other to clutch a copy of the school paper, ready to confront me.

"Um, just a second," I say. "I'm, uh, changing." Shit. Should not have said changing. Changing could possibly remind him of me changing in his bed, and that is the last thing I want to discuss. I rush to the mirror over my dresser and check my reflection. I run a brush through my hair and put on some lip gloss. Not that I care. What I look like, I mean. But since this could possibly be the last time Drew and I converse, since he obviously knows I'm "secretly obsessed" with him, I might as well look cute. I roll down the top of my gray pajama pants to show off a strip of my stomach. Although this may not be the best idea, after my recent brownie/Chinese food/pizza binges.

I've been drowning my sorrows in food, figuring it's a better drug than speed and/or Ecstasy. Although if I ever did decide to switch my drug of choice to either one of those, I wouldn't have a problem, since when I first got here, one of James's friends asked me if I wanted to score. I thought he was propositioning me for sex, until James cleared it up later. That was before he had sex with Simone and dumped her. I'm currently not speaking to him. Neither is Jasmine. We're all on asshole strike.

Drew knocks again. I leave the pants rolled down, deciding that exposed stomach is better than not, even if it's um, slightly larger than usual. I shut the light off to compensate, figuring the darkness will mask my bloated body.

"Hey!" I say brightly, throwing open the door. My new, just-decided-upon plan of attack is to pretend like everything's fine. I mean, really, who cares if I slept in his bed and then someone I thought was my good friend wrote something about how I secretly had a crush on him? I can be mature about this. I put on my best Katie Holmes in *First Daughter* face. "Where have you been?" I ask brilliantly, figuring it best to strike first, and make it out like he's been avoiding me.

"I was going to ask you the same thing," he says. He looks past me into the dark room. "Why'd you turn the light off?"

Shit. "Oh, uh, I was leaving the room," I say. "So, you know, saving electricity."

"Oh," he says uncertainly. "Where are you going?"

"To the living room," I say, rolling my eyes. "I'm going to watch, um, a movie." Duh.

"Oh, cool. Mind if I watch with you?"

"No." Yes. No.

He follows me downstairs and into the living room. "So

did you get the book?" Drew asks, sitting down next to me on the couch.

"Yeah. That was really nice of you." I look down and play with a stray thread that's popped free from the lining of the couch. I seriously cannot look at him for fear of my face revealing just how bad I want him. I think it's that fucking cologne he wears. It does something to me and makes me confuse my lust for a scent with lust for him. "I was going to thank you, but I've just been so busy with midterms and everything. . . ."

"That's okay. I just thought that maybe if you sold a picture or two, it might help your family come around and take this whole photography thing a little more seriously."

"How'd you know my family is freaked out about it?" I ask, finally looking up.

"Jasmine told me. Since, you know, you haven't really been around."

"Oh."

There's a silence, and I pick up the remote. "So, what should we watch?" I ask, wondering how long I actually have to watch TV with him before I can get out of here. I figure it's only a matter of time before he brings up Kelly's article and gives me the whole "I think we should only be friends" or "I think you're cool, but I could never date a roommate" speech. I glance nervously at Sam the cameraman, who's the one taping us right now. Getting humiliated is never cool, and is even worse when it could be broadcast to the nation. I wonder if I should bring it up first. You know, that whole "the best defense is a good offense" thing or whatever. Maybe I should say something like, "Can you believe all those LIES Kelly printed? NONE of it is true—she's such a LYING jerk. All she does is MAKE THINGS UP and LIE."

"Hey," Drew says, taking the remote out of my hand. I can feel my skin get hot where his hand touched mine. He looks at me seriously. "Are we cool?"

"Of course!" I say, thankful he's going to spare me the I-don't-like-you-in-that-way speech. "Are we cool?" is obviously code for "You know I could never date you, right, so we will never speak of this again, okay, you delusional fool?" "Why wouldn't we be?"

"I don't know. Things just seem kind of sketch since that one night." He waits for me to say something, but I keep quiet. "I don't want things to be weird between us," he finishes finally.

"Me neither," I say vehemently. "I'm totally fine, I swear."

"All right, cool," he says, switching on the TV. "Now is it gonna be Tom Cruise or John Travolta? Think carefully before you answer—our whole friendship could hinge on whether or not you answer this question correctly."

"It's gotta be John," I say. "Ever since *Grease* there has been no other choice."

"Good answer," Drew says, smiling at me. Heat rises through my body, and I'm not sure it's a good thing that I got the answer right.

NOW

So that was that. After we got the initial contact out of the way, I was able get back to avoiding him, only this time with a clear conscience. I mean, I had thanked him for the book, so I didn't owe him anything else.

The Kelly situation was slowly fading from my mind, I got the first post-sleeping-in-his-bed/post-newspaper-fiasco meeting with Drew out of the way, and Corey hadn't said anything about me sleeping in another guy's bed. It seemed like my life was on the upswing. And then something horrible happened, and things got worse than they'd ever been.

THEN

Two o'clock Wednesday afternoon, and I'm waiting outside Professor Lutkiss's office. He asked me to meet him during his office hours to talk about the photography project I turned in yesterday. If he likes the pictures I took, I'm pretty sure he's going to invite me to apply for the photography program. If he doesn't like them, well then, I'm not sure what will happen. I guess I'll take another photo class next semester, keep sending my stuff out, and hope that I eventually get invited to apply. Majoring in something else is not an option. I'm 100 percent sure this is what I want to do.

His secretary keeps giving me really weird looks, and she gave me shit about Frank coming in here. Apparently she's, like, the only person in the world who doesn't know that *In the House* is being filmed at Syracuse College. I swear she thinks I'm some sort of undercover journalist trying to smuggle in a camera to expose some horrid secret, which is completely ridiculous because a) I'm wearing black flare pants and a tight, low-cut white shirt, which is way too revealing for a professional journalist, and b) If I was going to try to expose some sort of secret and get proof on videotape, I most certainly would not do it with a huge handheld camera toted around by an even huger man decked out in various kinds of bling.

It does, however, make me wonder what sorts of secrets Professor Lutkiss is hiding that's making his secretary so worried. I saw this thing on *Dateline* once about a prominent lawyer who would go to Taiwan or something and participate in all kinds of illegal activity, including the sex trade and drug trafficking. *Dateline* totally busted him with their hidden cameras, and he was ruined. I think I remember seeing that his secretary knew about it too. Since she had to book his trips to Asia and all.

I pull out my psychology text and start reading, hoping this will give me a more authentic student air. I smile at the secretary. She glares at me and at Frank. Okay, then.

"Ally!" Professor Lutkiss says, coming out of his office. "Great to see you. Come in, come in, I'm sorry to keep you waiting."

"Oh, it's fine," I say, sliding my book into my bag and shooting the secretary a triumphant glance.

"Will your friend be joining us?" he asks, gesturing to Frank.

"He, um, kind of has to," I say. "Unless, of course, you have a problem with it, in which case he can just wait out here."

"It's fine," he says, running a hand nervously through his hair and straightening his tie. I try to hide my smile, thinking about how my first few days here I was so concerned about what I looked like, and now it doesn't even cross my mind.

"Sit," Professor Lutkiss says, gesturing to one of the chairs across from the desk in his office.

I sit down and wipe my palms on my pants.

"I've had a chance to look over your project," he says, laying out my pictures on the desk. For my project on where I am in my life, I've taken a picture of a broken magnifying glass lying on the steps outside the library, a guy and a girl walking away from each other on their way to class, and a picture of Drew, sleeping on the couch, his face covered by his arm, looking peaceful. The one of Drew is in black and white, except for his shirt, which I've colored blue. I hesitated about putting in the picture of Drew, but I wanted my project to be honest. Besides, it was a practice picture I took a long time ago, so it wasn't like I was stalking him down.

"Okay," I say, not sure if I'm supposed to say something.

"I think you have great potential," Professor Lutkiss says. "And I'd like to invite you to apply for the program. But only if you feel you're one hundred percent committed."

"I am," I say. "I'm positive."

"It's not going to be easy, Ally," he warns me. "And there's no guarantee you'll actually get in."

I nod seriously. I totally expected this. I mean, if it were easy, you wouldn't have to be invited, right?

"I think you have a lot of raw talent, but that can only take you so far. You have a lot to learn as far as technique, and you'll have to commit yourself to doing that."

"I will," I say, nodding to show that I recognized the seriousness of the situation.

"And please, please understand that you may have to resubmit your portfolio a few times before you're accepted."

"I understand," I say, nodding again, and trying not to freak out. YAY, YAY, YAY!

"That's great," Professor Lutkiss says. He stands up and shakes my hand. "You can get the application from my secretary."

"Thank you so much," I say, picking up my bag. That's it? I was expecting something a little more intense—hard questions that would leave me sweating and involved critiques of my pictures. I guess it's all dependent on my portfolio now, and how good it is. Which I'm kind of nervous about. But still! I got invited to apply!

I'm so excited that I don't even care that the secretary gives me attitude while she looks for the application. I don't care that I almost trip walking down the steps of the photography building and that Frank catches the whole thing.

I'm so caught up in the moment that I temporarily lose my mind and forget my vow to stay away from Drew. I run into the house, hoping he's home. No one else is going to understand this, and I have to share it with someone.

"Drew!" I yell, running up the stairs to the house. Frank rushes to keep up with me and is doing a pretty good job. Which is why I'm sure he catches the exact look on my face when I open the door to Drew's room. And find him in bed. With Kelly.

I look at Drew. Drew looks at me. I turn on my heel and run down the stairs and back out the front door. The cold air hits my face, and I'm gasping for breath. I feel like there's a rubber band around my chest.

"Ally!" Drew says, and from the sounds of footsteps behind me, I can tell he's coming after me. He catches me when I'm halfway across the lawn. "Ally!" he says, grabbing my arm.

"Don't touch me!" I yell, wrenching away from his grasp.

"Ally, nothing happened," he says.

I whirl around to face him. "Nothing happened? *Nothing happened?* You were in bed with Kelly and you expect me to believe nothing happened? I'm a little too smart for that, Drew."

I turn around and start to walk away from him, but he grabs my arm. "Ally, come on, I want to talk about this."

"There's nothing to talk about," I say, shaking him off.

"I told you, nothing happened. I don't even know her. I just met her yesterday."

"Oh, really?" I laugh loudly, throwing my head back. "Good to know that you let girls you've known less than twenty-four hours into your bed. And here I thought I was special."

Suddenly I have an awful thought. Why would Kelly write in her article that she'd never met Drew and then end up in his bed a week later? Did Drew know what she was doing? Did he *help* her write that article?

"How do you know her?" I ask, crossing my arms in front of my chest. I can feel the tears starting behind my eyes, and it takes everything I have to keep them from spilling over my cheeks. "How do you know Kelly?"

"I don't, really. I told you, I just met her yesterday. Ally, come on, let's go inside and talk about this. It's freezing out here." I look down and see that he's not wearing any shoes.

"Answer the question," I say, tapping my foot on the sidewalk. "How do you know Kelly, Drew?"

"We're working on an extra-credit research project for one of our professors. She came over to work on it, we were watching TV after we finished, and she fell asleep. That's it." He looks at me, his eyes pleading.

"I thought you just met her yesterday. If you were working on an extra-credit project, wouldn't she be in your class?"

"She's in a different class, same professor."

"Well, whatever. It doesn't matter." I turn and start to walk away. Frank turns to keep up with me, and Drew's cameraman turns back toward the house, ready to follow him back inside. But Drew's not finished, and he continues to follow me.

"What are you getting so upset about, anyway? I'm allowed to hang out with whoever I want. You have a boyfriend, Ally, remember?"

"Oh, please," I say, losing my battle with the tears. They start flowing down my face, making hot streaks on my cheeks. "Don't flatter yourself. This isn't about that, and you know it. It's about being a good friend and not messing around with someone who would write that kind of article."

He looks confused. "What article?" he asks.

"The article she wrote about us!" I throw my hands up in the air, amazed at his stupidity. He looks at me blankly. "Don't even tell me you didn't know, Drew. That girl pretended to be my friend for months just so she could write a stupid article about the show."

"Ally," he says, his voice softening. "I didn't know. I swear. Now, please, can we just go inside and talk about this?" He moves toward me, and for one awful and amazing second, I think he's going to put his arms around me. But I push him away.

"No," I say. "We can't talk about this. You expect me to believe you had no idea? I would think you'd realize that was the girl who printed all that shit about me, and about Jasmine and Simone! Come on, Drew, it was a pretty big goddamn deal."

"And when was I supposed to realize that? When you were ignoring me and blowing me off?"

"I wasn't ignoring you or blowing you off!" I'm sobbing now, and I reach up and wipe my tears away with the back of my hand angrily. "Besides, you said we were cool."

"Well, maybe we're not anymore," he says softly, his eyes meeting mine.

"Really? So you lied? Shocker."

"What's that supposed to mean?"

"Just that it seems pretty unlikely that you and psycho girl up there were just hanging out."

"We weren't hanging out! We were working on a group project, and she ended up falling asleep in my bed."

"Oh, okay, cool, and do you have a bridge you'd like to sell me while you're at it?"

"You know what?" he says, running his hands through his hair. "I don't need this right now. Not from you."

"Fine," I say, crossing my arms across my chest. "Then leave me alone."

"Fine," he says, turning around and starting back toward the house.

"Don't ever talk to me again!" I scream at his back. But he doesn't turn around.

I stand there for a few seconds, watching him disappear into the house. When he's gone, I sit on the sidewalk, pulling my knees up to my chest. I cry. And cry. And cry. I'm so sick of this. I'm sick of Frank, who's filming me right now. I'm sick of having to worry about what I say or what I do. I'm sick of being here. I'm sick of feeling the way I do about Corey and about Drew. I'm sick of people lying to me. I just want to go home.

I cry so hard, I feel like my body is going to break. I feel like I'm literally going to cry myself to death. That's how bad it hurts, physically and emotionally. I don't know when everything got so hard, but I've had enough. I stand up, wipe my eyes on the sleeve of my jacket, and march toward the house. I head up the stairs and right into my room, careful not to look in the direction of the boys' room.

I close the door behind me and throw myself onto my bed. Who the hell does he think he is? I mean, letting that girl in our house? That's so ridiculously fucked up. I can't even fathom how ridiculously fucked up that is. It's beyond fucked up. There are some things you just don't do. And messing around with someone who's done something so completely heinous to one of your friends is one of them.

I start crying again, the sobs making my body ache. What was I thinking, even comparing Corey and Drew? Corey would never, ever do something like that to me. He loves me. I'm so stupid. I pick up the phone next to my bed and dial quickly.

"Corey?" I say when he answers. "I need you to come here. Not Saturday. Now."

NOW

Yeah, so even I can admit that was pretty dramatic. I mean, "never talk to me again?" What was that about? I looked totally stupid, getting all upset and threatening when I had a boyfriend. It was like a scene from a bad TV movie. And watching it on the replays? Oh my God, forget about it. I saw it once and almost threw up.

I was upset, I was pissed, I was lonely. It was like everything was coming together in one moment—the way I was feeling about Drew, Kelly's betrayal, my problems with Corey, the fact that I was avoiding my mom, my photography, the cameras being in my face every single second. . . . I broke down. Of course, this is what I told myself, and to a point, it was true. Everything *was* coming down on me at once.

But most of it had to do with me. Not because I found

one of my friends in bed with a girl who had screwed me over. But because I started to think I'd almost wrecked my relationship with my boyfriend—arguably the most important person in my life—over a guy who would do something like that. And it scared the shit out of me. I felt like I'd come dangerously close to losing Corey, and I never wanted that to happen again. Ever.

THEN

"Ally, you know I can't come now," Corey says. He sounds exasperated, like he's explaining something to a little kid who's just not getting it.

"Why not?" I ask, starting to cry again. "You could get your flight changed. People do it all the time."

Corey sighs. "Ally, you can't just change a flight. Not two days before."

"Yes, you can," I insist. "You can!" Does he think I'm stupid? You can change a flight at a moment's notice, if you want. I mean, what if there's an emergency or something?

"Ally, I can't. It will cost a fortune. What's wrong? Why are you crying? Are you drunk again?" He says it like I'm drunk all the time instead of just that one time.

"No, I'm not drunk," I say, trying to sound haughty, which is hard because I'm crying.

"Then what's wrong?"

"I just miss you," I say. "I miss you so much. I'm having a really hard time here, Corey, and I need to see you." I curl the phone cord around my finger tight, watching my skin turn purple as I cut off my circulation. I wonder if you can die just from cutting off the blood to your finger. I pull the cord tighter.

"What's going on? Why are you so upset?"

"It's just everything. It's this whole Kelly thing, and the fact that these cameras won't leave me alone for one second," I say, glaring at Frank. He remains expressionless. I suppose I can forgive him for not being around when I got drunk and made a fool of myself, but can't he tell that my world is ending here? That I'm having major personal problems that I might not want BROADCAST TO MILLIONS OF COMPLETE STRANGERS? You'd think his morals would supercede his desire to do his job right. But no, he keeps filming, pimping me out to the world.

"Well," Corey says slowly. "I'm not sure I understand."

"What don't you understand?" I ask, trying to stop myself from screaming.

"I just don't get how you're so upset over some stupid newspaper article. I mean, Al, everything that girl wrote could probably be seen on the show, anyway."

"That's not the point, Corey," I say, wishing he would just be supportive instead of telling me how I'm supposed to feel.

"And," he goes on, completely ignoring me, "you *knew* what you were getting yourself into when you decided to go on the show. They told you everything was going to be broadcast. So I don't understand why you're complaining. I don't mean to sound like an asshole. I'm just saying."

When someone says "I don't mean to sound like an asshole," it totally means they're being an asshole. I concentrate on being completely silent, thinking maybe this is a more effective way to make my boyfriend realize that I need him to be supportive.

"Al? You there?" he asks finally.

"Yeah, I'm here."

"Look, I love you," he says. "Don't be upset. Everything's going to be fine, I promise." But it was easy for him to say, and way too hard to believe.

"Fine," I say, wiping my eyes with the back of my hand.

We hang up the phone, and I end up falling asleep on my bed. When I wake up a few hours later, it's dark out. I reach over and turn on the light, and then lie there, wondering how everything got to be such a complete mess, and wondering how I'm going to get dinner without actually getting out of bed.

I'm still lying there, staring at the ceiling, when Simone walks into our room a few minutes later. She's holding a piece of black cloth in one hand, and a pair of scissors in the other. She walks over to her bed and sets the objects down on her comforter. She looks down at them. She looks up at me. Then back down at the stuff.

"Hi," she says slowly.

"Uh, hi," I say, sliding out from under my comforter. "Whatcha got there?" I stand up and make my way over to her side of the room.

"I'm not sure," she says, looking confused.

"Well, it's definitely scissors," I say, getting a closer look. "And it looks like a shirt or something. Are you taking a design class? If you are, you should totally call Grant over. He's really good at stuff like that."

"It's James's."

"It's James's shirt?" I ask. It sounds kind of like a tongue twister.

"Yes."

"Okay." I'm not sure what to do with this. So I wait.

"I stole it."

"You stole it?"

"Out of the dryer. Downstairs."

"Okay." I wait.

"I think I want to cut it up." She looks at the shirt—which, under further inspection, turns out to be his trademark "outta my way or you're gonna get played" shirt—and then at the scissors, which are a tempting few inches away. "But I'm not sure."

"You're not sure if you should, or you're not sure if you want to?"

"If I should."

"Okay." I'm in a very I-hate-all-men-except-Corey-and-hope-they-die mood, so I don't want to encourage her, although inside I'm hoping she destroys the shirt, then hands me the scissors so that I can go rip up some of Drew's stuff, then catch a late-night flight to Florida and do the same to that wanna-be-boyfriend-stealing basketball groupie slut Jen's stuff. Like all of her short skirts.

But I don't say anything. I know I shouldn't convince my roommate to commit violence and vandalism. I don't want to corrupt her. I mean, she was a virgin when she got here. I don't want her developing anger issues or a criminal record on top of everything else.

She looks at me, her red hair messy around her face. "Maybe we should talk about this," I say, sitting down on the side of her bed.

"We should," she says, nodding. "It would be wrong."

"Very wrong."

"It's his favorite shirt."

"He wears it all the time."

"Plus, it's his property. It wouldn't matter if he hated it—it would still be wrong to destroy it. Because it doesn't belong to me."

"Right," I say, knowing she's right but at the same time being slightly disappointed that she's losing steam.

"What are you guys doing?" Jasmine asks, coming in to the room. She looks down at the scissors and the shirt lying on the bed. "Oh, please tell me you haven't bought a bedazzler or whatever the fuck those things are called." We look at her blankly. "You know, where you bead up purses and shirts and shit?"

"No," I tell her. "Simone was just considering committing a crime."

"Really!" Jasmine says, suddenly interested. "What sort?" She looks down at the shirt, getting the picture. "Simone, you bad, bad girl." She smiles.

"I'm not doing it," Simone says, pushing her hair back from her face. "It was a stupid idea. I'm gonna go put it back in the dryer right now."

"Okay," I say.

"Okay," Jasmine says.

"Okay." Simone.

"Okay." Jasmine.

"Right now." Simone.

No one moves.

"Of course," Jasmine says slowly. "If you did it, it's not like anyone would find out."

"Um, hello? In case you haven't noticed, we're on a reality show," I tell her, leaning back against the pillows on the bed. "People find out everything." Does she not notice the overhead cameras and the two cameramen who are in the room with us right now? I mean, really.

"I mean," Jasmine says impatiently, "that the only way James would find out is if one of his friends sees it on the show and tells him. And you'd have a couple days until that happens. Besides, he couldn't, like, get you arrested or anything. He could make you pay for the shirt, but how much could this thing really cost?" She holds it up disdainfully. "Twenty dollars at the most?"

"I would think that twenty dollars is definitely a pretty light punishment for what he did to you," I point out. I'm not sure about Jasmine's legal advice, but I know better than to say anything. I feel like we're in a movie where the women torch a guy's car or whatever. Only it's like the college reality-TV version.

"Twenty dollars *is* a pretty light punishment," Simone says, her eyes glistening. She picks up the scissors and runs her fingers over them, like they're some sort of precious heirloom. She picks up the shirt in her other hand.

Jasmine and I nod.

Simone then systematically begins shredding his shirt with the scissors, cutting it into strips. She's very calm as she does this. I expected maybe, like, screaming or some sort of angry rage or something, but it doesn't come.

When she's done, she makes a little pile of black cloth strips on the bed.

"Feel better?" Jasmine asks.

"I do, actually," she says.

"Good." I realize Jasmine and I may be accessories to the crime, since we were present and also encouraged Simone to do it. I'm surprised to find that this thought doesn't really scare me.

"I have to get rid of them now," she says, looking at the piles. "How am I going to do that without anyone knowing? Maybe take them to the dining hall and throw them out there?"

"Why do you have to throw them out?" Jasmine says, plopping down on her bed. "Stick them back in the dryer like that. It'll drive him nuts trying to figure out who did it."

Simone giggles. "Will you guys go with me?"

"Sure," Jasmine says. And that's how we end up sneaking down to the laundry room with strips of black fabric up our shirts, and putting them back in with James's clothes.

NOW

We never got caught. The producers never aired us doing it, which is totally weird when you think about it. I mean, it was complete drama. Little virgin girl gets dumped and then cuts up loser boy's shirt with scissors? They live for shit like that. But they didn't show it. Maybe there was too much going on with Corey's visit, or maybe someone took pity on us.

It was wrong, I know. I mean, just because James was a dick to Simone didn't give us any reason to destroy his property. But it certainly helped take my mind off the fact that in less than twenty-four hours, I was going to see my boyfriend for the first time in months. And I was scared to death. Not about seeing him, but about what could happen. Because even then, I think I knew.

THEN

Friday night, the night before Corey comes, I can't sleep. I know it sounds stupid, but I feel like this is our first date or something, and not just me seeing my boyfriend of two years. I feel like there's this huge pressure for things to be perfect. Things *have to* go back to normal when we see each other.

Corey's flight is getting in at one o'clock, and I spend three-and-a-half hours on Saturday morning getting ready. Which sounds pretty pathetic, I know, but like I said, I want everything to be perfect. I take a long, hot bath and use Jasmine's plumeria-scented bath salts. I stay in the tub for an hour, exfoliating my skin and deep-conditioning my hair.

It takes another hour to dry my hair and put on my makeup, since I'm attempting to recreate this smoky eye look that's in this month's *Cosmo*. It takes me a few tries, but eventually I get it right and am left with sexy, smoky eyes and kissable lips, thanks to the lip gloss I borrowed from Simone.

After forty-five minutes of trying on outfits in front of the mirror, I settle on a long-sleeved, low-cut black shirt, a pair of Kelly's Diesel dark jeans, and high black shoes. I don't want to be reminded of Kelly in any way, and was tempted to throw out and/or burn all her belongings (a.k.a. Pull A Simone), but Grant pointed out that a) if she tried to get them back and I'd destroyed them she could take me on *Judge Judy,* setting me up for more ridicule in front of a national television audience, and b) if she doesn't demand all her clothes back, the way to really get back at her would be to keep all the stuff, since it's worth a ton of money and makes me look hot. That way, at least I got something out of the friendship.

I spritz some perfume behind my wrists, loop a silver chain belt around my waist, and head outside to catch the bus. Yeah, I'm taking the bus. I figure it's way cheaper than a cab, and besides, Corey and I will probably end up taking a cab back from the airport. I would have liked to have been able to ask someone for a ride, but the only person I know who has a car here is Kelly. So, you know, not an option.

The bus turns out to be a horrible mistake. I figured there was a chance they wouldn't let Frank on with the handheld, which was my secret wish. But when the bus comes (after I've waited in the cold for fifteen minutes), the driver hardly gives Frank a second glance. She asks him for his dollar-fifty, and then ignores us.

No one else on the bus shares her view. They point and whisper, especially the teenagers who know who I am. This is a city bus, not a college bus, so the people aren't used to seeing me. I revert back to being A Spectacle.

By the time we get to the airport, I want to kill someone. Frank's not allowed in the airport, since they've been super security tight after September 11th, and I gladly leave him outside. I check the board to see which gate Corey's flight is arriving at, and head over there, trying to calm the butterflies in my stomach.

I'm a few minutes early, and I sit in one of the hard plastic chairs, savoring the moment with no cameras and wondering what I should be doing when Corey comes out of the gate. Should I be standing, looking around excitedly, or lounging in the chair, like I'm cool?

I finally settle on standing up, mostly because when I sit down, my mike pack digs into my back really hard and hurts like hell. I think it's because the pants I'm wearing are so low. Pretty soon, I start to see people coming through the gate, and I raise myself up on my toes, trying to spot him. And then, suddenly, there he is. He's carrying his iPod, the headphones hanging lazily around his neck. He looks tall, and more built than I remember. He's wearing a gray University of Miami basketball hoodie, and he's very, very tan. He doesn't see me yet, and he looks around, his hands gripping his carry-on.

"Corey!" I yell, like some kind of idiot. Yeah, okay, Ally, way to be cool. I immediately put a smile on my face to try to fix it, but then I remember the cameras aren't around and I can be as stupid as I want.

Corey hears his name and looks around, but he still

doesn't see me. I start weaving my way through the throng of people to get to him, and I'm practically in front of him before he finally notices.

"Hey!" he says, dropping his bag and throwing his arms around me. I lean into his body, and his smell brings back the memory of being close to him. To be honest, I kind of thought this would be one of those movie moments. You know, where everything's kind of a mess in the heroine's life, but she looks up to see her hero and everything becomes amazingly clear. In movies, these moments always happen after our heroine has been put through the ringer. Like things have gotten just so bad that she definitely is due for a moment of clarity. So I kind of expected that when I saw Corey, everything would be okay. That, you know, suddenly I'd have the strength to tell Kelly to fuck herself (and maybe bitch-slap her stunned face if I was feeling particularly feisty), hold my head high in the face of America's judgment, and realize everything with Corey was going to be fine.

I thought once I was in his arms things would feel perfect. But all it feels is awkward.

I can do this. I mean, this is Corey.

REASONS I SHOULDN'T FEEL AWKWARD AROUND HIM (A LIST):

1. He's my BOYFRIEND. And not, just like, a boyfriend of a couple weeks that you're supposed to feel awkward around, but my boyfriend of almost

TWO WHOLE YEARS. We're definitely past that stage.

2. Hmm. I can't think of any other reason. Except the fact that one time I had the flu and was, like, throwing up constantly and he came over and I accidentally threw up a little bit on his shoe. And he was really cool about it. So, it isn't like we haven't been in extremely awkward situations before. I mean, hello, puking on his shoe?

I should be totally comfortable right now.

We stand by the baggage claim, not really saying anything. That's the other thing. I figured once he got off the plane, we wouldn't be able to shut up. I mean, even when we saw each other every day, we'd still sometimes talk on the phone or instant messenger at night for hours. We never ran out of things to talk about: school, movies, politics, music, whatever.

"So, how was the flight?" I ask. I did not just say that. How corny. That's what you say to someone you've never met before, a friend of a friend that you're picking up at the airport or maybe an older cousin or something who's come for the holidays that you don't feel completely comfortable around. Definitely not something you say to your BOYFRIEND OF ALMOST TWO YEARS.

"It was good. I'm tired." He smiles and pulls me close. "But I'm glad I'm here."

"Me too," I say, wondering if it sounds fake. He grabs his bags when they come around on the baggage carousel, and we walk outside to where Frank is waiting with the camera. Frank straightens up immediately and zeroes in on us.

"Dude, that's your cameraman?" Corey asks, peering around the camera and trying to get a better look at Frank. Did my boyfriend just call me "dude"?

"Yeah, that's Frank," I say. "But you're really, um, just supposed to ignore the cameras."

"Right," Corey says, still staring at Frank. "So that dude just follows you around everywhere you go?"

"Yes," I say. "Did you think I was making it up?" It comes out meaner than I intended, and I keep talking in an effort to gloss over it. "So what's up with you saying 'dude' all the time? You never said that before."

"I don't know, " he says, grinning, and I smile back. "A lot of the guys on the team say it, so I must have just picked it up."

We wait on the sidewalk for a cab, and when one pulls up, we all pile in, Frank sitting in front next to the driver. Corey pulls me close to him, and I rest my head on his shoulder. He holds my hand and makes little circles with his finger on my palm.

"Did you get your hair cut?" Corey asks, running his fingers through it.

"Nope," I say, my words muffled against his shirt.

"Oh," he says thoughtfully. "It looks like it." I close my eyes sleepily and, the next thing I know, we're at the house and Corey's paying the driver.

"Are you excited to see the house?" I ask Corey as we climb the steps.

He shrugs. "I'm here to see you. Not the house."

"I know," I say, "but the house is pretty cool."

"Yeah," he says, sounding disinterested.

Jasmine's in the living room when we get inside, and she jumps up when she sees us. "Hey!" She's wearing ultra low-rise white pants and a tight pink T-shirt with *Playboy* Bunnies printed all over it in white and purple. Her hair's up in a ponytail. She looks hot, as always, and I look at Corey nervously, expecting him to be drooling and hoping that I don't notice. But he just looks bored.

"Hi, Jas," I say. "This is Corey. Corey, this is my roommate Jasmine."

"It's really great to meet you," Jasmine says. She smiles, revealing her perfect white teeth, and holds out her hand. "I've heard so much about you from Ally."

"Thanks," he says, ignoring her outstretched hand and looking around. "So this is the house!" he exclaims. "I'm excited for the tour, Al." Um, okay. Did he not just say two seconds ago that he didn't give a shit about the house?

"Yeah, the house is really cool," Jasmine says. "Definitely beats living in the dorms."

"So show me around, Al!" he says, still ignoring her. Is it possible that he's schizo? Can you develop multiple-personality disorder and not even know it? I mean, he'd have blackouts or something, right? I wonder if I should call him Corey just to make sure it's him and not some alternate personality that's taken over. A gay one, since, you know, he's being kind of rude to Jasmine and I don't know any straight guy who's intentionally mean to a hot girl. Unless the girl, like, dicked him over or something.

"Okay," I say slowly, looking at him carefully. He smiles. "Let's put your stuff in my room and then I'll give you the tour."

"Great!" he says.

"Um, see you in a few?" I say to Jasmine, shooting her an apologetic look.

"Sure," she says, looking confused.

"What was that about?" I ask Corey, once we're in my room with the door shut.

"What was what about?" he asks, dropping his stuff on the floor in front of my bed.

"Being rude to my roommate."

"I wasn't rude to her."

"Corey! You refused to shake her hand."

"Ally, please," he says, sitting down on my bed. "I'm tired. I've had a long flight. I don't need bullshit from you right now."

"I'm not giving you bullshit," I say, sitting down next to him. "I'm just wondering why you were mean to my roommate."

"Listen," he says, lying down on the bed. "I wasn't mean to her. I just don't think it's going to look that good if people see me talking to her."

If people see him talking to her? Why would people care if he talks to her? Because she's hot and he has a girlfriend? Did he not comprehend the fact that I was right there, and not only knew about the contact but was actually encouraging it? That it was, in fact, my idea that he talk to the hot girl in the *Playboy* shirt?

"But I was right there," I say. "I didn't care if you talked to her."

He pulls me down on the bed next to him and starts tickling my sides. "You think that's why I wasn't talking to her? Because my girlfriend wouldn't approve?" he says, teasing me. I laugh, and for a second, things feel completely normal.

"Yes," I say, trying to wriggle out from under his grasp. His hands feel good on my skin. "You shouldn't talk to any other girls except for me."

"Yes, master," he says, stopping with the tickling. He lies on top of me, brushing my hair away from my face with his fingers.

"No, but seriously," I say, closing my eyes and enjoying his touch. "Why were you mean to her? Are you really that tired? I'm tired too. We could take a nap."

"I'm not really that tired," he says. Okay, schizo. Did he not just tell me five seconds ago he was tired and didn't need my shit? I sigh. "And I told you. I don't think it's a good idea for people to see me talking to her."

"But why? I'm right here."

"I'm not talking about you," he says. "I'm talking about people. Like people who might be watching the show."

"But why would they care?" I ask. He's kissing the side of my neck now, and I can feel my body starting to respond to his. I'm aware of Frank in the corner, filming the whole thing, and it makes me a little creeped out. Kissing is okay, I guess, but what happens when Corey and I want to have sex? Will he leave? And what about the overhead cameras, the ones that are in the room all the time, no matter what? Will they shut those off in a sex situation?

I rack my brain, trying to remember what's happened on past seasons, if I've ever actually seen anyone having sex on the show. Too bad I'm on asshole strike and not talking to James. I'm sure he's had sex somewhere in this house at some point and could tell me what to expect.

"People would care," Corey says, kissing my forehead, "because I'm a basketball player for the University of Miami. We have a certain reputation to uphold. And that girl's a stripper."

He did not just say that. And how many times do I have to tell him that JASMINE IS NOT A STRIPPER. Is it possible that I've been telling that to his other personality? Note to self: Take abnormal psych next semester. I pull away from him and give him a disbelieving look.

"What?" he says, somehow misinterpreting my look of annoyance for one of lust. "God, I missed you so much, Al." He pulls me back toward him and tries to bite my earlobe.

"Wait a second," I say, rolling out from under him. "So what you're saying is that you were mean to Jasmine because you're afraid people will watch you talking to her and then they'll think badly of you?"

"Not badly," he says slowly. "It's just that I want to portray a good image to the public at all times. Which means I can't be hanging out with the wrong kinds of people." I look at him incredulously. Is this the same boy who didn't care what everyone thought when he started going out with me? The same one who told me not to worry about the mean things some of the girls at school said junior year when they found out Corey and I were together?

"It's nothing against her, personally," Corey says. "I just don't agree with what she does."

"Not everyone got a basketball scholarship, Corey," I say softly, looking up at the ceiling.

"God, Ally, it's no big deal," he says. "Are we fighting about this? Because that's pretty ridiculous. You don't even *like* girls, anyway, remember? They're all backstabbing bitches."

He pulls me close and kisses the side of my face. "I missed you. I want to spend time being with you, not fighting over stupid shit, okay?"

"Okay," I mumble into his shirt. But it's not.

We spend the rest of the afternoon walking around campus. "Kind of small," is all he has to say. He seems completely bored, especially when I show him the photography lab. He disregards my request to ignore the cameras and constantly talks directly to them. He also waves to people who stare at us, which pisses me off because it only encourages them. By the time we head to Ruby Tuesday for dinner, I'm exhausted from the stress of it all.

"What are you having?" Corey asks, looking at the menu.

"Cheeseburger," I say, scanning the appetizers.

"Cheeseburger?" he says, raising his eyebrows.

"Yes," I say, looking at him. "A cheeseburger. You know, it's a hamburger. Only with cheese."

"Oh."

"Why, what's wrong with that?" I say, wondering if he's heard something about mad cow disease. In which case, maybe I should have the chicken quesadillas.

"Nothing, I just figured you'd want to get a salad or something." He looks slightly uncomfortable.

"Why?" I ask, confused. I don't think I've ever ordered a salad in all the time we've been together. Salad, in my opinion, is not what you should have for a meal. I like salad, but only as a starter. Maybe that's what he means. "You mean, like, a salad as an appetizer or something?"

"No. I just thought you might want a salad, that's all." He looks away and down at his menu.

Oh my God. Is he—is he saying I'm fat? "Are you saying I'm *fat*?" I ask incredulously.

"No. No!" Corey says, reaching across the table and grabbing my hand. "I am not saying you're fat. I'm not."

"Then why did you ask me if I wanted a salad?" I ask him, pulling my hand away from his and leaning back in my chair.

Corey sighs. "I'm just used to eating healthy because of my coach," he says. "Besides, all the girls in Florida practically live on salad. That's all." He reaches for my hand again. "I did not mean you were fat. Besides, I like the fact that you love to eat." He says it like the girls in Florida are these hot models surviving on lettuce and broth and I'm this huge, sloppy dog who chows down on steaks while Corey looks on and says "Aww, isn't that cute?"

Plus, I wouldn't say that I *love* to eat. I mean, who doesn't like to eat? Well, some people, I guess. Like, sometimes Simone will say that she's been so busy, she forgot to eat. Which doesn't make much sense. How can you forget to eat? I consider ordering a salad just in case I really am fat, but stick with the cheeseburger just to spite him.

When the food comes, they screw up my order and give me cheddar cheese on my burger instead of American.

"They gave you the wrong cheese," Corey says as he takes a bite of his buffalo chicken sandwich. So much for healthy eating.

"It's okay," I shrug. "No big deal."

"Ally, send it back," he says.

"It's not a big deal," I say. "I'll eat it like this—it's the exact same thing."

"It's not the same thing. It's wrong." He turns to Frank. "Don't you think she should send it back?" Frank ignores him.

"I told you not to talk to him," I say. "He. Can't. Answer. Back. He'll be fired. And I'm not sending it back." I take a bite to emphasize my decision.

Corey signals the waiter, who comes rushing over.

"My girlfriend got the wrong order," Corey says, sounding stern.

"I'm very sorry, sir," the waiter says. He's young, about twenty, and pretty hot in an edgy, skater kind of way. It sounds funny hearing someone call Corey "sir," and I giggle.

"It's fine," I say. "It's not a big deal. Just the wrong cheese."

"Ally, it's not fine," Corey says, frowning. "It's not what you ordered."

"I'll take it back," the waiter says.

"Please do," Corey says, pushing my plate toward the waiter. "And I hope you'll adjust the check accordingly. Also, I'm not sure if you have any sort of discounts for college athletes, but I play basketball for the University of Miami." And then—*he winks.* The stunned waiter scampers off with my plate.

Oh my God. My boyfriend has become a diva, some sort of Jennifer Lopez/Whitney Houston wannabe. I stare at Corey, who picks up a fry and drags it through some ketchup, unaware of my disbelief. I don't know if I'm supposed to be mad that he sent my burger back, or amused at his inflated sense of self.

"You okay?" Corey asks, looking at me.

"Yeah, fine." No.

When the check comes—they take off my burger, but nothing else, which makes me secretly pleased—Corey pulls out a Visa card.

"Since when do you have a credit card?" I ask, picking it up. The signature on the back is kind of worn, making me think he's probably used it pretty frequently. I run my finger over the letters.

"Since school started," he says, taking the card out of my hand and putting it back on top of the check.

"Why?"

"Why what?"

"Why do you need a credit card?" Corey has a basketball

scholarship that covers all his tuition, plus room and board. Not to mention the fact that he's an only child and his parents pretty much give him whatever he wants. Including money.

"To build my credit," he says. "When I get my first NBA contract, I'm going to want to have good credit. So I can buy a house, a car, whatever."

"You already have a car," I point out.

"A better car," he says impatiently. Oh.

When we get back to the house, Corey heads to the bathroom to take a shower and get ready for bed. Simone and Jasmine are spending the night at one of Jasmine's friend's apartments so that Corey and I can have the room to ourselves. Which is pretty nice of them, seeing as how Corey was a dick to Jasmine earlier.

While I wait for Corey to get out of the shower, I decide to call Grant. I want to ask him what he thinks of the whole Corey-diva situation. I pick up the phone by my bed.

"Hello?" I say, not hearing a dial tone.

"Yo, I'm on dis phone," James says.

"Sorry," I say, rolling my eyes and putting the phone back down. Ugh. I didn't even know he was home. We didn't see anyone when we came in, which was just fine by me. My worst fear is running into Drew while Corey's here. I'm supposed to be never talking to Drew again, and it would definitely be awkward having to introduce him to my boyfriend. Although I'm sure America's secretly hoping there will be some sort of showdown.

What the fuck is taking Corey so long? Aren't guys

supposed to be, like, wicked fast in the bathroom? I get up and head to my dresser to pick out something to wear to bed. Corey's cell phone is lying on the top of it, so I pick it up to call Grant. But he doesn't answer. Probably out with Brett. Thanks for nothing, Grant, I think. I scroll down to the dialed calls menu so that I can delete Grant's number from Corey's call list. I don't want him getting confused and calling Grant to see whose number it is. The last thing I need is those two talking.

I hit the red button and delete Grant's number. And when I scroll back done to double-check that it's gone, my breath gets caught in my throat. Grant's number isn't there anymore, but the call that was made at three this afternoon is. And it was to Jen.

"Yeah, I called her," Corey says, sitting down on my bed. His hair's still wet from the shower, and he looks adorable. But I'm mad as hell, and his adorableness has no effect on me.

"Why?" I demand, pacing in front of my bed.

"Because she asked me to."

"And if she asked you to commit a murder, would you? If she asked you to have sex with her, would you?"

"Ally, come on, that's not fair," he says. "She's my friend. She wanted to make sure I got here okay. It's no big deal."

"I thought she was a basketball groupie headcase."

"I thought she was, too. But lately we've gotten to be better friends."

LAUREN BARNHOLDT

"Great. Such good friends that you have her number saved in your cell phone. How cozy." I stop pacing and cross my arms. This is unbelievable. Seriously, everyone knows the out-of-town phone call is one step away from getting naked. Is he delusional? Or is he secretly hoping for the nakedness?

"Ally," he says, standing up and putting his arms around me. "This is no big deal. We're friends. Like you and Grant are friends."

"Grant is gay."

"So?"

"So, it's completely different," I say, pushing him away. "And where was I when you called her?"

"In the bathroom."

"So if it was nothing, why'd you wait until I was in the bathroom? Why didn't you just tell me you were calling her?"

"Because I knew you would act like this," he says, pulling me toward him again. "And I don't want to fight with you."

"I'm not mad because you called her," I lie. "I'm mad because you didn't tell me."

"Oh, Ally," he says, pulling me close. I rest my head against his chest and try not to cry. "It's nothing. I love you. I would never do anything to hurt you or to hurt our relationship, okay?" He pulls away and looks at me. I nod silently, swallowing back my tears. "Good. Now what are we watching?"

We watch the new Shia LaBeouf movie, and after a few

minutes, I push it out of my mind, willing things back to normal. But later, when the lights are off and Corey starts to kiss my neck, I pretend to be asleep.

I wake him up at three in the morning. I can't not. It's like prolonging the inevitable.

"What's wrong?" he asks, sitting up in bed. "Did you have a bad dream?"

The overhead lights come on, flooding the room.

"Jesus," Corey asks, squinting. "What the fuck?"

"It's the overheard lights," I explain. "They come on when they think they're going to capture something good."

"Then go back to sleep," Corey says groggily. He tries to roll over, but I reach out and grab his arm. "What is it?" he asks again, and suddenly I can't say anything. He looks at me, and I look at him, and I can feel the tears already coming.

"Yeah," he says softly, and I know that he knows. He sits up and rubs his eyes. "Let's talk about it in the morning, Al. It's late." He looks at me, and a part of me wants to say no, forget it, let's not talk about it in the morning, or ever again. Let's just forget the whole thing. Part of me wants to pretend that things will get better, that once the show is over, or basketball is over, or we go home, everything will be fine. But to do that would be a lie. And I've been lying to everyone, including myself, way too much lately.

"No," I say, shaking my head. "Now."

He nods.

"I just—," I say.

"I think—," he says at the same time. We laugh, and he reaches out and takes my hand. "Go ahead."

"It's just different," I say, looking down at our hands. "Everything is just different."

He sighs. "I know," he says, "but we kind of expected that."

"I know." There's a huge lump in my throat, and it's hard to talk over it. "I thought it was going to be hard because of the show, and the distance, and just college in general. And I know that probably has something to do with it. But I don't think that's everything."

He looks at me and frowns. "What do you mean?"

I take a deep breath. "If I tell you something, will you promise not to get mad?"

He nods.

I clutch his hand tight and look at him. "Lately, something really weird has been going on. That night I got drunk. I ended up sleeping in my roommate's bed. In *Drew's* bed." He starts to say something, but I rush on. "And I know I was drunk, and it didn't mean anything, and nothing happened, but it's not just that. I've been having other feelings for him, too. More than friendship feelings. So much that I got upset when I found him with another girl, and I don't want you to be mad, because nothing happened. I would never—"

"Ally," he says, putting his finger to my lips. "It's okay. I know."

"You know?"

"Yeah," he says. He runs his free hand through his hair. "I saw it on the show. You telling Jasmine that you thought you might like him, and that whole sleeping in his bed thing."

"You did?" What the fuck? How could he see that and not say anything? "How come you didn't say anything?"

"I don't know," he says. "I guess I just figured it was normal, to a point." He doesn't say anything, and I wonder if he's thinking about Jen. I don't want to know.

"It is," I say. "It definitely is normal to a point. But there's a point where it becomes not normal. Corey, I got really upset over another guy."

"So what does that mean?"

"I don't know. I don't know what it means." I'm crying now, and he reaches up and brushes away one of my tears with his thumb. "I know that it doesn't feel like we're in a relationship anymore. I never get to see you, I don't know what's going on in your life, I've never met your friends or seen where you live. . . ."

"Al, that's not my fault," he says, propping himself up on an elbow and rubbing my arm.

"I know," I say. "It's no one's fault. But that doesn't change the fact that it's true."

"So what are we supposed to do?"

"Why are you asking me, like I have all the answers?"

He smiles. "Because you usually do."

"What do you mean?"

"I just mean that whenever I'm having a problem with something, you're usually the first one I tell."

"You do? How come you haven't told me about any problems lately?"

He shrugs. "I dunno. I guess I haven't really had any."

"Must be nice." I look at him, and I see the guilt flash across his face. He knows that I've been having a really hard time lately, and that he hasn't exactly been there for me. I suddenly realize that the one thing I thought I could always count on isn't there anymore.

"Ally, listen, I know I haven't exactly been the best boyfriend lately, but I've just been so busy with school, and practice. I don't think you realize the kind of pressure I'm under down there." He runs his hand through his hair and looks at me, and I can see in his eyes that he really is sorry.

"Enough pressure that you have to be mean to my friend because you're afraid what everyone else will think?" He looks away. And when he doesn't have an answer, he gives me mine. "Corey, this isn't working anymore."

"Ally—" I look at him, and he stops.

"Don't," I say. "I don't know what happened. But it did. Maybe we changed, maybe we grew up, or maybe it's just not the right time. I don't know. But I know it's not working." I'm crying hard now, and my tears have made a wet spot on Corey's shirt. It's almost surreal, actually. The whole thing: Corey being here at school with me, Sam being in the corner, Jasmine's and Simone's empty beds. It feels kind of like a nightmare—Corey and I breaking up while I'm far away from my family and my home, while some strange guy tapes the whole thing so that not only will there be a record of it, but everyone in America can see.

"I know it's been rough, Ally," Corey says, holding me close. "But I'm sure things will get better over semester break. I mean, I'll be home for a week , and we'll be able to spend time together and things will go back to normal."

"Corey," I say, propping myself up on my elbow. "I took a picture of another guy for my photo project on where we are in our lives. You called Jen to tell her you got here okay. This is . . ." I trail off, not really knowing what this is.

"Yeah," he says. He looks really sad, and for a second, I want to take the whole thing back. "You're right."

We don't say anything for a while, and there's no sound, just the quiet hum of the handheld camera and me sobbing quietly. After a few minutes, production turns the lights back off. Corey holds me, running his fingers through my hair. I know it sounds crazy, but as sad as I am right now, I don't want this moment to end. I can deal with this as long as he's here with me—it's the stuff that's going to come next that'll be the hardest.

It's Corey who speaks first. "You know we'll always be friends, Al. We'll always be in each other's lives." I look up and nod, unable to speak. "I think you're the most amazing girl I've ever met."

That's how we fall asleep. Him holding me tight as I cry into his shirt, and me wondering why he said all those things now, when it's too late, and why the right thing to do is always the hardest.

NOW

His flight wasn't leaving until Monday morning, and so we had all day Sunday to hang out while we were broken up. Surprisingly, it wasn't weird. We went out to eat, saw a movie, went to the mall, and didn't fight once. On Sunday night, he wanted to sleep on the couch, but I wanted him in my bed. We didn't have sex or anything—we didn't even kiss. I just wanted him there because it would feel even weirder if he wasn't.

On Monday morning I took him to the airport and watched him walk toward the gate. He turned around to wave, and I waved back. I know you're never supposed to look back, that that's the number one rule of any change, but I was glad he did.

Once he was completely out of sight, I went into the bathroom of that airport and cried for twenty minutes, harder than I'd ever cried before. I used a whole roll of toilet paper. My body was shaking so hard, I was afraid I would break.

I know, I know, I was having feelings for someone else and it was time for Corey and I to end. But that didn't make it any easier. He had been the biggest part of my life for two years. He was so hard to let go of, and I didn't know if my heart would ever feel better. If I wasn't Corey's Girlfriend, if I didn't have him, then who was I? I felt completely alone for the first time in a really long time. Maybe ever.

THEN

Reaction to Corey and I Breaking Up (a summary):

MY DAD: Maybe you guys could try relationship counseling.

MY MOM: Oh, honey, I'm so sorry. But what's meant to be will always be. Maybe it's for the best, anyway. You're so young.

GRANT: I told you. But seriously, Ally, that really sucks. Are you okay? He doesn't have any, like, naked pictures of you or anything, does he? Because that happened to this one friend of mine, Biscuit. Her ex-boyfriend posted all these pictures of her and her vibrator on the Internet.

MY BROTHER BRIAN: Do you want me to kick his ass?

* * * * * *

I stay in bed for two weeks. I skip school for the first three days, then finally drag myself to my classes, where I struggle to take notes and not throw up. Even though I'm not eating anything, I still constantly feel nauseated. I don't shower. I wear the same rotation of outfits every four days, which mostly consists of jeans and sweatshirts. I don't wear make-up. I definitely don't brush my hair. What's the point? It's not clean. I sleep. A lot. I watch TV. A lot.

On day fifteen, at around five o'clock in the afternoon, Jasmine and Simone stage an intervention. I've spent the day watching Lifetime movies, looking through my old high school yearbooks, and deciding what I'll do if I never get married.

Alternate life plan:

Get some sort of adventurous photography gig making tons of money where I'll be traveling around so much that I won't have time for love. Think Lisa Ling on that one adventure show. Only she's a broadcaster, and I'd be taking pictures. And she's engaged. Or married. Whatever. The specifics of this plan don't actually matter, since any of this happening is not all that likely, due to the fact that I don't plan on getting out of bed. Ever.

"This room is really starting to stink," Jasmine says pointedly, looking at my hair, clothes, and all-around disgusting appearance. I'm still brushing my teeth, at least, since I figure if I'm going to die alone and dirty, I might as well keep my dignity by not being toothless as well.

"I don't smell anything," I say. I'm lying on my bed

in the same flannel pants and Syracuse College sweatshirt that I've slept in for the past six days. I'm watching *Gracie's Choice*, this really good Lifetime movie starring Kristen Bell.

"That's because it's *you* that smells," Jasmine says, pulling the remote out of my hand and turning off the TV. "And everyone knows you can't smell yourself."

"That's not true," I say. "I can smell myself perfectly well. And I smell just fine, thank you very much. Simone?" I look to her for confirmation.

"Um"—she looks back and forth from me and Jasmine nervously—"well, Ally, it's not that you smell *bad* exactly, it's just that—"

"You reek!" Jasmine says, pulling the covers off me.

"I most certainly do not!" I say, grabbing the blanket before she can get the whole thing off the bed. We start a tug of war, which she wins, because a) she's tough, and b) I haven't eaten in days, so I'm weak and lethargic. I lie back down, sans covers.

"Leave me alone," I moan. "I'm upset."

"Ally, you can't keep this up," Simone says, sitting down on the side of my bed. She looks at me worriedly. "It's not good for you."

"I'm fine," I say. "Absolutely fine. Except for the fact that I'm cold." I glance pointedly at Jasmine, who's still holding my covers. She drops them on the floor. "Hey!"

"They need to be washed, Ally," she says. "And so do you. Now come on, you're taking a shower and then we're getting out of here. We're going to get dinner. You need to get out of the house. You're going to start growing mold or something."

"No," I tell them, reaching over and switching the TV back on. I can't believe they're doing this to me in the middle of *Gracie's Choice*. I mean, could they have picked a worse time? Gracie is just about to get custody of her brothers and sisters, which, hello, is, like, the point of the whole movie. "I'm watching something."

"You're getting out of bed, Ally," Jasmine says, switching the TV back off. "Don't make me pull you out of that bed and into the shower." I raise my eyebrows. "I'll do it. Think about how much shit you got for going to the strip club with me. What will everyone think if they see me putting you in the shower? Right after a breakup with your boyfriend? I mean, the lesbian rumors on the message boards alone would . . ."

Simone giggles. I glare at her.

"Fine. But I'm pissed at both of you." I grab my shower stuff and head to the bathroom.

An hour later, we're sitting in Pizzeria Uno with Sam the cameraman. Actually, he's sitting at the table across from us, but technically he's still there, so whatever. I'm showered, wearing clean clothes, and even have lip gloss on. Somehow, once I got clean and out of the house, my appetite came back, and I've eaten almost half of an Uno's pepperoni pizza all by myself.

"So then she grabs the tip right off the table in front of me. Off of my table!" Jasmine's saying. She takes a sip of her soda and swirls the straw around her glass. "So I was like, listen, I know you aren't pulling down the kind of shit I am, but that doesn't give you a right to steal." She looks at us over the top of her glass. "Seriously, sometimes I can't believe people."

"Wow," Simone says softly. "What a bitch." Jasmine and I look at her in shock.

"Did you just say 'bitch'?"

"I guess," she says, shrugging. "Why?"

"Nothing," I say. "It's just a very un-Simone-like thing to say, that's all."

"She's been doing a lot of un-Simone-like things lately," Jasmine reports.

"True."

"Did James ever ask you about the shirt?" Jasmine asks. She's wearing this see-through light blue top, and every time the waiter walks by, he looks like he's going to faint from wanting.

"No," Simone says. "He thinks some guy in his economics class did it. I guess James stole his girlfriend or something."

"Classy," I say, draining the last of my soda and looking around for the waiter so I can get another one.

"I can't believe I did that," Simone says, biting her lip. "I'm not going to do anything like that anymore. It's not worth it."

"Good for you," I say. I wish I could be so adjusted. Of course, I never got the chance to destroy anyone's property.

"Speaking of not being worth it, how's that bitch Kelly?" Jasmine asks me.

"Don't know." All the pizza I just ate shifts in my stomach. "I don't talk to her, she doesn't talk to me. And she didn't steal anyone away from me."

"Tried."

"She wasn't *trying* to do anything. Drew wasn't mine. I have—I mean, I *had* a boyfriend. She can do whatever she wants with whoever she wants."

"Oh, come on, Ally," Jasmine says, rolling her eyes. "It was so obvious that she was going to try to make a play for him. She knew you liked him. That girl is evil."

"I don't like him."

"You don't?" Simone asks, confused.

"No."

"Oh." Jasmine picks up the dessert menu and looks at it. "Well, then I guess you don't care that he asked about you the other day." She keeps her eyes on the menu.

"Oh?" I ask, trying to sound like I don't care.

IMAGINED CONVERSATIONS:

DREW: Is Ally dead yet? Because I really wish she were.

DREW: Hey, Jasmine, do you think Ally will be able to handle the fact that Kelly and I have decided to leave school after this semester and get married?

DREW: Listen, I've been meaning to ask you about Ally's mental health. I've been thinking maybe she should talk to someone about her obvious anger issues. Don't they do free counseling in Health Services?

"Yeah," Jasmine says. "So I think I'm going to have the

strawberry shortcake. Or maybe the huge peanut butter cup."

I look at her.

"He asked me how you were," she says, sliding the dessert menu back into the holder.

"Did you tell him I broke up with Corey?"

"No. I didn't think it was my place to tell him," Jasmine says. I nod. Not that it matters. I mean, why would Drew care if I broke up with Corey? All my Drew issues were totally self-inflicted. It wasn't like he was hitting on me all the time, or even showing the slightest interest. I've only seen Drew a few times since our big blow-up fight, due mostly to the fact that I've been a hermit for the past two weeks, hardly venturing out of my room. When I've seen him briefly in passing on campus or on my way to class, we ignore each other. Although one time I think he may have nodded at me, although I totally could have been imagining it.

The waiter comes back to take our dessert order, staring at Jasmine's breasts the whole time. She gets off on the attention, and asks him if she can have extra whipped cream on her strawberry shortcake. I order the giant peanut butter cup, figuring the extra calories won't make me fat since I have days of eating to make up for.

"So have you talked to him?" Simone asks me once our desserts come. The giant peanut butter cup turns out to be the size of Frank's neck and comes with an equal amount of ice cream and hot fudge. This makes me sublimely happy.

"Who?" I ask, spooning up some ice cream.

"Corey."

"No," I say. "I haven't talked to him since he left. I'm sure I will, at some point."

"Well, don't call him, whatever you do," Jasmine instructs. "You need time by yourself. And I don't mean time to lie around in your own filth, stinking up our bedroom."

"I wasn't that bad," I say.

"Yes, you were," Jasmine says. She looks to Simone, who nods.

"Whatever."

"So what about Drew?" Jasmine watches me carefully as she takes a bite of cheesecake.

"What about him?" I ask, feeling my stomach shift again. I take another bite of the warm peanut butter and chocolate in an effort to shut it up.

"Are you going to talk to him?"

"Why would I talk to him? I told him never to talk to me again. He hates me. Besides, I really don't think I need to torture myself by seeing him with Kelly." I'm suddenly not hungry. In fact, I kind of have a stomachache. I knew I shouldn't have ordered dessert. I put my spoon down.

"He's not with Kelly," Simone says.

"He's not?"

"Nope," Jasmine confirms. "He was never with her. They were working on some stupid project together." Oh. So he *was* telling the truth. "Actually, when he found out Kelly was the psycho who printed all that shit about us, he requested a new partner."

"Oh."

Jasmine and Simone look at each other. "So are you going to talk to him?" Jasmine asks.

"I don't know what I would say."

"You could start by apologizing for flipping out on him."

"I did not flip out on him! I thought he was hooking up with my archenemy!"

"Fair enough," Jasmine says. "But someone has to make the first move. And to tell you the truth, I think he thinks you hate him."

Simone nods. "He does. He thinks you hate him."

"He does?" I'm secretly pleased. Not that he thinks I hate him, but that he's thinking about me at all.

"You should talk to him, Ally," Simone says. "It's not worth it. I mean, you guys were friends."

"Yeah," I say. I pick up my spoon and drag it through the melted ice cream on my plate.

"Hey, Simone?"

She looks up.

"How come you're supposed to be the least experienced of all of us, yet I'm lying around in my bed, crying my eyes out for days like some kind of slug, and you're destroying James's property and moving on?"

She looks surprised. "Because," she says. "What else am I supposed to do? Being upset about it isn't going to help anything. I have to move on. I have no choice."

NOW

And neither did I.

THEN

Corey calls later that night. I'm in my room, lying on my bed, listening to music and catching up on my reading. My little journey into the land of no showering/no eating/ no studying has left me woefully behind on some of my homework.

No one else is home, and I reach over and grab the phone on my nightstand distractedly.

"Hello?"

"Hey," Corey says. "It's me." I fall back on the bed in surprise and my legs get tangled underneath me.

"Oh," I say. "Hi."

"Hi."

"Hi."

Pause. "I just wanted to call, you know, and say hi," Corey says. "And make sure you're doing okay."

"I'm fine," I say. "How are you?"

"Good," he says. "I'm good."

"Cool." I untangle my legs and sit on the edge of the bed. There's another pause, and I rack my brain for something to say. "Um, how's basketball?"

"It's going really well. I think I have a good chance of getting some really good playing time this season."

"That's great," I say. "I'm happy for you." I can hear the excitement in his voice, and I really am happy for him.

"So I was just calling to make sure you were okay," Corey says. "Plus, I didn't know what the rules were."

"The rules?"

"Yeah, if we're allowed to talk or not."

"Of course we're allowed to talk," I say, wondering how it got to this. I mean, is this us? Am I really making small talk with a boy I was with for two years? A boy I thought I was going to marry? I always wondered how that worked. Like, how can people be married for five, ten, however many years, fall asleep with the person every night, live with that person, and then get divorced and just have the person gone from their lives forever? It's really weird, when you think about it.

"So is the stripper pissed that I wouldn't talk to her?" Corey says.

I sigh. "No, Corey, I don't think she really cared."

"All right, cool. I didn't want to get you in trouble."

"You didn't." There's a silence.

"All right, well . . . I guess that's it. I just wanted to say hi. So hi."

"I'm glad you called," I tell him, meaning it.

"Yeah, me too. So, I guess I'm out."

I smile into the phone. "Hey, Corey?"

"Yeah?"

"I hope you have a great season. I know you're going to do really well."

"Thanks, Al," he says, and I know he'll always be the only one who's ever allowed to call me that. When I hang up the phone, I feel the tears behind my eyes, but it's only for a second, and then they're gone.

THEN

The next morning, I stand outside the door to Drew's room, taking deep breaths and talking to myself. I can do this. I mean, it's only *talking*. It's not like I've never *talked* to someone before. What's the worst thing that can happen? He slams the door in my face. He tells me to fuck off. He lets me say I'm sorry, then says, "Apology NOT accepted, and I never want to see you again." He asks me if I want to have sex, then after we do, he blows me off and never talks to me again. Okay, so the last one is pretty unlikely, but whatever.

Must. Stop. Negative. Self. Talk. Katie Holmes would totally suck it up and just knock on the door. Which is actually *easier* than talking, when you think about it. You just pick up your hand and knock on the door. Besides,

I've been standing here for two whole minutes, Frank is filming, and America probably thinks I'm stupid. For just standing here, I mean. Well, besides other things. So now it's sort of like I have to knock. Because, you know, if I don't, I'll look even stupider.

I raise my hand, ready to knock. On the count of three. One . . . two . . . two and a half . . . Suddenly there's a sound from inside the room. Shit. It has to be Drew, since I saw James leave for class about ten minutes ago. Fuck. The doorknob starts to turn, and I try to run. But Frank isn't as quick, and when Drew opens the door, Frank's standing in the hallway, and I'm standing in the doorway of the bathroom.

Drew looks at me. I look at Drew.

"Hey," he says.

"Uh, hi," I say, trying to sound nonchalant, like I'm always hanging out in bathroom doorways. His backpack is slung over his shoulder, and he's wearing a gray sweater and baggy jeans. I want to kiss him.

He turns toward his bedroom door, pulls his keys out of his pocket, and locks it. Fuck. He's locking his bedroom door because he thinks I'm a stalker! He thinks I want to, like, go in there and look in his underwear drawer or something. This is awful. Why didn't I just knock on the door when I had the chance? This is so much worse than that.

"Gotta lock it," Drew says, holding up the key. He shifts his backpack on his shoulder. "Some psycho cut up one of James's shirts, so we're not taking any chances."

Oh, thank God. It's Simone's psychosis that is causing

the locking of the door, not mine. "Good idea," I say, still standing in the bathroom doorway.

"Well, see ya," he says.

"Bye!" I say brilliantly. He disappears down the hall. Yup. Right on track.

Two hours later, I'm in photography and still analyzing the Drew encounter to death. If he hated me, he would have just ignored me, right? And, like, not said anything. Or given me a dirty look or something. He definitely wouldn't have explained why he was locking the door. I mean, if he *hadn't* explained, I would have thought it was because of me, and he *obviously* didn't want me to think that. Or he wouldn't have told me. Which means he doesn't hate me. Because if he hated me, he wouldn't care what I think. Right? Unless he just doesn't care either way. Like, maybe he doesn't care that we're fighting. Maybe he's just like, whatever, Ally can do what she wants.

I try to concentrate on Professor Lutkiss's lecture. I really need to stop thinking about this Drew thing, because I'm already slightly behind on my schoolwork, and I need to start getting my pictures ready to apply for the photo program for next semester. Which is why I should be listening to this lecture and not obsessing. Which is, you know, a waste of time. Obsessing, I mean.

I open my notebook to a fresh page, determined to take good notes. "Ally" I write on the top page. I do my best comprehending when I'm doodling. "Loves Drew" I write after it. And then cross it out. Because I don't love him. I don't even really *like* him, probably. I mean, he was just a distraction. To distract me from the problems I was having with Corey. So there's no reason to be getting all worked up.

I keep drawing lines through "Ally loves Drew" until it's obliterated in a sea of ink. Then, just to make the point, I rip the page out of my notebook and tear it into tiny pieces. There. Now I am ready to pay attention.

I poise my pen over the page just as Professor Lutkiss dismisses us. Oh. Well, whatever. I'll make up for it next time. I stand up and slide my notebook into my bag. When I look up, I catch Kelly's eye across the room. I look away quickly, and make my way toward the door.

"Ally!" she calls after me. I ignore her and walk faster. I'm out the door and halfway down the steps by the time she catches up with me.

"Ally!" she says again, grabbing my arm.

"Don't touch me!" I say, pulling out of her grasp. Does she want to fight? Is she really that stupid? Do college kids even fight? That seems so junior high. Not to mention now that we're out of the classroom, Frank's filming, and so I'll have videotaped proof of her assaulting me. I could totally press charges.

"Okay, okay," she says, dropping her arms. "Listen, we need to talk." She bites her lip, looking nervous. She's wearing tan pants and a dark purple shirt under her black wool coat. The shirt's kind of short, and you can see her belly piercing.

"We have nothing to talk about. Nice thought, though." I turn on my heel and continue down the steps. The bitch follows me.

"Ally, listen, I know you're mad, but—"

I turn around. "You know I'm *mad*?" I laugh at the obvious ridiculousness of this statement. "How could you possibly know I'm mad? Did your friend—oh no, wait, your *supposed* friend, write an exposé about you in the school newspaper while the whole nation watched?"

"Ally—"

"Did your *supposed* friend somehow weasel her way into the bed of the guy you liked?"

"Ally, you don't—"

"Stop saying my name!" She looks at the ground. "I have nothing to say to you. Not now. And not ever."

"This wasn't easy for me, you know." She looks like she's going to cry. Surprisingly, I don't feel like I'm going to cry at all. Maybe I'm done crying. Maybe I'm just pissed.

"Oh, I'm sorry, Kelly. Did my back hurt your knife?" She doesn't say anything. I tap my foot on the ground impatiently. "Come on. You wanted to talk, so let's talk. Why'd you do it?"

"I never meant to hurt you," she says. She shoves her hands in her pockets and looks at me. "At first, yeah, it was just kind of this game, you know? See if I could get into the house, how close I could get to the cast, see if I could get on TV. But then I really started to like you." She takes a deep breath. "I'm really sorry."

"That doesn't answer the question," I say. "Why'd you do it? If you got to like me so much, why'd you print the article?"

"You don't understand, Ally. Journalism is what I want to do. It's my dream. And it's a really hard field to break into. I figured if I had some good clips from national publications on my resume before graduation, I'd have a really good chance of getting into a good grad school."

I look at her blankly. Oh my God. The girl's lost it. "Did you really think that the *New York Times* was going to be interested in your little piece on some stupid reality TV show?" I almost scream. "Do you have any idea how humiliating that was for me? I thought you were my friend."

"I'm sorry."

"Yeah, I'm sorry, too. Sorry I ever believed you." I look down at the ground for a second, and then back up at her. "But mostly, I'm sorry that you're the kind of person that would let yourself get so caught up in some ridiculous delusions of grandeur that you'd sell out your friend. Because that must be really lonely for you."

She looks away. I start walking toward the house. "Oh," I say, turning back to face her. "One more thing. Stay away from me, and stay away from Drew, or I'll have Jasmine kick your ass." And with that, I turn around, walk quickly to the house, and right up to Drew's room.

NOW

I had no choice. I had just admitted on camera that I liked him. I could have let him hear about it or see it on a replay, but that's just ridiculous. I had to, at the very least, apologize to him for the way I acted. And depending on how he reacted, I figured I might just tell him how I felt. After all, things were already completely messed up. I had nothing to lose.

THEN

I knock on Drew's door quickly before I can change my mind.

"Come in!" Drew calls from the other side. Shit. I figured he would answer the door, and then possibly invite me in. That way, I'd be able to tell if he was really pissed or not. Because he obviously wouldn't let me in if he was pissed.

I debate running back to my room. But no one else in the house is home, which means it would be pretty obvious that it was me playing ding dong dash. Besides, I'm not chickening out. I pretend I don't hear him, and knock again.

"Come in!" he says. Shit, shit, shit. What is wrong with him? Who just says "come in" without asking who it is? I could be the crazy shirt ripper-upper, coming to do something worse. I'm debating whether or not I can get away with just knocking again when Drew opens the door.

"Oh," he says, looking surprised "Hi."

"Hi," I say. "I, um, wasn't sure you were here, since, um, no one said anything when I knocked."

"I said 'come in.'"

"Oh. I didn't hear you."

"Oh." Shit. Now what? For some reason, I forgot to rehearse what I was going to say, which was a terrible plan. Every teen movie I've ever seen shows the main character rehearsing what she's going to say before she enters a stressful situation. Even if she ends up actually saying what she rehearsed—which is inevitably very stupid—at least she's said *something* and isn't left just standing there looking ridiculous. Like I am right now.

"So, uh, how are you?" I ask. I'm trying to sound casual, but I can't take my eyes off his arms. He's holding the door, and his biceps are amazing. I can't focus on anything but how hot his arms are. In fact, I'm so focused on them, I don't know if he's said anything or not. I don't even know if he's answered my question.

"I'm good," I say, hoping that he's asked me how I am back. He nods and holds the door open.

"You wanna come in?"

"Sure," I say, shrugging. I walk into the room and sit down on the edge of his bed. He sits down on his desk chair.

"So. How have you been?" I ask him.

"You already asked me that." Okkaayy. Things are not

going according to plan. Not that I have a plan. But if I did, I'll bet this wouldn't be it.

"Listen," I say, taking a deep breath, "I wanted to talk to you."

He doesn't say anything. Yeah, definitely not off to a very good start.

"Look, I just wanted to say I was sorry for the way I acted the other day. Really, I totally overreacted, and I'm sorry. It's none of my business who you're dating or hooking up with or . . . or whatever," I finish lamely.

"I wasn't hooking up with her. I told you that." He looks at me, and I can't tell from his expression if he's pissed or not.

"I know you weren't," I say. "I know that now. But at the time, I was going through a lot of stuff, and it wouldn't have mattered what you said." Which isn't completely true. I mean, even if I wasn't going through all that shit with Corey and Kelly, I probably still would have been upset to find him in bed with another girl. But no need to mention that.

"Ally, it's important you know that I didn't know who that girl was. If I had, I would have never, ever let her in the house." He looks down at his hands. "My friends are the most important thing to me, and I would never jeopardize our friendship over something so stupid."

"Thanks," I say. "And I know you would never do anything like that."

"So, we're cool?" he asks, standing up. I look down at my hands quickly, and clutch the side of his mattress.

258

"Actually," I say. "There was, um, something else." He raises his eyebrows. "Corey and I broke up," I blurt. "I didn't know if you knew or not. . . ."

"No, I didn't." He sighs and runs his hands through his hair, leaving it a little rumpled. He walks over and sits down on the bed next to me. "I'm really sorry, Ally. Are you okay?"

"Yeah," I say. "It was the right thing to do. Just not meant to be, I guess." I don't mention the Lifetime movie marathons, the not eating, and the squalor that I lived in for two weeks. 'Cause, you know, it's not something that really needs to be talked about. He has enough examples of me being psychotic—he doesn't need another one.

"Yeah," he agrees, looking down at his hands. "Sometimes that happens. And it sucks. But I've realized that sometimes things happen, and if you ask yourself why, you'll just drive yourself crazy." I wonder if he's thinking about his dad. I want to kiss him. On his lips. And his arms. "But I'm glad you're okay." He looks at me and grins.

"What?" I ask. "Why are you looking at me like that?"

"I don't know." He shifts on the bed, and his leg brushes against mine. My stomach immediately begins to churn.

"That's what I love about you, Drew," I say, rolling my eyes. "You're so articulate."

"It's just funny, I guess," he says.

"Oh, good," I say. "I'm glad you find my love life so amusing." I push him playfully on his shoulder, and he reaches up and blocks my hand. Oh my God. Are we flirting?

"It's not that," he says, dropping my hand. Come back, hand, come back! I think, trying to focus on what he's saying. "I don't know. I guess I just always thought you and Corey would be together for a while."

"Why?"

"I don't know," he says, shrugging. "You just seemed so determined that you guys would be together no matter what." He studies me carefully.

"Well, yeah, kind of," I tell him. "It wasn't that I was determined to be with Corey, exactly. It's just that I didn't want the show to break us up."

"Did it?"

"No," I tell him. "The show didn't break us up. We grew apart, we changed, we started having different lives and needing different things. If I hadn't tried out for the show, we probably still would have broken up." As I'm saying the words, I realize they're true, and it makes me really sad—the thought that some things might be out of my control, that maybe nothing I could have done would have kept me and Corey together.

"Listen, Drew," I say. "I have to tell you something."

"What?" he asks, looking worried. His eyebrows knit together in concentration, and he looks adorable. I notice the scar on his chin again, and fight back the urge to kiss him.

"I just told someone on camera that I have a crush on you," I say slowly, figuring it's better to just get it out there.

"Oh," he says, swallowing. He looks . . . I don't know. Blank.

"Anyway," I say, rushing on, and taking his silence as a very, very bad thing, "I just wanted to tell you so you didn't hear it from a friend or anything. You know, who watches the show."

"Yeah," he says, shifting his weight on the bed again. "Um, actually, Ally, if we're being honest, someone told me about that a while ago."

"Wait, what?" I say, confused. Someone already told him about it? It just happened like five minutes ago.

"Yeah, you were in the bathroom, talking to Jasmine."

OH. MY. GOD. WHAT? He's known this whole time? Ever since I told Jasmine in the bathroom? And he never said anything? I rack my brain, trying to think of anything embarrassing I may have done since then, but breathe a sigh of relief once I realize I've basically been avoiding him. Well, besides that whole sleeping in his bed thing.

Oh my God. This is a disaster. If he's known this whole time and didn't say anything, then he's obviously not interested. This is horrible. Have I not learned anything? Never tell a boy you like him, never, ever, ever.

I take a deep breath and try to think about what Katie Holmes as First Daughter would do. "That's fine," I say haughtily. "I just wanted to tell you so you wouldn't freak out." I stand up to go, but he puts his hand on my arm and pulls me back down on the bed.

"Ally, I didn't say anything about you liking me because I didn't want to get in the way of you and Corey." He looks uncomfortable.

"Look, it's not a big deal," I say. "Seriously. I mean, I

know you have the Andrea girl at the gym or whatever, along with countless others, and I just didn't want—"

"Andrea at the gym?" He looks confused. "I don't go to the gym with anyone."

"But Kelly said . . . ," I trail off, feeling stupid. "But that girl you were talking to at the party that night? The night I slept in—the night I got drunk." He frowns. "She was blond," I offer helpfully.

"That's Tristan," he says. "She's my biology TA. I was asking her about an assignment, and then I just ended up hanging out with her and her boyfriend for the rest of the night."

"Oh," I say, looking at the ground. Great. So Kelly lied just to see if she could get a reaction out of me. Ugh. Suddenly I realize that I'm sitting on Drew's bed. The bed that I slept in. With him. The thought makes me hot, and I hope he can't tell by looking at my face.

"Anyway," Drew says. "The reason I didn't bring it up was because I didn't want you to like me just because you were confused about Corey." He's moved closer to me on the bed now, and his voice sounds huskier when it's right next to my ear.

Wait. Does that mean he *wants* me to like him?

I can smell his cologne and I can see his scruff and there's no Corey holding me back and he's wearing this blue T-shirt and I can't even think straight. I try to get it together.

"Drew," I say. "I just—" I turn my head toward him and I can't speak. We're so close together that we're almost kissing and my heart is pounding and I don't even care that there's a camera in the room.

I kiss him. It's a soft kiss on his lips, and I pull away quickly, not believing I just did that. My heart is pounding and my face feels hot. I try to pull away even more, in case he doesn't want to, but he pulls me back down toward him, and then suddenly his lips are back on mine and his hands are in my hair.

After what seems like forever, he finally pulls away. Our foreheads are still together, and I open my eyes.

"I wasn't sure . . . ," I say.

"Ally," he says, smiling. "Do you really think I would turn off ESPN for a Lifetime movie for just anyone?"

I smile back, and we're kissing again, and his hands are back in my hair and on my face, and for the first time in a long time, everything feels right.

NOW

The reporter from People.com smiles at me across the table of the café and picks up her pen. "So this is your last interview, huh? Are you excited?"

"A little," I say, trying not to sound like a bitch. "I'm really glad for my time on the show, but it's time to move on, you know?" This answer has been carefully rehearsed so that I come across as thankful and nostalgic about my time on the show, but not like I'm so screwed up that I can't imagine life without the cameras. The truth is, I'm really glad I don't have to suffer through another one of these. At first, I thought it would be really cool to have a chance to tell America my side of the story. But it's the same questions over and over, and really, no one wants to hear my story. Their minds are pretty much already made up.

The reporter smiles and tucks a stray strand of her blond hair behind her ear. She looks really young, probably just out of college. "So, the show's been over for two weeks," she says. "Has it been hard adjusting to not being around cameras anymore?"

"Well," I say, trying to look like I'm contemplating, even though I've been asked this question a million times. "It's been nice to be at home. And definitely nice not to have the cameras following me around. But as for adjusting, I don't know. Ask me next semester, when I'm back at school without them."

She writes something down and consults the sheet in front of her. "So while you were on the show you decided that you wanted to major in photography, even though your family didn't necessarily support that decision." She makes it sound like my family was about to disown me, which isn't exactly how it happened, but whatever. I'm used to the details of my life being exaggerated, so I just nod. "You ended up applying for the photography program. Any word on that?"

"Not yet," I say, crossing my fingers under the table, "but I'm really excited to hear. Hopefully in a couple of weeks. I have some photos under consideration at a few magazines, too, so . . . something may come of that, which would be really great." I give her a smile. She smiles back.

"What would you change about your time on the show?" the reporter asks, and I smile at the inevitability of the question.

"Nothing," I tell her. "I really think everything happens

for a reason. And I think everything that happened here these past few months was for the best." She writes something else on her pad, and I try to glance at what she's writing without her seeing. She seems cool, but I could be wrong. I mean, she could basically write whatever she wants, so the trick is to be open and approachable, but not to seem like you're trying too hard.

I made that mistake with my first interview, and the reporter wrote that I seemed kind of fake. Of course I was fake. What did she expect? Everyone's fake in certain situations. It's like when you go for a job interview and they ask you, "What would you do if you found one of your friends at work stealing?" and, let's face it, no one's going to tell on their friend. But of course you have to say, "I would tell IMMEDIATELY, because I don't think I could work in that kind of environment, it's not good for my morale." No one wants to look like an idiot.

"So what are you doing in Syracuse two weeks after the show stopped filming? Shouldn't you be at home, enjoying your semester break?"

In the past, I've told reporters that I'm here finishing up some last-minute stuff from the semester and working a little bit on my photography. Which is pretty much bullshit. But since this is my last interview, and I'm feeling a little reckless, I decide to tell her the truth.

"Actually," I say, shifting my weight underneath me, "I came up to help Drew move into his apartment. He's going to be living off-campus next semester, and he's moving his stuff in this weekend."

Her eyes light up at the mention of Drew, which I think is cute. She's too young to be that far up on the chain of command at People.com. I mean, let's face it—I'm not a super-celebrity. I'm just the newest in the batch of has-been reality TV stars. I'm sure no one at her magazine was clamoring to do the interview.

"Your castmate Drew?" she asks.

"Yup," I tell her, waiting for the question.

"Are you and Drew, like, a thing?" she asks, and it's probably the way she says it that makes me answer honestly. Everyone else has tried to word it all funny, like, "So, are you and Drew more than friends in any capacity?" It's a relief that someone's actually just coming out and being like, "So, what's the deal?" Plus, I can tell she's really trying to do a good job, and it makes me like her.

"Well," I say slowly, wondering if Drew reads *People. com*. "I guess you could say we're seeing each other. I want to take it slow, since I just got out of a long relationship. Plus, we haven't had time to really get to know each other without the cameras around, which is a huge part of it."

I start to blush talking about dating Drew, but she just nods and writes something on her pad. I wonder if she's noticing the blush and writing it down.

Imagined writings:

I fooled Ally with my innocent appearance and youthful, simple language and then got her to admit that she's dating Drew, blushing all the while.

"What does Corey think about the whole Drew thing?"

she asks, chewing thoughtfully on the tip of her pen. She looks really interested, and I'm shocked to realize that maybe she really is. It's so strange. When I'm home in Rochester, Grant and I will go out to dinner or something, and people I don't even know will come up to me and say hi or tell me they're sorry about Corey. Then, of course, there are the people from high school who do the same thing, which is totally embarrassing. I hate having everyone I graduated with know all the crap that's been going on the past few months.

"Well," I say slowly, taking a sip of my coffee. "Corey doesn't really know. I haven't talked to him lately, although I'm sure I will, at some point. Corey and I will always be in each other's lives in some capacity, but I think we just need a little space right now."

"And how are your roommates?" she asks. That's another question they always ask, even though the cast has done a bunch of group interviews. What they want us to do is break down and talk shit about each other, which totally worked when Jasmine told the YTV.com features editor that James has a small package and was overcompensating for it by sleeping with a ton of girls.

"They're good," I say. "Jasmine and Dale are officially a couple, although she still has a few problems actually saying the word 'boyfriend.'" She laughs. "Simone's dating this guy she met in her calculus class, and as for my friend Grant—who was practically a guest star—his parents actually agreed to have Brett over for dinner next week." I always add Grant in on that question—he likes the face-time.

"So things are good," she says.

"Yeah," I say, thinking about it. "Things are good."

"Are you happy?" she asks, studying my face. I try not to show my surprise. No one has ever asked me this before. Usually they don't care if I'm happy, and would actually prefer me to be miserable. Miserable = good story. Happy, well-adjusted Ally = boring.

"Yeah," I say, smiling as I realize it's true. "I really am."

She smiles back. "That's really all I have," she says, snapping her notebook shut. "Thanks so much for your time." She reaches out to shake my hand, and I shake it back.

"Write good things about me," I say, only half joking. She laughs and says she will.

I wrap my scarf around my neck and walk out of the coffee shop. The cold air hits my face, and I shove my hands in my pockets and start walking back to Drew's apartment. I'm hoping by the time I get there, he'll have finished setting up his bookshelf so that we can just order pizza and hang out.

As I walk, I start wondering what Drew told the reporters that asked *him* about *me.* His interviews have been done for almost a week now. For some reason, I got more interview requests, which makes no sense. You'd think that the guy hottie of the house would get the most press. Note to self: Find out every publication that interviewed Drew and buy copy ASAP. Thinking about Drew telling some reporter that we're dating makes me flush, even though it's cold out. I pull my coat tighter around me, and start walking faster.

It's not until I reach the sidewalk of Drew's apartment building that it hits me—the show is really over. No more cameras, no more interviews. Just getting back to real life. I think about how excited I was when I first found out I was going to be cast, and how so much can change in just a few months. And finally, I think about how even though so many things have ended—the show, Corey and I, my first semester of college—I can't help but feel like something's just starting. Only this time, the credits say, "Ally Cavanaugh, as herself." I run up the stairs and knock on Drew's door.

Turn the page for a peek at another novel
by Lauren Barnholdt:

7:00 P.M.

I lose everything. Keys, my wallet, money, library books. People don't even take it seriously anymore. Like when I lost the hundred dollars my grandma gave me for back-to-school shopping, my mom didn't blink an eye. She was all, "Oh, Eliza, you should have given it to me to hold on to" and then she just went on with her day.

I try not to really stress out about it anymore. I mean, the things I lose eventually show up. And if they don't, I can always replace them.

Except for my purple notebook. My purple notebook is completely and totally irreplaceable. It's not like I can just march into the Apple store and buy another one. Which is why it totally figures that after five years of keeping very close tabs on it (Five years! I've never done anything consistently for five years!) I've lost it.

"What are you doing?" my best friend Clarice asks. She's sitting at my computer in the corner of my room, IMing with her cousin Jamie. Clarice showed up at nine o'clock this morning, with a huge bag of Cheetos and a six-pack of soda. "I'm ready to party," she announced when I opened my front door. Then she pushed past me and marched up to my room.

I tried to point out that it was way too early to be up on a Saturday, but Clarice didn't care because: (a) she's a morning person and (b) she thought the weekend needed to start asap, since my parents are away for the night, and she figured we should maximize the thirty-six-hour window of their absence.

"I'm looking for something," I say from under my bed. My body is shoved halfway under, rooting around through the clothes, papers, and books that have somehow accumulated under there since the last time I cleaned. Which was, you know, months ago. My hand brushes against something wet and hard. Hmm.

"What could you possibly be looking for?" she asks. "We have everything we need right here."

"If you're referring to the Cheetos," I say, "I'm sorry, but I think I'm going to need a little more than that."

"No one," Clarice declares, "needs more than Cheetos." She takes one out of the bag and slides it into her mouth, chewing delicately. Clarice is from the South, and for some reason, when she moved here a couple of years ago, she'd never had Cheetos. We totally bonded over them one day in the cafeteria, and ever since then, we've been inseparable. Me, Clarice, and Cheetos. Not necessarily in that order.

"So what are you looking for?" she asks again.

"Just my notebook," I say. "The purple one."

"Oooh," she says. "Is that your science notebook?"

"No," I say.

"Math?" she tries.

"No," I say.

"Then what?"

"It's just this notebook I need," I say. I abandon the wet, hard mystery object under the bed, deciding I can deal with it later. And by later, I mean, you know, never.

"What kind of notebook?" she presses.

"Just, you know, a notebook," I lie. My face gets hot, and I hurry over to my closet and open the door, turning my back to her so that she can't see I'm getting all flushed.

The thing is, no one really knows the truth about what's in my purple notebook. Not Clarice, not my other best friend, Marissa, not even my sister, Kate. The whole thing is just way too embarrassing. I mean, a notebook that lists every thing that you're afraid of doing? Like, written down? In *ink*? Who does that? It might be a little bit crazy, even. Like, for real crazy. Not just "oh isn't that charming and endearing" crazy but "wow that might be a deep-seated psychological issue" crazy.

But I started the notebook when I was twelve, so I

figure I have a little bit of wiggle room in the psychiatric disorders department. And besides, it was totally started under duress. There was this whole situation, this very real possibility that my dad was going to get a job transfer to a town fifty miles away. My whole family was going to move to a place where no one knew us.

So of course in my deluded little twelve-year-old brain, I became convinced that if I could just move to a different house and a different town, I'd be a totally different person. I'd leave my braces and frizzy hair behind, and turn myself into a goddess. No one would know me at my new school, so I could be anyone I wanted, not just "Kate Sellman's little sister, Eliza." I bought a purple notebook at the drugstore with my allowance, and I started writing down all the things I was afraid to do at the time, but would of course be able to do in my new school.

They were actually pretty lame at first, like French kiss a boy, or ask a boy to the dance, or wear these ridiculous tight pants that all the girls were wearing that year. But somehow putting them down on paper made me feel better, and after my dad's job transfer fell through, I kept writing in it. And writing in it, and writing in it, and writing in it. And, um, I still write in it. Not every day or anything. Just occasionally.

Of course, the things I list have morphed a little over the years from silly to serious. I still put dumb things in, like wanting to wear a certain outfit, but I have more complicated things in there too. Like how I wish I had the nerve to go to a political rally, or how I wish I could feel okay about not knowing what I want to major in when I go to college. And the fact that these very embarrassing and current things are WRITTEN DOWN IN MY NOTEBOOK means I have to find it. Like, now.

The doorbell rings as I'm debating whether or not the notebook could be in my parents' car, traveling merrily on its way to the antique furniture conference they went to. This would be good, since (a) it would at least be safe, but bad because (a) what if my parents read it and (b) I won't be able to check the car until they get home, which means I will spend the entire weekend on edge and freaking out.

"That's probably Marissa," I say to Clarice.

Clarice groans and rolls her blue eyes. "Why is *she* coming over?" she asks. She pouts out her pink-glossed bottom lip.

"Because she's our friend," I say. Which is only a half truth. Marissa is my friend, and Clarice is my friend, and Marissa and Clarice . . . well . . . they have this weird sort of love/hate relationship. They both really love each other deep down (at least, I think they do), but Marissa thinks Clarice is a little bit of an airhead and kind of a tease, and Clarice thinks Marissa is a little crazy and slightly slutty. They're both kind of right.

Marissa must have gotten tired of waiting and just let herself in, because a second later she appears in my doorway.

"What are you doing in there?" she asks.

"I'm looking for something," I say from inside my closet, where I'm throwing bags, sweaters, belts, and shoes over my shoulder in an effort to see if my notebook has somehow been buried at the bottom. I try to remember the last time I wrote in it. I think it was last week. I had dinner with my sister and then I wrote about what I would say to . . . Well. What I would say to a certain person. If I had the guts to, I mean. And if I ever wanted to even think or talk about that person again, which I totally don't.

"What something?" Marissa asks. She steps gingerly through the disaster area that is now my room and plops down on the bed.

"A notebook," Clarice says. Her fingers are flying over the keyboard of my laptop as she IMs.

"You mean like for school?" Marissa asks. "You said this was going to be our party weekend! No studying allowed!"

"Yeah!" Clarice says, agreeing with Marissa for once. She holds the bag out to her. "You want a Cheeto?" Marissa takes one.

"No," I say, "*You guys* said this was going to be our party weekend." Although, honestly, we don't really party all that much. At least, I don't. "All I said was, 'My parents are going away on Saturday, do you want to come over and keep me company?'"

"Yes," Clarice says. "And that implies party weekend."

"Yeah," Marissa says. "Come on, Eliza, we have to at least do *something*."

"Like what?" I ask.

"Like invite some guys over," Clarice says.

Marissa nods in agreement, then adds, "And go skinny dipping and get drunk."

And then Clarice gets a super-nervous look on her face, and she quickly rushes on to add, "I mean, not *guys* guys. I mean, not guys to like date or anything. Just to . . . I mean, I don't know if you're ready to, or if you even want to—oh, crap, Eliza, I'm sorry." She bites her lip, and Marissa shoots her a death glare, her brown eyes boring into Clarice's blue ones.

"It's fine," I say. "You guys don't have to keep tiptoeing around it. I am completely and totally over him." I'm totally lying, and they totally know it. The thing is, three and a half weeks ago, I got dumped by Cooper Marriatti, *a.k.a.* the last person I wrote about in my notebook, *a.k.a.* the person who I never, ever want to talk about again. (Obviously I can say his name while defending myself from the allegation that I still like him—that is a total exception to the "never bring his name up again" rule.) I really liked him, but it didn't work out. To put it mildly. Cooper did something really despicable to me, and for that reason, I am totally over it.

"Of course you are," Clarice says, nodding her head up and down. "And of course I know we don't have to tiptoe around it."

"I heard he didn't get into Brown," Marissa announces.

I snap my head up and step out of my closet, interested in spite of myself.

"What do you mean?" I ask. Cooper is a senior, a year older than us, and his big dream was to get into Brown. Seriously, it was all his family could talk about. It was pretty annoying, actually, now that I think about it. I mean, I don't think he even really *wanted* to go to Brown. He just applied because his parents wanted him to, and the only reason *they* even wanted him to go was because his dad went there, and his grandpa went there, and maybe even his great-grandpa went there. If Brown was even around then. Anyway, the point is, the fact that he didn't get in is a big deal. To him and his family, I mean. Obviously, I could care less.

"Yeah," Marissa says. "Isabella Royce told me." She quickly averts her eyes. Ugh. Isabella Royce. She's the girl Cooper is now rumored to be dating, this totally ridiculous sophomore. She's very exotic-looking with long, straight dark hair, perfect almond-shaped eyes, and dark skin. I hate her.

"Anyway," I say.

"Yeah, anyway," Clarice says. She holds out the bag of Cheetos, and this time I take one. "Oooh," she says as I crunch away. "Looks like Jeremiah added some new Facebook pictures." She leans over and squints at the screen of my laptop. She's saying this just to mess with Marissa. Jeremiah is the guy Marissa likes. They hook up once in a while, and it's kind of a . . . I guess you would say, booty-call situation. Meaning that, you know,

Jeremiah calls her when he wants to hook up, and Marissa keeps waiting for it to turn into something else.

"That's nice," Marissa says, trying to pretend she doesn't care. "Here," she says, picking a stack of letters up off the bed and holding them out to me. "I brought you your mail."

"Thanks," I say, flipping through it aimlessly. I hardly ever get mail, but sometimes my sister, Kate, will get a catalog or something sent to her, and since she's away at college, I can hijack it. But today there actually is a letter for me. Well, to me and my parents. It's from the school.

"What's that?" Marissa asks, noticing me looking at it. She's off the bed now and over in the corner, picking through the mound of clothes I hefted out of my closet. She picks a shirt off the pile on the floor, holds it in front of herself, and studies her reflection in the full-length mirror. "Are my boobs crooked?" she asks suddenly. She grabs them and pushes them together through her shirt. "I think maybe my boobs are crooked."

"Your boobs," I say, rolling my eyes, "are not crooked." Clarice stays noticeably quiet and Marissa frowns.

"They're definitely crooked," Marissa says. I slide my finger under the envelope flap and pull out the piece of paper.

"You should really hope that's not true," Clarice says sagely. She whirls around on my desk chair and studies Marissa.

"Why not?" Marissa asks.

"Because there's no way to really correct that," Clarice

says. "Like, if your boobs are too big, you can get them reduced; if they're too droopy, you can get them lifted. But for crooked boobs, I dunno." She looks really worried, like Marissa's crooked boobs might mean the end of her. "Although I guess maybe you could get them, like, balanced or something." She grins, totally proud of herself for coming up with this idea.

"Hmm," Marissa says. She smoothes her long brown hair back from her face. "You're right. There's no, like, boob-straightening operation."

"You guys," I say, "are nuts." I look down at the folded piece of paper in my hand, which is probably some kind of invitation to Meet-the-Teacher-Night or something.

Dear Eliza, Mr. and Mrs. Sellman,

This letter is to advise you that we will be having a preliminary hearing on Tuesday, November 17, at 2:00 p.m., to discuss Eliza's response to the recent slander complaint that has been filed against her. Eliza will be called on to talk about her experience with the website LanesboroLosers.com including her involvement and
participation in the comments that were posted on October 21, about a student, Cooper Marriatti.

Please be advised that all of you will be allowed to speak.

If you have any questions, please feel free to give me a call at 555-0189, ext. 541.

Sincerely,
Graham Myers, Dean of Students

Oh. My. God.

"What the hell," I say, "is this?" I start waving the paper around, flapping it back and forth in the air, not unlike the way a crazy person might do.

"What the hell is what?" Marissa asks. She drops her boobs, crosses the room in two strides, and plucks the paper out of my hand. She scans it, then looks at Clarice.

"Oh," she says. Clarice jumps up off her perch at my desk and takes the paper from Marissa. She reads it, and then Clarice and Marissa exchange a look. One of those looks you never, ever want to see your best friends exchanging. One of those, "Uh-oh, we have a secret and do we really want to tell her?" looks.

"What?" I demand. I narrow my eyes at the both of them. "What do you two know about this?"

Marissa bites her lip. "Wel-l-l-l," she says. "I'm not sure if it's true."

"Not sure if what's true?" I say.

"It's nothing," Clarice says. She gives Marissa another look, one that says, "Let's not tell her, we're going to freak her out too much."

"Totally," Marissa says. "It's nothing."

"Someone," I say, "had better tell me exactly what this nothing is." I put my hands on my hips and try to look menacing.

"I heard it from Marissa," Clarice says, sounding nervous.

"I heard it from Kelsey Marshall," Marissa says.

"HEARD WHAT?" I almost scream. I mean, honestly.

"Wel-l-l-l," Marissa says again. "The rumor is that Cooper didn't get into Brown because of what you wrote about him on Lanesboro Losers."

"But that's . . . that doesn't make any sense." I frown, and Marissa and Clarice exchange another disconcerting look.

Lanesboro Losers is a website that my older sister, Kate, started last year when she was a senior. The concept is simple: Every guy in our school is listed and has a profile. Kind of like Facebook, except Kate set up profiles for every guy—so basically they're on there, whether they like it or not. Under each guy's picture is a place for people to leave comments with information they may have about that guy and how he is when it comes to girls.

So, like, for example—if you date a guy and then you find out he has a girlfriend who goes to another school, you can log on, find his profile, and write, "You should be careful about this guy since the ass has a girlfriend who goes to another school."

It's pretty genius when you think about it. Kate got the idea when a bunch of the boys at our school started this list ranking the hottest girls in school. Only it wasn't just like "the top eight hottest girls" or whatever. They ranked them all the way down to the very last one. Kate, who was number 1 on the list, was outraged. So she decided to fight back and started Lanesboro Losers. Even though she's at college now, she keeps up with the hosting and has a bunch of girls from our school acting as moderators. (I would totally be a moderator if I could, but again, another thing I'm afraid of—the moderators take a certain amount of abuse at school from the guys who know what they do.)

"What do you mean he didn't get into Brown because of what I wrote about him?" I ask now, mulling this new information over in my head.

"He didn't get into Brown because of what you wrote about him," Marissa repeats.

"I heard you the first time," I say. "But that makes zero sense."

"It totally makes sense," Clarice says. "Apparently the Brown recruiter Googled him, and when they read what you wrote about his math test, they brought it up at his interview and basically told him his early decision application was getting rejected."

I sit down on the bed. "That thing I wrote about his math test was true," I say defensively.

Well. Sort of. Last year before his math final, Cooper got a bunch of study questions from his friend Tyler, and when he showed up to take the test, it turned out they weren't just study questions—it was the actual test. Cooper had already given the packet back to Tyler, and for some ridiculous reason, he didn't want to get Tyler into trouble, so he didn't tell anyone. So see? He *did* cheat, even though it was unintentional.

"It was totally true," Marissa says, nodding up and

down. "Which is why you shouldn't feel bad about what you wrote." She gives Clarice a pointed look.

"Totally," Clarice says. "You shouldn't feel bad about it." She keeps nodding her head up and down, the way people do when they don't really believe what they're saying.

I close my eyes, lean back on my bed, and think about what I wrote about Cooper on Lanesboro Losers. I have pretty much every word memorized, since I spent a couple of hours obsessing over what I should write. (It couldn't be too bitter, but it couldn't look like I was trying *not* to be too bitter either. It was a very delicate balance that needed to be struck. Also, I couldn't post the truth about what really happened between me and Cooper, since it was way too humiliating.) I finally settled on, "Cooper Marriatti is a total and complete jerk. He cheated on his final math test junior year just so he could pass, and he also might have herpes." The herpes thing was of course made up, but I couldn't help myself. (And, as you can see, despite my best efforts, I totally missed the balance.)

Anyway, the thing about Lanesboro Losers is that once you post something on there, they won't take it down. It's a fail-safe, just in case you end up posting something about a guy when he's being a jerk to you and then try to log on and erase it when you guys are back together. Kate set it up so that it's totally not allowed.

"Whatever," I say, my heart beating fast. "I don't feel

bad." I hope saying the words out loud will make them true. And for a second, it works. I mean, who cares about dumb Cooper and dumb Brown? It's his own fault. If he hadn't done something totally disgusting and despicable to me, if he hadn't lied to me and been a complete and total jerk, I wouldn't have written that, and he would be going to Brown. So it's totally his own fault, and if he wants to blame anyone, he should blame himself, really, because it's no concern to me if he wants to—

My cell phone starts ringing then, and I claw through the blankets on my bed, looking for it. Some books clatter onto the floor, and Clarice jumps back. She's wearing open-toed silver sparkly shoes, and one of the books comes dangerously close to falling on her foot.

"Hello," I say. The number on the caller ID is one I don't recognize, so I try to sound super-professional and innocent, just in case it's someone from the dean's office.

There's a commotion on the other end, something that sounds like voices and music, then the sound of something crinkling, and then finally, I hear a male voice say, "Eliza?"

"Yeah?" I say.

"Eliza, listen, I didn't . . ." Whoever it is is keeping their voice really low and quiet, and I'm having a lot of trouble hearing what they're saying.

"Hello!" I repeat.

"Who is it?" Marissa asks. "Is it Jeremiah?" Sometimes Jeremiah calls me looking for Marissa, if he thinks we might be together, or if he can't get through to her for some reason. Clarice's theory is that he does this so he can relay messages to me instructing Marissa to come over for a hookup, while not having to actually talk to her.

"Hello?" I say again into the phone. I put my finger in my other ear the way they do sometimes on TV, and it seems to help a little.

"Eliza, it's me," the voice says, and this time I hear it loud and clear. Cooper. "Eliza, you have to listen to me, the 318s and Tyler . . ." There's a burst of static, and the rest of what he's saying gets cut off.

"Cooper?" I ask, and my heart starts to beat a little faster.

Marissa and Clarice look at each other. Then in one fast springlike movement, they're on the bed next to me, huddled around the phone.

"Yeah, it's me," he says. There's another burst of commotion on the other end of the line.

"Eliza, listen to me . . ." he says. "You're going to have to—" And then I hear him talking to someone else in the background.

"What do you want?" I ask, my stomach dropping into my shoes. "If this is about you not getting into Brown, then honestly, I don't even care. It's all your own fault that you didn't get into Brown, and I don't regret—"

"Eliza," Cooper says. "Listen. To. Me. You have to meet me." His voice is low now, serious and dark. "Right now. At Cure."

Marissa and Clarice are falling all over themselves and

me, trying to get at the phone, and Clarice's earring gets caught on my sweater. "OW, OW, MY EAR!" she screams, then reaches down and sets it free. I pull the phone away from my ear and put it on speaker in an effort to get them to calm down.

"Cure?" I repeat to Cooper incredulously. Cure is a nightclub in Boston, and they're notorious for not IDing. I've never been there. But Kate used to go all the time, and most of the kids at my school have gone at least once or twice.

"Yeah," he says. "Eliza . . ." I hear someone say something to him in the background, and then suddenly his tone changes. "Meet me there. At Cure. In an hour."

"Tell him no," Marissa whispers, her brown eyes flashing. "Tell him that you never want to see him again!"

"Ask him if he really turned you in to the dean's office!" Clarice says. She picks up the letter from the dean's office and waves it in the air in front of me.

"Are you there?" Cooper asks, all snottylike.

"Yes, I'm here," I say. "Look, why do you want to meet me at Cure?"

"Don't ask questions," he says. "You'll find out when you get there. And make sure you wear something sexy."

I pull the phone away from my ear and look at it for a second, sure I've misheard him. " *Wear something sexy*? Are you *crazy*?" I ask. "I'm not going." This doesn't sound like a "Come to Cure so I can apologize to you and make sure you forgive me for the horrible things I've done" kind of request. It sounds like a "Come to Cure so that something horrible can happen that may involve humiliating you further."

Marissa nods her head and gives me a "You go, girl" look.

"Yes, you are," Cooper says.

"No, I'm not," I say.

"Yes, you are," Cooper says. And then he says something horrible. Something I wouldn't ever even imagine he would say in a million years. Something that is maybe quite possibly the worst thing he could ever say ever, ever, *ever*. "Because I have your purple notebook." And then he hangs up.

About the Author

LAUREN BARNHOLDT is also the author of *Two-Way Street*, *The Secret Identity of Devon Delaney*, *Four Truths and a Lie*, and *One Night That Changes Everything*. She lives in Waltham, Massachusetts. Visit her website and say hello at www.laurenbarnholdt.com.

Girls you like. Emotions you know. Outcomes that make you think.

ALL BY

DEBCALETTI

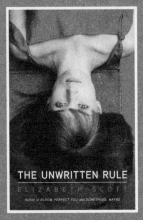

SiMONTEEN

Simon & Schuster's **Simon Teen**
e-newsletter delivers current updates on
the hottest titles, exciting sweepstakes, and
exclusive content from your favorite authors.

Visit **TEEN.SimonandSchuster.com** to
sign up, post your thoughts, and find out what
every avid reader is talking about!